ROMANTIC TIMES PRAISES JANEEN O'KERRY!

KEEPER OF THE LIGHT

"O'Kerry's world and characters are likeable. If you are a fan of [this author] you will enjoy *Keeper of the Light*."

SPIRIT OF THE MIST

"Janeen O'Kerry breathes the misty atmosphere of ancient Celtic Ireland into a tale that mixes warriors, magic, legend, and a love that will not be denied into a romance that satisfies."

SISTER OF THE MOON

"Janeen O'Kerry casts a delicate spell of wonder and wishing in this tale of ancient Ireland."

MISTRESS OF THE WATERS

"*Mistress of the Waters* is a moving tale of ancient rites and beliefs. . . . Readers who like Gothic and magic will love this story."

LADY OF FIRE

"Readers are whisked into the land of mists and warriors, druids and legends, as Ms. O'Kerry spins a delightful yarn of undeniable love."

QUEEN OF THE SUN

"Ms. O'Kerry draws the reader into the midst of her tale with accurate historical detail and well-crafted characters."

THE MAN WHO WOULD SHOW HER LOVE

There was a great creaking and rustling from inside the house; then the door opened wide and another man appeared. He was so tall, and his shoulders so wide, that he all but blocked out the soft light coming from within. In the wavering torchlight Keavy could see his face once again, and this time her impression was rather different.

The eyes were the same. Again Keavy saw the gold-hazel gaze boring right through her, the gaze of a man accustomed to making decisions and being obeyed. But while she and the others had been dining hungrily at the long-delayed feast, this man had been bathing and changing into fresh clothes.

His long hair, clean and damp and combed out smooth, fell down past his shoulders and was a vibrant brown. His smooth beard and thick mustache, equally clean, were of the same shade and set off his ruddy skin. He wore a new linen tunic over trews of heavy dark-green wool and soft boots of folded dark brown leather. His torque—made from a twisted ribbon of shining gold bent into a near-complete circle, and capped at each end with the fierce gold likeness of an eagle's head—rested at his neck. His iron sword was in place in a plain leather scabbard at his belt.

"Good evening to you, Lady Keavy," he said. It was the same low, quiet voice she had heard earlier. "You are welcome here. Please, come inside the house of the king."

Other *Love Spell* books by Janeen O'Kerry:

KEEPER OF THE LIGHT
SPIRIT OF THE MIST
SISTER OF THE MOON
MISTRESS OF THE WATERS
LADY OF FIRE
QUEEN OF THE SUN

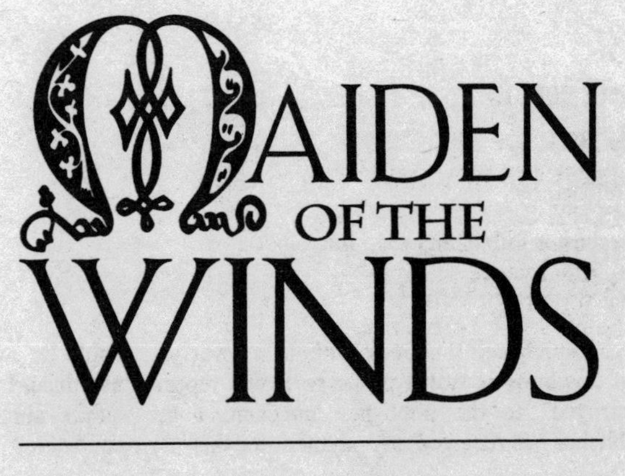

LOVE SPELL

NEW YORK CITY

. . . for every man whose lady's love has given him wings.

LOVE SPELL®

July 2003

Published by

Dorchester Publishing Co., Inc.
276 Fifth Avenue
New York, NY 10001

ISBN 0-505-52534-8

Printed in the United States of America.

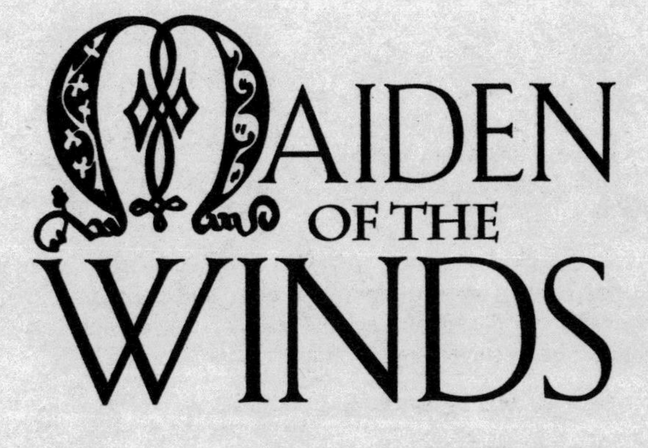
MAIDEN
OF THE
WINDS

PRONUNCIATION GUIDE

Aengus—ANG-gus
coibche—KAH-ib-keh
Coilean—KAH-lin
Dun Gaoth—dun ghee (hard g)
fidchell—fik-YEL
Keavy—KEE-vee (from the old Irish name *Caoimhe*)
Maille—MAH-lee
Samhaim—SOW-when
Seabhac—SHAH-vak
Seanan—SHAH-nen
Sorcha—SOR-kah

Chapter One

The first winds of spring blew cold and fresh over the forests of eastern Eire, lifting a soaring golden eagle high on outstretched wings. The bird could see all of his kingdom and more from up there, and he took the time to inspect his every wheat field, beehive, and farmer's house, every apple tree and glittering stream, and every grassy, flowering meadow. It was an annual task after the long, cold nights of winter.

Reveling in his power, the eagle soared through the sky examining his kingly domain.

A motion far below caught his sharp eye. There, running and dancing along a sunlit brook and weaving in and out of a row of silvery birch trees, was a group of young women. Each wore a soft linen gown of yellow or green or blue, and each carried a small basket. Their feet were bare in the soft new grass, and their hair streamed long and loose down slender backs.

The eagle circled once above them and then

flew down to perch high in one of the birches. The young women did not notice him as he watched and listened.

Their laughter reached him first. They were five in number, all young, all tall, all slender, all beautiful—yet one of them stood out among even such a gathering as this.

"Keavy! Keavy!" called the others, laughing as they tried to keep up with the long-legged girl who led them in their playful dance. "Wait for us! How will we ever find any primrose or watercress when you go so fast?"

The one called Keavy stopped at last and turned to face them, her long fair hair shining with silvery light like a river in bright sunshine. She set down her basket in the grass and waited for them with her hands on her hips, frowning in mock impatience.

"How can I stay still on a day like this?" she asked, then burst out giggling. She caught up her basket and dashed away again, her simple green gown swinging around her legs and billowing out behind her in the wind.

The rest of the girls squealed with laughter and raced in pursuit. All of them ran until they reached an open, sunny spot by the edge of the stream, where they dropped down to sit breathless in the grass, surrounded by the calling and singing of the wrens and the larks.

"The servants will be waiting for their watercress," said one girl.

"And the healers did ask for more primrose," warned another.

"We said we would bring these things for them if only we might be allowed outside the fortress gates for a little while, so we'd better fetch them back if we ever want to go beyond the walls of Dun Mor again!"

"They will have them, they will have them," Keavy said with a laugh. "Though I'd have said I'd bring them all the gold in Eire if it meant being outside on a day such as this, after staying inside all winter!" She threw back her head so that her hair formed a shining pool in the grass behind her, and closed her eyes as the warmth of the spring sun caressed her face.

The eagle spread his wings and flew to another birch tree, just above the place where the young women rested. None of them noticed he was there.

"Are you ready to go on yet?" Keavy asked, reaching for her empty basket.

But her companions only moaned in protest and stayed where they were. "It is not fair, Keavy—you are older than the rest of us and can go farther than we can!"

Keavy only laughed again. "I have only just reached seventeen years. The rest of you are all sixteen, are you not? I am not so much older."

"But you are taller and stronger, no matter what your age, and you have tired me out!" complained another of the girls. All of them laughed.

Still smiling, Keavy caught up her basket and

got to her feet. "Stay here, then, and rest. I cannot sit still! I'll get the watercress, and perhaps by the time I do that you will be ready to go on and look for primrose."

"Go, go!" they agreed. "But not too far."

"Not too far," Keavy promised.

As she started along the stream, her hair flowing down nearly to her ankles as she walked, the eagle left his perch and followed, wheeling high above the trees in the bright blue sky. Even with his sharp eyes, it was sometimes difficult to see her as she walked. Through the sunlit trees far below, her skin was nearly as white as the bark of the birches, her gown nearly the same shade of green as the leaves and grass. Yet he could easily find her pale golden hair with its silvery highlights, and when at last she stopped to search out some watercress at the edge of the stream, the eagle flew down to a branch just above her.

The sound of his great wings made her look up.

Keavy nearly dropped her basket. "Oh," she whispered, and took a step forward.

The eagle folded his wings and remained very still.

"Well, beautiful eagle," Keavy said, also standing still. "I am happy to share this day with you. I find that I am often followed by wild birds, who seem to like my company for some reason—but they are usually wrens or larks or sparrows. Never have I been in the company of a golden eagle."

She took another careful step forward, and another, until she stood just in front of the low branch. The kingly bird was almost near enough to reach up and touch.

The eagle watched her closely as she approached, tilting his head and fixing her with his deep amber stare. She was even more beautiful up close than she had been from the sky: tall and slender, graceful and fair, with light green eyes and her long hair streaming in the fresh spring winds. And she was still young enough to fly from him like the maiden she was if he were to show himself to her in his true form. But a creature of nature, even one as powerful as a golden eagle, would not frighten the maid at all.

"I hope we have not intruded on your territory," Keavy was saying. "My friends and I simply could not stay in any longer on a day such as this, the first day to bring a little of the warmth and sunlight of spring with it." She smiled. "You seem to have felt the same way."

The bird drew himself up and ruffled his feathers, never taking his fierce gaze from her. Keavy took one last step forward. "I want to remember this," she said, lifting one hand a little, as though she longed to reach out for him but dared not. "Already this was a special day, and now it is even more so. . . ."

Then Keavy did raise her hand, slowly and cautiously, clearly hoping to touch his soft golden-brown feathers. Yet she did not have to reach far. The eagle raised himself up and stretched out, extending the tip of one great wing straight toward Keavy's face.

She closed her eyes as the smooth dark gold feathers brushed gently over her cheek and the surface of her hair. Then the bird settled back onto his branch, still watching her.

Keavy could not speak for a moment. She could only gaze back with a look of wonder in her green eyes, clearly understanding that she stood in the presence of something magical. "All my life I have heard the tales of such things as this," she whispered. "Tales of those who had the power to change their shape if they chose—into a hunting wolf or a leaping salmon or even a great golden eagle. I can only believe that this must be what you are."

The bird ruffled his feathers again and opened and closed his sharp, curving beak, though he made no sound. "And if you have power enough to take the form of one so magnificent as the eagle, you must be a great druid—or maybe even a king."

The bird gave a short cry and cocked his head.

"Always I will remember this," Keavy said, her eyes shining, and took a step back.

The eagle raised his wings as though ready to take flight; but instead he carefully preened the feathers of his right wing and then dropped one golden-brown feather to the fresh new grass below the birch tree. As Keavy watched, entranced, the eagle did the same with his left wing, and a second gold-brown feather fell to earth. At last the great bird ducked his head and ran his curving black beak through the plumage over his heart, and dropped a third and final feather to the grass.

Then, with a loud cry, the eagle leaped up from his branch and climbed into the air on great strokes of his powerful wings. Keavy swung her head to follow his flight, her pale hair heavy as it swept behind her. The eagle circled overhead, waiting until she picked up the three feathers from the grass; and then, with a last cry of farewell, he soared away on the currents of the sky until he was lost from sight.

Chapter Two

Another spring came and went, and another and another, until eight years had passed from the day Keavy had encountered the golden eagle in the forest. On this new morning in early spring, she crossed the busy yard within the enormous circular earthen walls of the fortress called Dun Mor with a basket of clean new wool. It was already combed and ready for spinning, and Keavy smiled as she thought of the fine new fabrics she could weave from it and of how she might embroider them.

She smoothed her soft yellow wool gown a little as she walked, proud of how nicely it had turned out. Her green-and-white-plaid rectangular cloak, also of the best wool, was pleasing as well. Perhaps she could start another piece of embroidery for the yellow gown—she could do birds again, always a favorite, sewn from the best linen threads in blue and purple and green. . . .

"Keavy! Keavy!"

She stopped and turned at the sound of a young woman's voice calling her name, her long gold braids swinging behind her back. "What is it, Doreen?"

Doreen hurried out from behind one of the many round houses and ran up to Keavy. She was only a servant girl, but her hair was braided as prettily as Keavy's, and she had a little simple embroidery on the sleeves of her plain wool gown.

"You have done very well with the embroidery!" Keavy noted. "You have been practicing. You will be a noble lady someday, if you are not careful."

"Oh, I *have* been practicing, and I thank you again for showing me. But that is not why I called out to you! They're here! Did you know? They're here for you!"

"What are you talking about?" Keavy asked with a laugh, walking across the yard once more.

"The travelers from Dun Gaoth!" Doreen was breathless and excited at the thought of visitors. "They're your distant cousins—second or third or something, I can't remember. Didn't you know they were coming?"

"I did not," Keavy said, stopping to look at her young friend. "But if they're here to visit my father and mother, I can guess why they have come. Did you see them?"

"I did! First I saw a few servants, and then the warriors who formed an escort. And then a father, and a mother, and their grown son!"

Keavy closed her eyes. "It is the beginning of spring, and my father is trying to marry me off again. It could be nothing else." She sighed, and continued walking toward her home.

Doreen hurried after her. "But Keavy—don't you *want* to be married?"

Keavy raised her head and smiled a little as she walked with long strides. "I'm sure I will want to marry someday," she admitted. "But there is plenty of time yet."

"You are all of twenty-five! Most girls are married long before then. Why, I—"

"You are not yet sixteen." Keavy laughed. "Do not worry. You will marry when the time is right for you to do so. As for me, I will do the same—but I assure you it will not be today."

"I would not be so sure this time, if I were you," Doreen warned, in a worried voice. "Your parents seemed very determined when they greeted this young man's family at the gates."

Keavy glanced at her. "I can handle my parents. I've done it many times before. I simply have to remind them that I am waiting for the right man to come. *I* will be the one to know who that man is . . . for I am certain, somehow, that I have yet to find him."

She touched her fingertips to the three feathers she always wore in her bronze brooch with its fine inlay of white enamel—the three feathers left as a gift for her by the magnificent golden eagle on that bright spring day so many years before. "But thank you for telling me, Doreen. I will see you later today."

"I hope so. I want to learn as much as I can from you, before . . . before you—"

"Before dark," Keavy interrupted, trying to smile. "I'm sure that is what you mean. I do not intend to go anywhere." She smoothed her yellow gown, straightened her cloak, and then walked back to her family's round house.

As she pushed open the door, a voice rang out. "Keavy! Ah, I am so glad you are finally back!" said the silver-haired Finola, frantically polishing the gold cups lined up on the central stone hearth. "Come here, come here! You must change into your best gown and touch some rowan to your cheeks. There is someone very special here to see you!"

Keavy glanced at her mother and nodded, then walked across the clean, dry rushes on the floor until she reached her sleeping ledge. Setting down her basket of wool, she turned and smiled politely at her parents. "Well, now. Who is it today?"

Her father sat on a thick cushion tossed down on the rushes. He looked up and frowned at his daughter, his iron-gray hair falling past his shoulders and his thick beard and mustache all but hiding his face. "This is nothing to smile at. It is a very serious matter, and one which is long overdue."

"Are you in such a hurry to be rid of me?" Keavy asked lightly, sitting down on the ledge.

Now it was her mother's turn to frown. "Daughter, you are past twenty-five years of age! You should have at least three children by now. It is a scandal to us that you are not yet married!"

"A scandal? How could that be?"

Her mother placed her hands on her hips. "Because it looks as if no one wants my daughter! As if the girl I raised is somehow flawed and not good enough for any man to make his wife!"

"Do you truly think I am flawed?"

Her mother sighed and lowered her arms. "Of course I don't. There was never a girl as pretty or as lively or as accomplished as you. But if you cannot make a match—why, what will people think?"

"Perhaps they will think I wait for the man I truly love," Keavy said.

"Perhaps they will think no man wants you," said her father from his cushion with a grunt.

Keavy stood and walked away from her sleeping ledge to the round stone-walled hearth at the center of the house. "Do I not help to make our lives more comfortable here?" she asked, as she had so many times before. "Do I not earn my place in your house with all that I do?"

"Oh, Keavy, it is not that," her mother began.

"Look around you, at this house," Keavy continued, walking in a large circle around the fire. "I made many of the cushions you sit on, stuffed with the cleanest straw and made from the very best hides. I cut and sewed these fur cloaks for the sleeping ledges. I made many of the fine clothes you both wear—I spun the thread, I wove the cloth, I sewed the garments, and I embroidered them as well as anyone has ever seen. And the food—you know well that no one can prepare foods the way I can prepare them, especially dainty things made with honey. Do you not agree?"

"You are not a servant!" her mother protested. "You are a lady of the noble class and should behave like one!"

"Your mother is right. You are not a servant," said her father. "And because you are so skilled at all those things, that is all the more reason why you should spend your talents on a family of your own. I will not have it said that your father somehow prevented his skilled and beautiful daughter from marrying, thinking to keep her home and have her work only for him instead of for a husband, as she should."

"But I am perfectly content to live here and do these things! I enjoy my life very much the way it is and have no desire to change it."

"It is time for you to make your own life and your own family," commanded her mother, with a tone in her voice that Keavy had not heard before.

"We have indulged you far too much, we know," her father admitted. "But that will be remedied now. As pleasant as it is to have you here and doing all of these things for us, I must insist that you do them for your own husband and your own children. That is only right and proper, and that is how it will be."

Keavy folded her arms. "And if I refuse? If I

wish to stay here until I myself can find the man I want?"

Her father got to his feet and looked down at her with equal determination. "You will *not* stay here," he said. "Something must be done to break you out of the comfortable pattern of your life. I fear you will wake up one day still living here but long past the age of having children, and you will wonder why your parents did nothing to push you out of your too-comfortable nest. Did they prefer to selfishly keep your talents at home for themselves? You will wonder."

He shook his head. "That will not happen. I swear it. If you refuse yet another husband, I will send you away to live among the servants until you change your mind and at least attempt to make a match."

Keavy glanced from her father to her mother and then back again. This was quite different from the way these discussions usually went, and for the first time she began to feel apprehensive. "Surely you would not truly send me away," she whispered. "Surely you would not—"

"We will do whatever is necessary to set you on the proper path," her father said. "And we will discuss the matter no further. Go with your mother now, and prepare yourself to meet this man."

"Oh, and he is quite a nice man," her mother added, trying to be helpful. "Training to be a bard, he is, and quite handsome. He will make you a very good husband; I am sure of it!"

But Keavy only backed away from them. "I cannot do this," she said through gritted teeth. "I *will* not do this!" She clenched her fists, turned away from her parents, walked straight to the door, and pulled it open—

And there stood a short, slim, round-shouldered youth, staring down at the ground while his two beaming parents stood on either side of him. "Oh, you must be the Lady Keavy!" said the woman with a delighted giggle. "I am Sorcha, and this is my husband, Dallan. And this"—she dug her elbow furiously into the young man's side until he briefly looked up from beneath his mop of brown hair, revealing sullen eyes and a downturned mouth—"this is our son, Coilean. The man who is to be your husband!"

Keavy could only stand with her hand on the heavy wooden frame of the doorway and stare. *They can't be serious,* she thought, looking down at the unpromising suitor called Coilean. *My parents could not possibly be serious about this!*

"Your mother is my second cousin, Keavy," continued the woman, "and so I knew, even at Dun Gaoth, that she had a daughter of marriageable age."

"And then some," said her husband under his breath.

The woman seemed not to have heard. "May we come inside and speak to Finola and Egan?" she asked, still smiling brightly.

"Of course, of course," Keavy murmured. She

stepped back to let them come inside; there seemed to be little else to do.

The visitors gave their son a firm push forward and all but lifted him up the step into the house. Then Keavy saw they had not come alone. She frowned as Oran, a solemn, serious druid who was a master of the law, stepped out from beside the doorway and walked silently into the house as well.

Keavy's hopes fell even further. Her parents had arranged for prospective husbands and their families to call on her before, but never had they brought along a druid—especially not a druid well trained in law and contracts. *Marriage contracts.* Keavy sighed and closed the door.

Her mother was busy setting the very best leather cushions down on the rushes for her guests and pouring honey wine into their small, flat golden cups. "Sit down, all of you; sit down and be welcome!" Finola said, handing around the cups and taking her own place on her favorite feather-stuffed cushion. "Keavy, you must sit, too! The time has come to discuss the contract!"

Slowly, reluctantly, Keavy sat down on the only remaining cushion—which happened to be the one beside Coilean. Even sitting down she was taller than he. Coilean merely held his cup with both of his slender, delicate hands with their long, perfect fingernails, and gazed down at the wine. He seemed to be trying his best to take no notice of anything.

"Now, then! If all of you are comfortable," began Keavy's mother, "let me introduce you to our beautiful daughter, our only daughter, our only child. This is Keavy, the most beautiful lady at Dun Mor."

"And soon to be the most beautiful at Dun Gaoth, I am certain," said Keavy's father, Egan, with a slow smile for Coilean's parents.

"Do you see all of these beautiful things we have about our house?" said Finola. "The stitched furs, the soft cushions, the fine fabrics of our clothes, the beautiful embroidery that covers them? All of that is Keavy's work. Think what a valuable addition she will be to the people of Dun Gaoth—and to your home, Coilean, as your wife!"

Coilean slowly raised his eyes and peered up from beneath his flopping mass of brown hair, but he remained silent.

"Your daughter is indeed a lady of great beauty and many talents," said Dallan. "Coilean, now, is a bard. He's already quite good on the harp and the flute, and is learning to create his own poems as well as singing those that the poets have written."

"Why, how nice! How very nice," enthused Finola. "I'm sure Keavy would enjoy having such an artistic man as her husband! Oh, they make such a lovely couple, do they not—two such creative young people!"

"May I ask . . . how young?" inquired Dallan, as delicately as he could.

Egan sat up a little straighter. "Our daughter is just past the age of twenty-five years."

"And your son?" inquired Finola.

"Coilean is twenty-two years of age," answered Sorcha.

"A perfect match!" cried Finola, and clapped her hands together, looking at each of the other people and clearly hoping all would join in. But there was only silence, broken by the sound of Coilean taking a hasty gulp of his wine.

"Twenty-two years?" asked Keavy's father. "Coilean, you have made no match though you are from a fine family and you are twenty-two years of age?"

Coilean raised his head a little and managed to meet Egan's eyes for a fleeting moment. "I . . . I have—"

"It is true he has made no match," said Dallan quickly. "But that is only because there have been so many possibilities no single choice could be made! Until now, of course."

"There is Maille." Coilean seemed to find his voice at last. "I wished to make a match with Maille, but you—"

"Of course you did not wish for any such thing!" interrupted Dallan, a little too hotly. He looked at his hosts and smiled tightly. "A mere dalliance, as young men are wont to do. It means nothing. She's just a servant girl, born among the rock men, the lowest of the low. She's nothing at all. While your daughter Keavy is from a noble family just as Coilean is. They are, as my wife said, a perfect match."

But Coilean shot a brief glare at his father before looking away, and Keavy began to feel a little hope. Clearly the young man already had someone else, and his parents were simply trying to get him away from what they saw as an unsuitable match.

Keavy almost smiled. Coilean did not want this marriage any more than she did.

"Ah—shall we offer what we have brought?" said Sorcha to her husband.

"Of course. Finola and Egan, we hope you will accept this as a *coibche* for your daughter, Keavy, on behalf of our son, Coilean, who wishes to contract a marriage with her."

Keavy felt as though she were watching all this from a distance, as though it were happening to someone else. She certainly wished it were. If this family were offering a *coibche* for her, they were serious about marriage.

Too serious.

Finola quickly accepted the heavy, carved wooden box that Coilean's father handed to her. She set it down in the rushes and removed the lid, and as she did so Keavy saw her face light up.

Keavy's eyes flicked to the box. It held a nice collection of gold rings, plates, and cups. There was nothing out of the ordinary, but it was indeed all of gold—she saw no bronze or copper among the pieces. Her mother seemed quite pleased at the gleaming treasure that had come to her, even though it was supposed to go to the bride. She looked up at her husband and nodded quickly, and he mirrored the gesture.

"Oh!" said Finola, suddenly remembering that Keavy was sitting beside her. She turned the box and held back the lid, proudly displaying the contents. "Does this *coibche* meet with your approval, my daughter?"

Keavy hardly spared a glance for it. She could feel her face reddening. "I feel as though I'm being traded like a milk cow," she said under her breath, trying to keep her rising temper under control.

Her father looked up at her. "Not like a milk cow at all," he said, glancing at their guests. "More like a virgin heifer!"

Keavy's mouth fell open in shock. Her father must be serious about her leaving if he would say such a thing about her, but their guests laughed uproariously—all except Coilean, who only sighed impatiently and clearly wished he were anywhere else.

Never had she been so pleased to see that a man had absolutely no interest in her!

Seeing the look on Keavy's face, her father stopped laughing and turned to the silent druid. "Oran, we accept the *coibche* that Coilean has offered our daughter. We are ready to discuss the contract for the marriage."

Oran nodded and got to his feet, and all of them shifted about on their cushions so they could see him. "In some ways, this is quite a typical marriage," he began. "A man and woman brought together with the intent of making a match. *Coibche* offered and accepted. A contract of marriage arranged. Yet it is clear to me that in some other ways, this particular marriage will be anything but typical."

All remained silent as Oran paced slowly over the rushes. Both sets of parents looked apprehensive, while Keavy and Coilean both glowered up at him. "None could fail to see that this bride and this groom are nothing if not reluctant. They *could* make a match with each other if they truly wished, but it will be difficult. And so I would propose that a special condition be included for this particular contract of marriage."

The four parents all looked at each other, and then turned back to Oran. "What do you propose?" asked Egan.

The druid folded his hands behind his back and stood still, gazing down at his little audience. "I would propose that unless this marriage lasts until the full moon after Beltane—three full moons from the one that occurs seven nights from now—it will be declared never to have existed at all, and the *coibche* will be returned to Coilean's family."

Finola's eyes widened. She clutched the prettily carved wooden box sitting in the rushes before her and drew it closer, apparently speechless at the thought of having to return it.

Finally Egan spoke. "I think that is a very wise idea, Oran. After that length of time, there is a good chance that a bond will have formed between the bride and her husband, and they will be reluctant to end their marriage."

"And an even better chance that a child will be on the way," added Finola, nodding in agreement. "They'll be even more reluctant to part if that happens."

"Oh, so true, so true," agreed Sorcha. "Once Keavy knows she will have a baby to hold, she will not want to leave her husband."

The parents all looked at each other, nodding and smiling. "No doubt three months of marriage with a woman like Keavy would be enough to change any man's mind!" said Dallan, and all of them laughed.

Oran sat down again on his cushion. Finola drew the box holding the *coibche* even closer. "Then it is settled!" she said. "Keavy and Coilean will be wed in seven nights' time."

Keavy shot a glance at Coilean, only to see that he was staring at her with what must have been the same expression of disbelief that was on her own face. In an instant she was on her feet.

"You cannot be serious!" she cried, her voice trembling with outrage. "I do not know this man! He does not know me! He says he loves another. Do our feelings count for nothing?"

"Keavy," her father said, getting slowly to his feet. "We will, of course, give you a little time to get to know each other before the wedding day."

"A little time?"

"You and Coilean may walk outside now while we finish making the arrangements. When you come back in, you may tell us that you accept, and that the two of you will be married in seven nights' time."

Keavy looked from one face to another, simply aghast. "I can give you my answer now," she said. "I will have none of this."

"We have already discussed it. If you refuse to marry this man, you will find every one of your possessions sitting outside the door so that you might take them with you when you go to find your place among the servants—if they will have you."

He shook his head. "This is your last chance, Keavy. You have refused all other offers of marriage. No longer will you stay here with your parents like a child, when you should be caring for a family of your own."

Dallan, too, got to his feet. "And you, Coilean? Will you walk out with this lady and then come back and accept your marriage?"

The man's son glared up at him, sullen as ever. "I, too, can give you your answer now. I want no part of any marriage unless it is to Maille. You have known this all along."

"And I will tell you again: if you refuse to marry this highborn woman, this beautiful lady we have been so fortunate to find for you, you will not find that servant girl waiting for you. We will have her sent away where you will never find her."

"As you have told me many times," Coilean muttered. He looked away, and his gaze caught Keavy's.

She raised her chin. "We seem to have little

choice," she said to him. "Will you walk with me?"

After only a moment, he got up from the cushion and moved to the door. Keavy followed, and as they went outside she pulled the heavy door closed behind them.

Keavy walked steadily across the grounds of Dun Mor, keeping her head down and her hands folded in front of her. She could hear Coilean as he trailed along a few paces back, and found herself fervently hoping no one would think they were a couple.

Yet she knew it might already be too late to worry about such things.

She led him along the high, curving, grass-covered inner wall of the fortress until they reached the armorer's workshop near the back. The place was quiet; the craftsmen were out in the surrounding fields testing their newly made weapons, and few other people passed by. Three shaggy brown sheep and their wary lambs, safe within wooden pens along the back of the fortress, were the only ones to see them.

Keavy placed one hand on the rough wall of the building and turned to Coilean. At that moment a wren came down to alight on her arm, but she paid it no mind. Her spirits sank even further at the sight of her betrothed's pale and sullen face, but she went ahead anyway with what she had to say.

"Coilean . . ."

His gaze shifted briefly from the ground to her

hands . . . and then to her arm, where the bright-eyed wren perched. He blinked at the sight, and began to look almost frightened, but kept silent.

"We do not seem to have much choice before us."

The young man looked away again and gave a heavy sigh.

"Your family will send away the woman you love if you do not accept this arrangement. And *my* family will send *me* away if I refuse it. I think we both know that they are quite serious this time—all of them."

Coilean gave a quick nod and went back to studying the bare ground at the base of the armorer's house, trying not to look at the wild bird that had come to rest on Keavy's arm.

She frowned. He seemed determined to say nothing at all about anything. "Coilean, do you *want* to wake up married to me?"

He looked up at her, his eyes huge and staring. Her words seemed to have caught his attention. "You are a beautiful and accomplished lady," he said. "But I have no wish to marry anyone unless I can marry Maille. I have known for a long time that she is the only one I would ever want to wed."

"Then I am glad for you, to know such a thing," Keavy said. "But your family does not think she is a suitable match for you. She's going to be sent away if you try to contract a marriage with her. I am sure you would not want to see that happen."

"I would not," he agreed quickly. "I would do anything—"

Keavy gave him a wry smile. "It looks as though you may have to do just that. Are you truly willing?"

He glanced up. "Surely you don't want to marry me any more than—"

"Oh, you are right. I do not want to marry you. Though I am sure you are a good man and an accomplished bard, from what your parents said. And it is true that a bard is likely to be a gentler man—and live a longer life—than a single-minded warrior or a pre-occupied king. For just those reasons, some women actually prefer to marry a poet or a druid."

"But you are not one of those women."

She shook her head and tried to smile a little. "I have not yet found the one I wish to marry at all, though I've always felt he was out there, somewhere. I will know him when I see him, and I will find him if only I keep waiting and do not give up."

Coilean barely seemed to have heard. "My parents only hope to keep me away from Maille, while still pushing me out of their house," he muttered.

"We are both in that situation. And so it seems to me that we have no choice, Coilean, but to marry each other."

This time he met her eyes. "No choice?" he asked, his voice rising and his face getting redder. "No choice but to marry each other? You are willing to go along with this?"

"Not willing," she explained. "But I am beginning to see that by marrying each other, we may each gain what we want: the freedom to do as we wish with no further interference from our families."

Coilean shook his head, looking completely baffled. "How is that possible?"

She grinned. "It seems to me that if our parents had searched out every last unmarried man and woman in the entire land of Eire, they could not have found a poorer match than you and me.

"Look at us! We have nothing in common. You are a bard. I have only a passing interest in poetry and music, and much prefer the tangible arts of fabric and thread. I love the outdoor life and all the creatures in it, especially the birds, while I suspect you prefer the quiet of a house where you can compose your poems with no distraction.

"I am so tall and strong that I am constantly mocked for it, while you are . . . ah, you are made for the gentler pursuits of language. And most of all, you love another, while I have long felt that the man I am meant for is far away and as yet undiscovered. Do you not agree that this is true, Coilean?"

"I do agree," he said. "It is a mystery to me why our families cannot see it."

She waved her hand impatiently. "They care nothing for how we might feel about each other, or whether we would have chosen each other on our own. All that matters to our parents is that you do not marry beneath you, and that I marry . . .

well, that I marry someone. And that is exactly what they have arranged."

"That is what they have forced on us," he muttered, turning away again.

"So they have. But sometimes it is better to bend a little with the wind, rather than trying to stand against it and breaking."

He glowered at her once more, but managed to keep his gaze level with hers. "Please explain."

She folded her hands. "The stipulation on this marriage is that it must last for at least three full moons past the one marking the ceremony. After that—well, after that we are free to do as we will, and that would include being divorced, if that is what we wish."

"Our families believe that after three months, we may not want to part from each other."

"With any other marriage, that might well be true. But I propose that we accept this marriage, to please our families—all the while living together as any brother and sister might do, of course—and then, at the end of the specified time, be divorced under the laws on grounds that I am barren.

"Since there will be no child, none can say that you must continue to live with me. The husband of a barren woman is always free to leave her and take another wife if he wishes."

"Free after one year's time," Coilean said. "I, too, know something of the law."

"The legalities will have to wait for one year, that is true. But in the meantime we can return to our lives free of our parents' interference, having done exactly as they asked."

"But . . . will any accept our reasons for parting only three months after the marriage?"

Keavy laughed. "The people of both our fortresses will only be surprised that it would last even that long, between two who are as poorly matched as we. Then you will be free to wed your servant girl, and I can go on with my life as I wish."

He sighed, and slowly nodded his head. "It seems we have little choice. I cannot let them send Maille away."

"And I cannot let my parents send me away. It seems a fair enough trade—a few fortnights spent together to please our families, and then we are free to do as we wish for the remainder of our lives."

"All right, then. It sounds quite reasonable when you put it that way. We may as well go and tell them we will be married in seven nights' time."

She nodded slowly. "Time enough for me to travel to Dun Gaoth."

"Seven nights," he repeated. "So soon . . ."

Keavy shrugged. "The sooner the wedding, the sooner the divorce. Do you see?"

He gave her a wan smile. "I see. Let's go now, then, without any further delay."

Keavy nodded and started off across the grounds of Dun Mor with Coilean following a little way behind her. She drew a deep breath and told herself that one could tolerate almost anything for three months, if it meant having freedom after that . . . and she could not help but think, yet again, that somewhere beyond the walls of Dun Mor there must be the man that she was meant to marry. The man whom she could truly love.

The wren flew away just as she reached her house.

Chapter Three

King Aengus hated mud. Really hated it. He especially hated it when it was well churned with horse manure, and hated it most of all when he had just been kicked facedown in it.

Across the valley from him the warrior men of Dun Mor roared with laughter, even as his own men—the men of Dun Gaoth—shouted in fury at this outrageous, unthinkable insult to their king. Only the fact that he was unable to signal an attack kept them from charging across the valley to unload their resentment on their enemy.

The three men of Dun Mor, who had come to Aengus to negotiate an end to the long day's battle, had apparently not yet had enough fighting to satisfy themselves—even though the sun was beginning to set. Knowing King Aengus was inclined to make a bargain so all could go home, the three of them had dared to walk out to face him, kicked his feet out from under him, then dashed back to their own side before the men of Dun Gaoth could catch them.

"Face me; come back and face me!" shouted Parlan, the king's champion, even as he hauled his mud-soaked king to his feet with one hand and shook his iron sword with the other. "You are the worst cowards ever to fight in Eire! How *dare* you do such a thing!"

Parlan's voice shook with rage, but also with anticipation. Now the fighting would be even more satisfactory, for they had vengeance on their side. He paced back and forth in front of his laughing enemy even as the warriors of Dun Gaoth, lined up behind him, began pounding their long wooden shields with the hilts of their swords and shouting out the worst insults they could manage. "Face me!" Parlan cried again. "Send your champion out to face me!"

"Parlan," Aengus said to him, leaning down close to his ear. "It is near dark. There is hardly time for another battle. We have five men so badly wounded they cannot fight any longer. Dun Mor has at least that many. Just let them finish shouting their best obscenities and then we can all go home."

But Parlan seemed not to hear. "Send your champion out! Send him out here, if he's even worthy of the name!" His normally fair face was flushed with anger. "I will show them what happens when they dare to shove our king into the mud like he is a dog! I will . . . *show them!*"

Unable to contain himself any longer, he

charged headlong into the line of warriors and was immediately followed by the shouting men of Dun Gaoth, pushing past their filth-spattered king in their eagerness to resume the battle.

Almost falling down again as his men stormed past, Aengus picked himself up and limped slowly away from the battlefield. He climbed up the shallow side of the valley and stood at the top, where his three druids waited among the servant boys who held the horses.

He tried to brush off the mud as best he could, but it was only becoming colder and drier in the rising wind. Instead he looked down upon the battle where the men shouted and swore and smashed down swords upon shields, driving each other back first one way and then the other.

"Trouble is, we're an even match," Aengus mused, trying to catch his breath. "Neither side wants to give in."

"The light is fading," remarked Nessan. "They'll be calling for torches soon."

"Torches will not bring this battle to an end." King Aengus shook his head. "They simply want to fight. There is no real reason. They are all just wild young men spoiling for battle, so they might have something to brag about over the next feast. They need no other reason."

"Oh, but that is not altogether true, King Aengus," protested Sean. "They are fighting over this long-contested piece of land. They were willing to attack our border sentries for it, and I suppose I can understand why. Look. A more beautiful place I have never seen."

Aengus could only nod, dismally aware of the mud drying on his light brown hair and beard. Sean was right. If ever a place was worth fighting over, it was this one.

He and his druids and servants looked down through the gathering twilight into a long, slender valley whose level floor and gently rising sides were lush with green grass. Winding along its length was a clear rocky brook, and widely scattered near the brook were heavily branching apple trees. New green buds were just beginning to show on their bare branches. Farmers had placed a few large, oval-shaped straw beehives on wooden platforms beneath the branches, an ideal location in the spring when the apple trees would blossom.

But the whirling, skirmishing fighters noticed none of the beauty around them. Their boots tore and trampled the fresh new grass and turned it into bare patches of mud. Their swords nicked and hacked the newly budding trees. Their wild lunges overturned the heavy beehives and sent them crashing to the ground. "Torches!" shouted Parlan, even as he continued to swing his sword beneath the trees.

"Torches! Torches!" shouted the other men, never missing a blow as they cried out to their servants. They slipped and slid in the increasingly barren and muddy ground, already low and wet and now chewed up by nearly an entire day of fighting between some sixty men. "Bring the torches!"

"The land suffers, King Aengus," said Finbar quietly. "It is an unfortunate strip lying between two kingdoms that claim it—but like a beautiful woman caught between two men who want her, she ends up neglected and hurt while they fight. If you cannot win this contest—which it appears will go on forever, between two evenly matched and equally determined foes who enjoy the battle far more than the spoils—I fear there may be little left to fight over."

Aengus continued to watch his men, even as a few of the servants began to light the torches they had brought. "I would give this little valley to Dun Mor if I thought it would stop this . . . but it will not. Dun Mor is a large and wealthy kingdom. They are fighting for sport and for challenge and to remind us of how powerful they are. They do not need this valley."

"Perhaps not. But they will take it if they can," said Nessan, frowning at Aengus. "All men fight for sport, but you are right when you say that Dun Mor fights as a show of strength. They are indeed large and wealthy, and they got that way by looking for any weakness that would let them take a little more of someone else's land—grove by grove and valley by valley.

"You had no choice but to meet them here today," the druid continued. "They nearly killed the sentries keeping watch here at our border and thought nothing about it. If you do not push these men back, you will find them at the fortress walls of Dun Gaoth before you know it."

Aengus continued to watch the raging fighters. "Trying to take a small border valley, and reveling in the fight that follows, is one thing. Trying to invade our home is quite another. They do not want a true killing war any more than we do. There would be few men left in Eire if every battle was to the death."

"We can only hope you are right, King Aengus," said Sean. "The men of Dun Mor are well known for their arrogance and aggression. Are you willing to take such a risk, by allowing them to intrude on your valley instead of fighting until you succeed in beating them back? Or perhaps you would prefer to simply call your men back and go home to Dun Gaoth?"

Aengus glanced at the druid. "And abandon this valley to Dun Mor? As you say, that would only encourage them to try to take more and more and more of our land. The battles would only get more desperate. Yet if I should encourage my men to continue this fight, that will only goad Dun Mor into battling right back." He took a deep breath and looked back down into the twilight valley. "It seems that whatever path I choose leads only to a fight."

"But is it not the duty of any king to lead his men into battle and inspire them to great feats?" asked Sean. "From just such tests as these come great warriors, next champions, future kings. Are not battles such as these necessary to find the best and strongest men?"

Aengus shrugged. "It is only a matter of time before another man is killed, and then a blood feud will spill over far beyond this place. There will never be an end to it. I will admit that once I was no different from the men we stand here watching . . . but that seems long ago."

He shook his head. "Battling for the sake of having something to brag about over your next cup of wine, and destroying what you claim to be defending, should not be the goal of a king. Or of any worthy man. But as I stand here, I do not know how to stop it."

The druids had no answer for him. All of them stood in silence as the night descended. The full moon would be rising soon, but the clouds were so thick that it would give them no light. The servants walked down near the battlefield with their torches held high, casting spots of wavering, glaring light across the little valley so that the determined fighters could continue with their battle.

Keavy stood in the heavy twilight on a hill outside Dun Gaoth. Somewhere behind the thick gray wall of cloud, the sun was setting. Before long the full moon would rise, but it would not be visible tonight—not behind those clouds.

She was surrounded by her family and by Coilean and his family, and by a number of the other highborn men and women who lived at the fortress and who had come out to witness this final agreement of Coilean and Keavy's contract of marriage—though she noticed that there seemed to be very few warriors among them. While they waited for the druids to arrive and perform the recitation of the contract, Keavy's mother wasted no time busying herself in conversation with the other women and learning all she could about the local gossip and customs.

Keavy gazed down at the lonely stone fortress that was Dun Gaoth. It was not at all like Dun Mor. Her familiar home was safely tucked away in the sheltering forest, surrounded only by a few small fields where the trees had been cleared away. It was well protected and would never be seen unless one knew exactly where to look.

Dun Gaoth sat wide-open to the sky on the crown of a wide, smooth hill. Its bright gray-white stone stood out against the grass as clearly as a white cloud against the sky, and it was just as vulnerable to the winds and rain.

Dun Mor was surrounded by two thick earthen walls, filled in between with the sharp broken branches of blackthorn trees. Anyone or anything that tried to climb over would instantly regret the attempt. But this place had only one single wall made from loose stones of all sizes, piled up so high that three men would have to stand on each other's shoulders just to peer over the top.

Strangest of all was Dun Gaoth's entrance. Instead of Dun Mor's tall wooden gates that could be thrown open wide to the world, this odd stone fortress had only a single narrow tunnel through one section of the southern wall. It was just large enough to allow one horse or cow to walk through, but that was all. Wooden wagons and fine chariots would have to be left outside, and so they were, sitting along the fortress's stone wall with their shafts resting on the damp bare ground.

There was little chance of anyone making off with them, she supposed. The fortress had no need for any sort of gate on either side of the tunnel, for the bare, treeless hills offered no place to hide for any who might try to creep up on it; they would be seen long before they could ever get close, since the inside walls had stone steps built into them all the way around. Lookouts could move about over any part of the wall whenever they wished—and so could the fortress's warriors if need be.

This circle of stone was so wide that some twenty neat stone buildings with thatched straw roofs were scattered across the ground it enclosed. There were rectangular houses large and small, and several wooden sheds where animals were sheltered or where the craftsmen worked in wood and metal. There was also one very large rectangular wood-and-stone building that must be the great hall, for it was so large that the entire population of the fortress could gather within it if they wished.

Beyond the huge fortress the hills rolled away to a partly tree-lined lake, scattered with small islands and narrowing at its far end to form a river that disappeared into the distance. Past the lake the dense forest began, and none could see any farther than that.

It was all far too open and unprotected for Keavy. She was very glad she would not be staying here beyond a few full moons. After that, her part of the bargain would be satisfied, her family could not say she had not attempted a marriage, and she would be able to return home and resume her peaceful, creative, and very comfortable life, waiting for the true husband fate would provide her.

Aengus knew the battle could not go on much longer. The men were exhausted, boastful as they were, and the torches would not burn forever. He began to feel cold as the wind picked up and sent a chill through his muddy clothes—a wind that sent up a great rattling through the bare branches of the oak and birch trees above them in the forest, and then through the bare apple trees, and finally struck them full-force.

The sudden wild wind whipped the warriors' cloaks about them and set their horses to stirring and moving about. It also made short work of blowing out the torches.

In the darkness, the battle's clanging and bashing ceased. Each war party withdrew to its own side of the valley. "Light the torches. Light the torches!" the men all shouted. "Hurry!" But try as they would, none of the servants could get another fire started. Each spark they managed to strike over their little pile of dry twigs and bits of straw torn from the fallen beehives was instantly extinguished by the driving winds.

Aengus saw his chance. "Come with me," he said to his three druids, and together they marched through the dark down the damp and muddy hillside to the very edge of the erstwhile battlefield.

"Men of Dun Gaoth!" he shouted. "I say to you that the battle is over for today. The light has gone and the winds have decided that there will be no more this night. Let us leave this place and return to our home!"

Voices floated out of the hazy darkness. "End the battle?"

"We've nearly won!"

"I need no light to fight the men of Dun Mor!"

"Neither do I! I can find them by their reeking stench alone!"

Now it was his warriors' turn to laugh, but Aengus shouted them down. "Listen to your druids! Their word on this is final. All three of them are in agreement, as well as I. You defy both your king and your druids if you do not obey!"

At last the men shut their mouths and listened to him. "Finbar! Nessan! Sean!" Aengus cried. "What say you to the warriors of Dun Gaoth?"

The three druids stepped forward to stand just before him. "We say that this battle is over," called Finbar. "The torches have gone out and will not be relit. This will have to be settled on another day."

"I agree," called Nessan.

"As do I," shouted Sean.

"Come with us, then, men of Dun Gaoth," Aengus commanded, turning away from the dark valley. "Your king and his druids are going home."

Slowly, reluctantly, his men obeyed, and began trudging up out of the valley. But, "Beware of us, scum of Dun Mor! There will be another time!" they called back over their shoulders. "We will come back and meet again. This valley is ours, not yours! And next time we will start at dawn, so there will be no torches for the wind to blow out!"

"Come on, come on," Aengus said in a growl as each hiked past him. "Get your horses and go. It's going to be a long ride home." He was as tired as he ever remembered being, not to mention covered with mud, and he wanted nothing more than to get to his house, bathe in the steaming tub of water his servants would have ready for him, sit down with a dish of beef and wheat bread and a cup of good wine, and fall asleep until sunrise on a stack of furs and soft cushions.

Yet such basic comforts were far from the thoughts of his men, Aengus knew. Already they were boasting of the stories they would tell—some true, some not entirely true—and thinking of the beer they would drink and the women they would brag to and sleep with.

Once, Aengus knew, he had been like them: full of life, and eager and hungry for all the thrills it had to offer. But that had been long ago in another time, almost in another life. He was thirty-eight years of age and felt far older, and he woke up each day to find that though he was a king, he was entirely alone.

The wind, which never seemed to cease in this place, set Keavy's dark red gown to flapping about her legs and nearly tore her blue-and-red cloak from the heavy bronze brooch that pinned it at her shoulder. She almost wished she had not worn the brooch, with its eagle feathers; wearing it to a marriage she had no wish to make seemed to dishonor the magical memory. But it was too late to do anything about it now. Keavy turned away from the winds, away from the sight of the lonely stone fortress of Dun Gaoth and the lake beyond it, and back to the gathering of people on the gently sloping side of the hill.

Her mother came hurrying over with a worried look. "What is it?" Keavy asked. "It will be dark soon. Why do they wait?"

Finola sighed. "It's the king," she said, her glance flicking over the crowd of people. "They're waiting for the king."

Keavy shrugged. "It is only a recitation of a contract. As long as the druids are here, why do we need the king?"

"I do not know. They're so different here from the people at home! They will say only that the king is a very important part of the marriage ritual in this place." She spread her hands. "Strange people, strange ways. It is simply what they do."

"Well, then, where is he? Did he not know that our contract was to be recited this day?"

Finola continued to glance around nervously. "It seems there is a battle going on," she whispered. "Between the warriors of Dun Gaoth and our warriors of Dun Mor. And you know how men are: when given the choice between fighting or listening to a marriage contract, which do you think they will choose?"

Keavy drew back and looked at her. "A battle? Is it anything serious?"

Finola threw up her hands and turned Keavy away from the crowds. "Quietly, quietly! Our men are fighting theirs right now!" she said in a hiss. "And we are all alone here, defenseless!"

"It is nothing new for the men of two tribes to fight each other for no purpose, especially on a fine day in early spring," Keavy said with a wry smile. "Hunting, gaming, drinking, fighting—it is all the same sport to them. I'm sure they will be back soon."

"Oh, I hope you are right." Finola sighed. "It's probably nothing serious. It just doesn't seem like a good omen on the day of a contract between two kingdoms!"

Keavy could only shake her head and try to smile a little.

The sun could not be seen, hidden as it was behind the heavy gray clouds, but Keavy knew it must have finally slipped below the horizon—the light quickly began to fade. Three long torches were carried to the top of the hill and lit against the gathering twilight. The assembled group would either have to have the ceremony now or else go inside and have it tomorrow. The dark of night was no time to start a marriage.

At last the two druids—one from Dun Mor and one from Dun Gaoth—walked out through the narrow tunnel in the huge stone wall of the fortress and made their way up the hill to the waiting crowd. "Gather 'round," they called, standing near the torches at the very highest point. "Gather 'round. This contract of marriage must not be delayed. The king will return when he returns. Coilean of Dun Gaoth, and Keavy of Dun Mor—come forward together and stand here before us."

Slowly, picking up the hem of her skirts, Keavy walked to the top of the hill. The torches snapped and guttered in the wind and did little to keep the gloom away. The only thing their light showed her was Coilean's pale face, as still and sullen as ever as he paced across the windblown hilltop to stand beside her and face the waiting druids.

Keavy closed her eyes as the recitation of the contract of marriage began. It was a cold and eerie scene, and nothing at all as she had imagined. No matter how many times she told herself this was only a formality so that she and Coilean might please their families and thus gain their own freedom, a feeling of despair began to creep over her. This was not how she had ever thought her wedding would be.

No, not like this—not out here on this barren, windy hilltop with not a tree in sight save for the very distant forest beyond the lake, disappearing now into the darkness; not standing in a bloodred gown beneath a cold, dark sky for this dull listing of her property and his property and how this would be a marriage of equals who would live together at Dun Gaoth, a place she had never seen before and that only felt cold and exposed when compared to her familiar forest home; and especially not standing beside this pale and sullen young man who had no more love for her than she did for him.

Mercifully, the recitation did not take long. "So, with this agreement, Coilean and Keavy are now husband and wife. The feast is ready for them in the great hall. Go there now and await the arrival of King Aengus." Just that quickly it was over, and everyone turned and left the windswept hill for the stone fortress below.

Keavy could only watch them go, staring down again at that cold and lonely place where almost everyone was a complete stranger to her . . . and where the man she had just married was anyone but the man she loved.

Chapter Four

Flying over the dense forests of Dun Mor to the open hills of Dun Gaoth took, it seemed to the great golden eagle, no time at all. His powerful wings would carry him high on the winds, where he could look down on all of his tired men as they rode slowly home after a long day's battle.

Even in the darkness he would have no trouble seeing them. The light of the rising full moon would show him every detail, every tired face, and every horse, but he did not have to travel at their slow and plodding pace. He could soar high above it all, the king of all he surveyed, with the freedom to go where he liked in the blink of an eye—

"Wouldn't it be fine if we could fly home the way *they* can fly home?"

Aengus blinked at the sound of Parlan's voice, coming out of his reverie. He glanced up into the deepening darkness just in time to see a pair of crows fly into the nearby forest for the night. "I suppose it would," he said, sitting up straighter on his horse and stretching his tired arms and legs as he rode.

The fatigue after the long day, the quiet darkness surrounding his men, the steady, rocking strides of his horse, and the warmth of his thick wool cloak had all combined to lull him to sleep . . . or, perhaps, into something like a dream state, where he remembered things from very far away and very long ago.

"It would be a fine thing indeed," Aengus said. "At this pace, the moon will be high by the time we get home."

It seemed that his every joint ached and his every muscle was sore, far beyond the way they should feel for a man of thirty-eight years. He stretched one arm and felt only discomfort. Once he would have felt strength and power in this arm, power enough to let him soar above the earth . . . but that had been very long ago, and on this night he had no reason to believe such a thing would ever happen again.

Following behind her new husband, Keavy walked through the cold, damp, stone-lined tunnel that ran through the enormous stone wall of Dun Gaoth and stepped into the bare earth of the fortress yard. The white clay of the small rectangular houses seemed to leap and jump in the wavering light of the scattered torches, and the entire place was filled with ominous shadows as she walked across the grounds. Keavy was very glad to reach the doorway of the large hall that sat across the center of the fortress, and walked inside hoping to see something like normalcy.

She was relieved to see that the Great Hall of Dun Gaoth was much like the one at Dun Mor, though this building was rectangular instead of round. There was an enormous circular stone hearth in the center with a good hot fire burning in it to cook the two whole sheep turning above on iron spits. The sweet-smelling smoke rose up to the hole cut in the thatched-straw roof high above their heads and vanished into the night.

It seemed to be a fine place where a king would conduct business and invite guests to enjoy his hospitality. Yet at the same time there was a feeling of everything being slightly worn—a little old—and somehow not quite cared for as it should be. The floor was thick with straw, but that straw was a little gray. There were two neat rows of wooden slabs sitting on the straw, with cushions and fleeces and furs placed on either side of those slabs—but a second look showed that the wooden slabs were scratched and dull, the cushions were in need of repair, and the fleeces and furs were bare in spots and not entirely clean.

Keavy told herself that this was simply normal wear. No doubt no one would notice such things but her. Perhaps guests were simply more frequent here at Dun Gaoth than at Dun Mor, and items would need repair more often—but she could not help but feel that these things had never known the touch of a craftsman's hand, nor the needle of a seamstress, since the day they were first made.

She looked away. In the rear of the hall, servants hurried back and forth as they prepared food, and they began bringing out leather skins of wine and stacks of battered bronze plates and nicked wooden cups for their guests.

People took their places on furs and cushions, and Keavy began to relax a bit. It had been a long and nerve-racking day, and a good meal and a little wine was exactly what she needed right now. That and perhaps some pleasant conversation with a few of the others here in this new place would be most welcome—and she would not notice how bare the fleeces might be in spots.

She found a place on a soft gray fur near the end of the first row of wooden slabs. Coilean sat down beside her, and her parents and his took their places across from them. "There. You see, dear, it is not so very different from the king's hall at home," her mother said. "I'm sure you will be very happy here."

Keavy could only smile politely, glance briefly at Coilean—who looked nowhere but at his plate—and take the first sip of her wine from the wooden cup.

The blackberry wine tasted very good indeed, though she could not help but wonder why such important folk as wedding guests would not merit the use of golden plates and cups. Ah, well, it was not her place to ask. Keavy set down her half-empty cup and began to realize how hungry she was, but a quick look around showed her that no one was yet being served. The servants all hovered anxiously near the back of the hall, hurrying about and whispering together but making no move to bring out any of the food.

Keavy caught her father's eye. "Why are we waiting?" she whispered.

Her father glanced at the place at the very end of the row, just across the corner from Keavy. It was set with a bronze plate and cup that were only a little better than the ones passed out to the guests, but no one was yet sitting there. She also realized that though everyone was seated, a number of the places were still empty.

"They're still waiting for the king and his men," her father said. "They should all be returning home soon, and these people are determined to wait until they do."

"They are certainly determined," Keavy remarked with a sigh, glancing over her shoulder again toward the hearth, where the sheep turned on spits. The delicious smell of roasting meat filled the hall, and Keavy was as hungry as she had ever been in her life. "I do hope the king comes back soon," she added.

A short way down the row, she noticed that a few of the women were giving her knowing smiles as they looked at her, even laughing and giggling behind their hands. They nudged each other and glanced back at her.

Keavy frowned, wondering what they found so amusing. Weren't they hungry too? Then she looked over at Coilean, who had already drained his wine cup and sat looking furtively around for more. He paid no attention at all to her or to anyone else.

The women at the table must be thinking of the wedding night to come. Of course, they did not know that she and Coilean had made an agreement to have a marriage in name only and would be going their separate ways just as soon as three full moons had come and gone. Keavy smiled back at them, as prettily as she could manage, and then quickly drank down the last of her blackberry wine.

The thick clouds overhead had begun to break up. As the line of weary riders approached the stone tunnel of Dun Gaoth, the moon shone down from the highest point of the sky, and its faint white light alternated with deep shadow. King Aengus rode at the head of his men through the tunnel leading inside his fortress, and when he came out the other side he saw Seanan, his personal servant, waiting for him.

"Ah, Seanan, there is no one here that I am happier to see," Aengus said, sliding down from his weary horse. He began pulling off his mud-caked leather armor and boots and dropped them in a heap on the ground, not caring that he was left standing barefoot in only his stained linen tunic and woolen trews. "When I see you, I see good food and a hot bath and a comfortable bed beside my own hearthfire. And I don't mind saying I cannot get to them soon enough."

Seanan smiled as one of the horse boys led away the king's mount, and handed his master an enormous thick rib of hot mutton dripping with grease. "I do have all of those things ready for you, my king," he said. "But I must also tell you that another task awaits you this night. There has been a contract of marriage made between a man of Dun Gaoth and a woman of Dun Mor."

"From Dun Mor." Aengus drew a deep breath and closed his eyes. "Good. Good. All the more reason for them to avoid a killing war with us. Where is she now?"

Seanan began to walk toward the king's house, and Aengus went along with him. "All are still in the hall awaiting your return so that they might begin the feast."

Aengus stopped short. "Still waiting? They have not yet begun to eat?"

"They are patiently waiting for you and your warriors to return, King Aengus."

Aengus stared at his servant, and then set off walking again toward his house. "Send someone to tell them that the feast is to be served at once! And kindly remind me to leave word, should I be away on another such occasion, that there is no need for them to wait for me again. A battle to defend our kingdom cannot be planned for the most convenient time! It is hardly the best way to start off married life together, waiting and waiting while the food grows cold and the guests grow hungry and bored. And it will not make the new bride look kindly on the king."

Seanan smiled as he closed the door after Aengus. "She will look upon you kindly enough, as all brides do."

He glanced at his servant. "What man was it who married today?"

"It was Coilean, my king."

"Coilean? Coilean the bard, the son of Dallan and Sorcha?"

"The very same."

Aengus almost laughed, and he took a large bite out of the mutton rib. "I thought I heard some rumor of a match being arranged for him, but I thought it to be only gossip. I can only imagine what sort of woman would agree to marry a pup like Coilean."

Seanan glanced at him with raised eyebrows. "This one might surprise you. She is . . . not what one might expect a wife of Coilean's to be. She—"

Aengus raised his hand. "Please, tell me no more. I will see her when I see her, and that will be soon enough, I know, for me and for this lady."

Suddenly there was a great rustling and stirring among the guests. Keavy looked up to see that all of the others were quickly getting to their feet and walking toward the wide center doors. "What has happened?" she asked, looking from her parents to the departing crowd and back again. "Where is everyone going?"

Her mother stood up and took a few steps toward the crowd, listening closely to its conversations. Then she hurried back, beckoning to Keavy. "Come, come! It's the king and his men. They've returned! Hurry, now!"

Keavy got to her feet, paying no attention at all to Coilean, and started toward the door. "I'd be happy to see every wolf and warrior in Eire gathered together at the gates, if it means we can eat," she murmured. Lifting the hem of her heavy red skirts, she walked outside with the others into the cool damp air of the spring night.

She raised her cloak up over her head as a light rain began to fall, tucking her long braids beneath the heavy brown-and-purple plaid. The torchlit yards of Dun Gaoth now teemed with activity as men dismounted from their horses, servants led the animals away, and the men milled about talking with each other and with their families before starting toward their houses to wash and find clean clothes so they could join the feast in the hall.

Keavy stood near the back of the throng, near her parents, watching yet another crowd of strangers of which she was now expected to be a part. She tried to tell herself that they were undoubtedly much like the men and the families of her own home at Dun Mor, and that she would manage to live among them for the short space of three full moons. Yet it was strange to see so many unfamiliar faces in a fortress so very different from her own, and she pulled her heavy cloak even higher up so that the edge of it fell down over her eyes and left her face in shadow.

Then she looked up to see that two men, one very tall and broad-shouldered and heavily muscled, and the other small and gray-haired and dressed in plain servant's garb, walked very close to where she stood. The tall man wore a long iron sword at his hip but there was nothing else about him to say who he was . . . and then he turned to look at her as he and his servant walked past, and both of them slowed and stopped.

At first he was only a figure of shadow, a tall silhouette in the torchlight whose broad shoulders and great, deep chest nearly blocked out the soft light coming from the torches behind him. He must surely be the king, Keavy thought, for he was one of the largest men she had ever seen.

Then he took another step forward, coming to stand within the wavering torchlight—and what she saw resembled anything but a king.

He wore a filthy, mud-stained, long plain linen tunic, with brown woolen trews that were equally crusted with mud. His feet were bare save for the dirt on them. His hair and beard seemed to be dark brown, but she could not tell if that was its natural color or if it was just more mud. He held an enormous rib of mutton in one hand and wiped the greasy fingers of the other on whatever edge of his linen tunic held the least amount of dirt.

Keavy made herself look up and meet his gaze. The face was that of a man somewhere near the age of forty, perhaps, but who looked and plainly felt far older. His eyes held weariness and even a touch of boredom as he gazed out at this little party that had interrupted his supper after his long day, merely to pay him their respects when he would no doubt have preferred to be left in peace to eat and rest.

Keavy almost giggled at the sight of him. The wine and the fatigue were beginning to make her feel a bit light-headed. This king was certainly not very impressive! *Ah, well.* He would not be her king for long.

"My lord, this is the Lady Keavy from Dun Mor, newly married to Coilean of Dun Gaoth," said the gray-haired serving man. "And my lady, before you stands Aengus, our king."

"Good evening to you, King Aengus," Keavy said, bowing her head to him. "I am sorry we have disturbed you this night."

"It is no trouble, my lady." He tried to hide the half-eaten mutton rib behind his tunic, but it was far too late for such niceties. "You have not disturbed me at all."

His voice surprised her. It was quiet and measured, not at all gruff, as she had expected. From the sound of him he was a courteous and educated man of high station, entirely at odds with his coarse and dirty appearance. Yet she could hear the patient weariness in his voice, and noted how his broad shoulders were heavy with fatigue.

Yet tired though he was, his eyes were as sharp and clear and aware as those of any man she had ever seen . . . large gold-hazel eyes with thick, dark eyebrows and heavy lashes. Had she seen nothing but those eyes alone, she might have known she was looking at a king.

As he held her gaze, a silence fell around them. No one moved or spoke or even breathed, it seemed, as those sharp eyes flicked from her face to her neck to her shoulder to her—

Keavy drew herself up tall as indignation set in. Even though she was hidden beneath the heavy cloak, he was looking her up and down as though she were a mare he'd been offered to ride. She held his gaze until at last his eyes flicked away, and then she too looked away, though she held her head high. Those eyes and that voice had indeed fooled her, but it was clear to her now that the king of Dun Gaoth was just as coarse and common as his appearance made him out to be.

"I must apologize for staring at you, Lady Keavy," the king said then. "It is not every day that such a lovely bride comes to Dun Gaoth. Let me offer good wishes to you and to your husband, Coilean the bard."

She nodded once, still holding him off with her steady gaze. "Thank you."

He glanced down at himself, suddenly seeming self-conscious about his grimy state. "I must again apologize, this time for the way I look. It was a long day of battle for me and my men." He tried to smile at her. "I promise you that when next we meet, I will be bathed and fit for your company."

She gave him a polite smile in return. "Of course," she agreed, wondering why he thought she would care. "I wish you good evening, King Aengus."

"Good evening to you, Lady Keavy," he said, and then he continued on his way with his servant.

Keavy let out her breath and turned to follow the others inside the hall, where at last they would be allowed to eat. The smell of the roasting mutton drifted out through the open doors, making her ever more ravenous—but she found her way was blocked, yet again, by the two druids who had recited her marriage contract.

"We will be back for you after the feast," said the first.

"It is our charge to escort the bride to the marriage bed," said the second.

Feeling the smiling glances of the crowd as they walked past her, Keavy began to blush. Did the druids have to be so very obvious and public about the fact that this was the first night of her marriage—as if no one knew what a married couple did on that night? Well, they would soon be proved wrong about this particular couple, though they would never know it!

She looked around for her mother, and saw that Finola had wasted no time in finding a group of women with whom to gossip. Several of them were gathered around her, talking away and apparently telling a most interesting story, for Finola listened intently and then looked somewhat shocked and surprised, though she recovered quickly and went on chatting in her typical animated fashion.

Keavy went over to her mother and took her arm, smiling as she drew Finola away from her newfound friends. "Come inside, Mother; you must be as hungry as I am. The feast is finally ready for us."

"Oh, Keavy, you are such a good girl," her mother said with something like sympathy. "You saw the king, did you not? I am sure he will be quite presentable before . . . before he sees you again."

Keavy almost laughed again. "I'm sure he will—though I'm not sure why everyone seems to think that should be so important to me."

Her mother glanced up at her and seemed to be about to say something, but then changed her mind and patted her daughter's arm instead. "There's a good girl, Keavy," she said. "After all, it's only for one night."

One night? Keavy continued on her way to the hall, covering her mother's hand with her own and smiling a little to herself. She and Coilean would not have even that much, though she saw no reason why anyone needed to know about that!

Chapter Five

Aengus walked across the straw to the back of his rectangular stone house, moved aside the tall leather screen, and stood beside his fur-covered sleeping ledge. Unstrapping his sword belt and dropping it, he sat down on the ledge and reveled in the feel of the warm, dry straw against his cold, tired, mud-stained feet.

"She is an uncommonly lovely bride, if I may say so, my king."

Aengus glanced up. Seanan stood beside the central stone hearth arranging plates and cups and good hot food. "With her heavy cloak pulled up, I could scarcely see her face—though she was quite tall and her voice rather pretty, I will admit."

"She seemed to . . . ah . . . look forward to seeing you later this evening."

He laughed a little. "Seanan, I have been a king for some fifteen years, and that is long enough for me to know that no bride looks forward to this aspect of her marriage ritual. And neither does her husband."

"She was quite at ease when she spoke to you . . . and yet you do not sound as though you look forward to it either, my king," said Seanan, carefully lifting a wooden plate and cup. "Surely you know that you are the envy of every other man at Dun Gaoth. Any of them would eagerly change places with you this night."

"And none more so than Coilean, I am sure." He took the plate of roasted strips and chunks of mutton, watercress rolled in meat drippings, and hot wheat bread thick with butter that Seanan handed to him, and set it down on the ledge before him, quickly picking up the dagger that lay across the plate and stabbing a thick chunk of meat with it.

"So at last Coilean's family has managed to find him a wife," he said, holding up the dagger and chewing off a large bite of the meat. "Dallan was a fearless fighter and ever a tireless servant of Dun Gaoth . . . yet as sometimes happens, his son simply has no talent for either."

He accepted a cup of beer from Seanan and went on eating. "I expect no trouble from Coilean tonight. He will do whatever he is told to do without protest—at least, no public protest—even to the point of marrying whatever woman his family chooses for him." Aengus sighed. "Well, no matter. She will be here soon enough. Just prepare me a hot bath with plenty of soap, good Seanan, so that I might do my duty without offending this new bride of Coilean's."

Given permission to eat at last, the hungry diners made short work of the whole roast sheep and the watercress and wheat bread and butter. The food was adequate, but like the furnishings, it too seemed to suffer for lack of proper attention. The meat tended to be either nearly burned or still cold, and the bread was blackened on the outside and too thick and soft on the inside. But everyone was so hungry that Keavy heard no murmur of complaint.

Soon—for it was very late, so late that Keavy could actually see the full moon through the hole cut in the high straw roof above the enormous hearth—the people began to rise from their cushions and furs and leave the great hall for their houses and the warmth of their own beds.

Keavy now wanted nothing more than sleep—a good night's sleep alone on her own private ledge, as she and Coilean had agreed. And she was more certain than ever that she would have no desire to break that agreement. He still barely glanced at her, or at his parents, and looked every bit as tired as she felt.

Strangely, she felt a twinge of disappointment. She would have nothing to look forward to on this night save a pile of soft furs in a strange house. Never had she thought to spend the night of her wedding like this! But one more look at Coilean's sullen face was all it took to convince her that the furs were definitely the better choice, wedding night or not.

"Shall we go to our house, my husband?" she asked politely. "I am sure you must be as weary and as anxious for sleep as I am."

He glanced up quickly. His expression was blank, even for Coilean, as though he did not understand what she was saying. And then Keavy became aware that the two druids from Dun Mor—one of whom had recited the contract at her hilltop marriage ceremony—stood directly across from her.

"Lady Keavy," the first one said, "it is time. You may come with us now."

Keavy frowned and looked at her family, then at Coilean—but all four of them had gotten to their feet and stepped back to stand quietly behind the druids. Her mother gave a little smile, and for a moment looked as though she might actually giggle—but mercifully remained quiet.

Her own husband, Keavy noted, had walked right past her to stand with his parents and study the straw on the floor.

Strange people, strange ways, Keavy thought, remembering what her mother had said earlier that day. Well, she would go along with almost anything right now if it meant she could get out of this awful red gown, lie down, and go to sleep. She folded her hands and turned to the druids. "You wish to escort my husband and me to our home?"

But the druids only stared at her as though she

were a simple child who did not understand their language. "We are here to take you to the king's house," the second druid said, and the two of them stepped back and bowed as though politely allowing her to go first.

"The *king's* house? Why would I go there?" Keavy looked at the two of them, puzzled for a moment. "I have already greeted him this evening."

"Because," said the first druid, with heavy patience, "this is your wedding night."

Keavy looked from one to the other, her expression unwavering. "I am aware of what night it is. My husband will await me at our home. Should I not go to him?"

"Lady Keavy," the second druid said gently, "you do not seem to understand. You are not simply going to the king's house. You are going to the king's bed."

For a long moment Keavy could only stare at them.

"The king's . . . bed?" She blinked, looking at each of the druids. "I could not possibly have heard you correctly. I thought you said I was to go to the king's bed."

Again she looked from one to the other, but both men remained silent. Then she turned to her mother.

"Oh . . . ah . . . now, Keavy, there's a good girl," Finola said with some anxiety, twisting her hands together and trying to smile at her daughter. "As

I said, it's only for one night. It's the custom here, you see, and—"

"Custom? You are telling me I am expected to spend the night of my wedding with the king instead of my husband, that this is simply the 'custom,' as though that were all the explanation I might require?" Keavy could only stare as the realization began to sink in. "Did you know of this?"

"I did not!" her mother protested, throwing up her hands. "I knew nothing of this until just a short time ago, when I spoke to the other women while you were being introduced to the king. They told me of it."

"Have you so much as *heard* of such a thing before?" Keavy asked.

"Why . . . I suppose I have, in some of the old stories. But—"

"I have never heard of this before," Keavy whispered, "except in an ancient tale or two that I took to be just that—simply tales. But you are telling me this is actually done in this place?"

Her mother held out her hands in a gesture of helplessness, and then shrugged. "It is a very old custom, my daughter, one that is no longer followed at Dun Mor—but as you see, some of the older kingdoms still keep to it. Such things are not easily changed."

"But why?" Keavy asked. "Why would anyone want to force a bride away from her husband on her wedding night and expect her to . . . to sleep with another man?"

The first druid drew himself up with some indignation. "The king is not just another man. He is the king. He—"

"He is not my husband!"

"But he is the king, and you are a bride from outside these walls, and so for this night he is indeed your husband," said the second druid. "You may have discarded the ancient and lawful ways at your home of Dun Mor, but we can assure you they are most certainly still practiced here."

"As well they should be," said the first. "You asked why we should follow such a custom, Lady Keavy, and so I will tell you." He held her gaze, speaking all the while in a low and serious tone. "The ancients knew how important—how *powerful*—is the virginity of any bride. Should the taking of such be left to just any man—a man who may not himself possess the wisdom or the strength of spirit to give the task the respect and the attention it deserves? The ancients found a better and more respectful way, and we follow their example to this day."

"Far better a king than an awkward, drunken husband at such a time, would you not agree, Lady Keavy?"

"Far better a man who loves me," she answered faintly, and started to back away from them.

But she soon found herself up against the solid inner wall of the great hall. "You already have the love of your husband," said the first druid. "And he will have all the rest of your days together to show you that love."

"On this night you have an ancient duty, and

so does the king," said the second. "And now it is time to go to the house of the king."

Keavy could only stare at them in shock. She wanted desperately to tell them that it was not a true marriage, it was only a harmless sham to let her and Coilean please their families and then move on with their lives as they wished. But how could she tell these druids that her marriage was nothing but a lie?

She tried to simply raise her head and stare coolly back at them. "What if I refuse?" she asked, her voice shaking only a little. "Will your king force me, if I refuse?"

"He will not—but neither will your marriage be recognized as valid. You would again be an unmarried woman of Dun Mor, just as you were when you arrived here, and you and your family would have to renegotiate your contract of marriage with Coilean."

Keavy closed her eyes. She had done all of this solely to keep the life she wanted for herself, and Coilean had done the same. And now it had come to this!

"I wish to stay married to Coilean, but I will not go to the bed of another man," she insisted again, though the trembling in her voice was becoming more obvious. "I will not."

"Then you have no marriage at all, for it will not have been consummated, and you will return to Dun Mor at sunrise."

The druid's voice was final. Keavy cast about for some way out, for some other choice, some way to escape this awful predicament—but the two druids came to stand on either side of her, and her mother and father stood with them, and Coilean and his family and a small group of people from Dun Gaoth crowded around. Keavy was entirely surrounded and found herself being urged and pushed and all but carried to the door of the hall.

There was no way out. Strong hands held her by the arms in a polite but very firm escort across the yard. "You cannot mean to make me do this!" she said in a hiss between clenched teeth. "You cannot be serious about this! And surely that man I met in the yard—that old, tired man, as filthy as any brute farmer—could not possibly be your king!"

No one made any answer. Behind them, in the crowd, Keavy thought she heard a few snickering laughs and a few whispered comments. "It's to be expected. . . ." "A young bride, she's frightened of the king—she'll come around soon enough. . . ." "She just needs a bit of encouragement. . . ."

Keavy tried to pull her arms away from the tight grip on either side of her, but it was no use. "At least show me the real king!" she pleaded. "I know it cannot be the man I saw in the yard! Please, at least take me to the real king, whoever he is!"

Fear gave way to anger as her temper reached the boiling point. "I knew nothing of this! I never agreed to this! I've been deceived and I've been sold to a old man dirtier than any brute rock man, but who still managed to look me up and down with the eyes of an eagle!"

There came only more laughter and whispers from behind her as she was carried along by her unrelenting escort. Before she knew it she was standing in front of the largest of Dun Gaoth's houses, where a torch sputtered and flared in the heavy dampness of the night air.

One of the druids rapped on the wooden door. After a few moments it swung slowly open, and a small gray-haired man peered out at the visiting crowd.

"Good evening to you, Seanan," said the first druid. "Please tell King Aengus that we are here with the new bride."

The gray-haired man bowed and then disappeared back inside, leaving the door partly open. The guests fell silent as they waited. And to Keavy's astonishment, from within the quiet house came the loud, rasping, raucous sound of snoring.

Keavy tried to look at the two druids who still held her arms, but they only stared straight ahead as though they heard nothing at all.

"Your king certainly does seem anxious to see me," she said, finding it impossible to keep silent. "You say he has this great solemn duty to perform, yet we arrive to find him asleep and *snoring*."

"Lady Keavy," said the first druid, still watching the house, "please prepare yourself. The king will be here in a moment."

The snoring suddenly stopped. There was a

great creaking and rustling from inside the house. Then the door opened wide and another man appeared in the doorway.

He was so tall, and his shoulders so wide, that he all but blocked out the soft light coming from within. In the wavering torchlight she could see his face once again, and this time the impression was rather different.

The eyes were the same. Again Keavy saw the gold-hazel gaze boring right through her, the gaze of a man accustomed to making decisions and being obeyed. But while the rest of them had been dining hungrily at the long-delayed feast, the king had been bathing and changing into fresh clothes.

His long hair, clean and damp and combed out smooth, fell down past his shoulders and was a vibrant brown. His smooth beard and thick mustache, equally clean, were of the same shade and set off his ruddy skin. He wore a new linen tunic over trews of heavy dark green wool and soft boots of folded dark brown leather. The king's torque—made from a twisted ribbon of shining gold bent into a near-complete circle, and capped at each end with the fierce gold likeness of an eagle's head—rested at his neck. His iron sword was in place in a plain leather scabbard at his belt.

At least he was clean now.

"Good evening to you, Lady Keavy," he said. It was the same low, quiet voice she had heard earlier. "You are welcome here. Please come inside the house of the king."

He stepped back, and the two druids practically lifted Keavy up the two steps into the house. They walked her in, past the raised square hearth in the center, over the fresh, thick straw on the floor, and all the way to the back of the dwelling where tall screens of leather painted with trees, clouds, and birds concealed the king's sleeping ledge.

Keavy's family and Coilean's quickly crowded in behind them, along with as many of the other men and women as could manage to jam themselves inside. Finally the two druids eased their grip on Keavy's arms, and she rubbed the bruised skin where they had held her for so long. But as she looked at the crowd behind her, she realized she still could not escape—not with a mob like that between her and the door.

The heat was rising inside the packed house. Keavy pushed back the top of her cloak from her head and let it fall back on her shoulders, struggling to catch a breath of air inside the stifling house. She stole a glance back at the king. Perhaps she would be able to reason with him, since it was plain there would be no talking to the druids.

But whereas before the king had merely regarded her with polite interest, he was now staring openly at her with confusion in his eyes—as if he knew her, or thought he knew her, but could not remember where or when.

His gaze flicked to the brooch she wore, more easily seen now that the top of her cloak rested on her shoulders instead of bunching in heavy brown-and-purple folds where she had clutched it close to her neck against the rain. His eyes narrowed as he looked at the brooch, its gold with white enameling that she always wore, its three feathers that had been a gift from the golden eagle so many years before.

She saw him look again from the feathers to her face, and it seemed that his breath caught. He opened his mouth as if to speak to her—but then the druid beside her began to speak, and Keavy made herself look away from the frankly staring man.

"Aengus, king of Dun Gaoth, we have brought to your house this night a woman who has married a man of your kingdom. As was the law and custom of the ancients, who taught us to do the same, we have brought this new-made bride to the king under the law of the First Night.

"This is not a duty to be undertaken lightly, or by just any man. The blood of a woman is a powerful thing, a thing to be respected, and so the ancients taught us that it is best for a king to be the man to take a woman's blood, for no man has more power."

With that the druid stepped back—as much as he could in the overly crowded house—and placed Aengus's hand over Keavy's. Her eyes widened at the sight of her slender white fingers disappearing beneath his large hand, roughened by sun and wind and weapons and with strength enough to crush her if he chose. The two of them stood unmoving, hand in hand, while everyone slowly filed out of the house.

Keavy's parents, among the last to leave, gave her a small wave as they started out the door. "Remember your duty to your husband, daughter," her father said.

"Oh, you'll make a wonderful wife," her mother added with a beaming smile. "Remember your duty, as your father said, and we will see you once or twice each year."

Then the door closed and the house was empty, save for Keavy and Aengus still standing together with her hand covered by his.

Chapter Six

Instantly Keavy pulled her hand away. She was a little surprised, and relieved, to find that the king made no attempt at all to hold her, but simply let her go with no resistance. Yet Keavy's heart was beginning to pound and her anxiety continued to rise, even though all the king did was sit down on the edge of his stone hearth and fold his hands together in front of him.

She began moving toward the door. How could she possibly escape this? No doubt the house was surrounded by the same mob that had brought her here. She was alone in this home with this man, this powerful man who was a complete stranger to her but with whom she was expected to—

"Lady Keavy," he said quietly. "Will you come and talk with me for a time, that I might get to know you better?"

She whirled to face him. "I will not. I cannot do this," she cried. Her voice shook but she did not care if he noticed. "I cannot! I knew nothing of this custom before I came here. No one said anything about this to me!"

"I understand," he said, still sitting quietly. "You thought to spend this night with your husband. But this is only one night out of all that you and he will have together. I assure you I have done this many times, and I understand how you feel. I will do my best to make certain the experience is . . . not unpleasant for you."

Keavy almost laughed. "I am afraid you do not understand at all," she murmured, looking away from him. Then she raised her head and stared straight at him. "I cannot do this. You may send me away, King Aengus, or make me a servant or a slave—I do not care—but I will not have this!"

She turned toward the door. She thought he would get up and try to stop her. But all she heard was his calm voice from where he sat on the hearth. "You are not a prisoner here. I will not force you to do anything. If you are not willing to stay, no one will attempt to make you."

Quickly she turned and reached for the iron latch of the door with shaking hands, hoping she could get through the crowd outside. They might not be as accommodating as the king seemed to think they would be. But just as she got hold of the latch, Aengus spoke again.

"You may go if you wish, Lady Keavy. But you must understand that if you leave this house with your marriage unconsummated, the law of Dun Gaoth requires that the contract of marriage that you have made with Coilean this day be declared invalid. You will immediately be escorted back to Dun Mor, back to the home of your parents."

He smiled a little, though he was not mocking her. "And you and Coilean and your families would no doubt be the subjects of poems and satires and gossip for many years to come. Would you risk so much just to avoid a custom that is strange to you but has been observed here for longer than any can recall?"

Keavy lowered her hand. Slowly she turned until she faced him again. "It is more than just having to return home in disgrace," she admitted, "for both me and for Coilean."

A flicker of interest showed in his eyes. "How is that?" he asked. He gave her a wise look. "Surely you will not tell me that you love him."

She clasped her hands in front of her and took one step—but only one—in his direction. "I see no reason why I should not tell you the entire story. It will all come out anyway once I am sent back to Dun Mor."

She drew a deep breath. "You are right. Coilean and I did not choose to marry each another. We were all but forced to marry by our families. Mine insisted that I was spending my life caring for them when I should be starting my own family, and Coilean . . . well, his parents were determined to keep him away from a certain servant girl. He wished to marry her, but they would never approve of such a match."

"Forced to marry? I do not see how urging a

grown daughter to devote herself to her own family instead of to her parents, and encouraging a son to make a good match, could force two people to marry against their wills."

Keavy looked away. "My parents insisted they would send me to live among the servants if I did not accept this match, for I have refused all others. And Coilean's family threatened to have his servant girl sent away where he would never find her—and he believed them."

"As you believed your own family."

She nodded. "I did. Coilean and I both knew they would not relent this time."

"Would your parents truly send you away to live as a servant?"

"Worse. Not only would they send me away, but while I was there, they would find me another husband and force me to accept a match one way or another."

"So . . ." The king stood up and moved a pace toward her, stopping to run his fingers over the stones of his hearth. "Both you and Coilean found yourselves in the position of having to marry, or else face severe consequences—and so you agreed to marry each other in order to appease your families."

She looked away. "We did."

"And I suppose the two of you intended to live out your lives with a sham of a marriage, and simply take what lovers you wished in secret?"

Keavy raised her chin. "We had no such intention. Our contract of marriage required us to stay together for at least the duration of three full moons, and we agreed between ourselves to accept this. After that time we would request that the marriage be dissolved on the grounds that I am barren, since there was no chance of there ever being children between us. We would have therefore kept to the agreement with our parents and then been free to live our lives as we wished. Coilean could go and marry his servant girl, whom he loves, and I would be left in peace to pursue the arts of fabric and embroidery and live as I wished, free to . . . to . . ."

"To do what, Lady Keavy?"

She stared into his eyes for a moment as she searched for an answer, then finally looked away. "To look for the one man whom I might truly love," she whispered.

"I do find it difficult to believe that no other man has ever wanted to take you for his wife," Aengus said. "To believe that no man has ever loved you . . . or that you have never loved any man."

She smiled a little. "There have been other offers of marriage—but I was never drawn to any of those who made them."

He nodded. "I would have been quite surprised had you told me no man ever wanted you. Surprised . . . and disbelieving." He took another step toward her, and then leaned back against the hearth again with his hands resting on the stone on either side of him. He fixed her with his steady, level gaze.

"I will not hesitate to tell you that you are among the most beautiful of women," he said. "Never have I seen skin so fair, hair so—"

But Keavy whirled away from him and faced the door, crossing her arms over her chest. "I can only imagine how many women you must have seen, King Aengus, alone with you here in your house, whether by their own choice or no," she said, her voice shaking again. "I can only wonder how many times you have said these same words to those same women."

All she heard from him was a gentle sigh. "I had no more choice in the matter than did any of the women. I was just doing my duty as king, and nothing more."

Keavy snorted.

"And I told you the truth when I said how beautiful you were. Your name means one who is slender, tall, and graceful, and so you are . . . as slender and graceful as a young willow tree, and so tall that your eyes and mine would nearly be level with each other. And such beautiful eyes they are, pale green like the new grass in early spring, and it distresses me to see them as they are now, filled with anger and with fear, because I believe I have seen those eyes before . . . and they held only happiness and curiosity on that spring day so long ago."

She looked up at him, studying his face a little more closely. "What do you mean? I am certain we have never met. Why do you believe you saw me years ago?"

He smiled at her, a gentle expression, with an equally gentle and patient look in his hazel eyes. "You are right that I have seen many beautiful women in my life, but none so beautiful as the young and graceful spirit I saw near the stream at Dun Mor some eight years ago. She ran and danced and laughed there with her young companions, all in their lovely linen gowns dyed bright as spring flowers, and not minding the cold of the fresh new grass on their bare feet."

Her lips parted as the memory came back. "I do remember a day such as that. But the young women would often go out together on fine spring days, eager for the fresh air and freedom after a long winter spent confined within the fortress walls. Never do I recall meeting any man, especially not a king."

"I am sure the young maidens of Dun Mor were not in the habit of meeting strange men while out searching for herbs and primrose," he said, and for just a moment Keavy thought she saw a gleam in his eye. "But tell me, Lady Keavy . . . do you ever recall being visited by a bird on one of your springtime outings?"

She smiled, beginning to relax just a little. "I am often to be found in the company of birds. They seem to like me, probably because I like them, and follow me almost everywhere. Whenever I go out, it seems, there will be a wren or a lark or a sparrow or two that will fly after me and perch nearby, and sometimes fly down to my wrist or shoulder. It would be stranger for me to be without the birds than it would be for me to be with them."

"I see. But tell me . . . having a wren come down to sing to you and sit on your hand is one thing. Do you ever remember having a golden eagle appear to you?"

She thought her heart would stop. "An eagle?" she said under her breath. Her hand reached up of its own accord to touch the soft, faded feathers of her brooch. "How—I mean, why do you believe such a thing?"

How could he have known about the eagle that came to her that day and made her a gift of its feathers? She had never told anyone what really happened. She had said only that she had found the feathers out in the forest, and would never say anything more.

He held her gaze for a long time, and as she looked into his golden eyes it seemed that all the world hung still, suspended, the way a hawk hovered in flight, the way her own breath held steady as though she had forgotten how to breathe. . . .

"Would you care for some honeyed wine, Lady Keavy?" the king asked, and he stepped toward the leather screens behind which, Keavy knew, his sleeping ledge was hidden.

She began to breathe again, but pressed herself very close to the solid stones of the hearth, as though hoping she could sink into them. If she could, then no one could make her do anything she did not wish to do, or go anywhere she did not wish to go. But as Aengus lifted the heavy leather screen aside with one hand as though it weighed nothing at all, she could not help but notice just how wide his shoulders truly were and how strong his arms must be . . . and the way his long golden-brown hair fell soft and shining over his neck.

Briefly the image of Coilean came into her mind. She saw his slight form and quiet manner, and his limp brown hair that always lay on his neck wrapped in an old leather cord. That weak and passive male was now her husband, and even though she had told herself she had good reason to go along with the decidedly unamusing game of marrying him, the fact remained that she *was* married and this *was* her wedding night . . . and as she stood alone beside the hearth an overwhelming feeling of disappointment came over her.

She bit her lip and looked away as Aengus came back from behind the screens, for she knew her eyes were bright and wet. "Thank you," she whispered, accepting a copper cup filled with wine and quickly taking a drink. And along with her disappointment came an awful feeling of guilt, for she could not help but notice how very different this tall and powerful man really was from her unwanted and unwilling husband.

She turned away not only so he would not see the emotions that must be plain on her face, but also so she would not have to look at his great height and strong shoulders and kind but piercing eyes. But she could not escape that voice—a voice that held a surprising and unnerving power over her now that it was directed at her and her alone.

"Again, I am sorry," he said. "You should have been told of this custom before the marriage took place. I suppose everyone just assumed you already knew."

Keavy's eyes burned, and she kept her back to him as a tear ran down her cheek. "I should have learned it for myself. I should have asked. I should have known," she said. "And I should have prepared myself for having to spend my wedding night knowing that I have no love for my lawful husband, and he has none for me, and that I had nothing more to look forward to on this night than solitary sleep."

"I thought this was just a ruse, a mere formality, so that the two of you could please your families and then have the freedom to make marriages of your own choosing. Is that not what you told me?"

"It was . . . but there will never be another wedding night, not like this one . . . this night that I should have saved for my true husband, and not spent either alone or with . . . with . . ."

"With a man you do not know and do not love," Aengus finished.

"With a man who gives me no choice."

He set down his copper cup. "You do have a choice. As I said, I will not force you."

"But if I do not . . . consummate with the king the marriage I made today with Coilean, I will have to go back home, to be bartered away to the next man my parents can find for me . . . or I can go and live among the servants of Dun Mor, little better than a slave." She brushed away another tear, but then raised her chin and drew a deep breath, determined not to let him see just how shaken she truly was.

"Lady Keavy . . . perhaps it is too much to think of all at once. You do not have to decide at this moment. Please. Come and sit with me on the furs, and we can talk, and eat the bread and honey that Seanan has left for me, and drink a little blackberry wine. I would be happy to see you enjoy it."

She turned back to face him, suddenly filled once again with apprehension. Sit with him on the sleeping ledge? His own sleeping ledge, alone there with him on the soft and inviting furs?

Casually, as if he were alone, Aengus walked to the ledge and sat down on it. On the furs rested a large wooden plate stacked with flatbread made from wheat, dripping with butter and honey. He took a bite, and then another, and then happened to glance up and see Keavy still standing at the hearth. "May I offer you some of this?" he asked, holding out the wooden plate. "It's quite good. There is plenty of blackberry wine as well. I will share my cup with you."

You do not have to decide at this moment. . . .

The day had been long and wearying enough without the added shock of learning about the wedding-night customs of Dun Gaoth, and her resistance was giving way. Just sitting down in a quiet place with no one staring at her and pointing at her and whispering about her, and enjoying a little wine and bread and sweet honey, was very tempting.

The king had said he would not force her. Slowly, keeping her heavy cloak pulled close around her, Keavy walked across the thick straw, moved past the leather screens, and found herself standing beside the sleeping ledge of the king.

Chapter Seven

She sat down on the very edge of King Aengus's sleeping ledge, perching as far away from him as she could in the shadows cast by the tall leather screens. "It is quite comfortably warm in the house tonight," he said. "Your cloak is heavy. Perhaps you would like to take it off while you have your wine and honey bread."

She shot a glance at him, but he was occupied with pouring more wine from a leather skin into the plain copper cup. It would be a relief to take off the heavy, scratchy, and hideously dyed brown-and-purple-plaid cloak, which was all but suffocating her now in the close warmth of the house. Careful as always of the eagle feathers, Keavy pulled off the white enameled brooch and then dropped the heavy wool into a pile on the straw at her feet, gently placing the brooch on top of it. She adjusted the equally heavy dark red wool gown so that it sat a bit more comfortably on her shoulders and then reached for the cup of blackberry wine that Aengus offered.

"Beautiful clothes," he said politely. "Did you make them yourself? I believe you said that you enjoyed the arts of fabric and embroidery."

Keavy shrugged, looking down at the bloodred gown and the brown-and-purple cloak. "I did make them, but I can tell you they are not the sort of clothes I usually wear. They are too heavy and too dark. I much prefer lighter colors and softer fabrics."

He nodded, giving her a gentle smile. "I would have been quite surprised to hear you say otherwise. I do remember a young woman in a soft linen gown the color of springtime grass. Heavy reds and browns simply do not suit you. Why did you choose such clothes for the day of your wedding?"

She took a deep breath. "Because . . . I suppose . . . I knew only too well that this contract of marriage was not a true one. I could not bring myself to wear the beautiful things I had hoped to one day wear on the day of my wedding, and so—at my family's prodding—I made the red gown that most brides wear, though I do not like the color, and a cloak made in the last colors I would ever wear by choice."

"So it was as if Coilean married someone else, and not Keavy, for she was nowhere to be seen."

She nodded, gazing into the shadows. "I would like to think that this was so—but the fact remains that Keavy was there, and Keavy is now married to Coilean. And there is nothing she can do, this night, to change that—not without severe consequences for herself and her husband."

"Three full moons is not such a long time," Aengus said.

"It is not. I said that to myself many times, while contemplating this marriage. I thought I could do this thing. I thought that three full moons of pretending to be married was a small price to pay. But that was before I knew how long this first night would really be."

Aengus was silent. Keavy turned away from him again as the darkness, the silence, the emptiness of the house closed in on her. Then she raised her head as another thought occurred to her.

"Where is *your* wife, King Aengus?" she asked. "Or perhaps I should say 'wives'? Have they all been sent away, since the king is expected to be otherwise occupied this night?"

"I have no wife at all," he answered, his voice quiet once more. "It has been more than a year since the death of Queen Deirdre, and I have had no wish to take another. Walk through the house if you wish; you will see none of the clothes or ornaments or other fine things that a woman would own or use. Ask any of the people of Dun Gaoth. They will tell you of her passing and that their king has no wish ever to marry again, even though we had no child—and that he ordered all the gold in the kingdom put away, out of respect for a young queen who died long before her time."

Keavy nodded. So that was why there were no fine gold plates or cups at the feast, not even at the king's place. "I am sorry to hear of the loss of your queen. Yet . . . I am surprised that you would never want another wife, even after many months. Does not every man want a son?"

"I have already had a queen—a wise queen who always did her duty, even as I have always tried to do. I have no need, and no wish, to ever take another."

His voice carried such a note of finality that Keavy could not bring herself to ask him any more about it. She took another deep drink of the sweet blackberry wine and held tight to the cup as the silence closed in around her again. Very soon she would have to make a decision about whether to get up and leave this house, and face all the consequences that would follow such an action, or whether she would stay in her marriage with Coilean, which meant she would have to stay here—in this house, for this night—with Aengus.

Aengus stood up and turned toward her. Keavy froze, staring up at him, drawing back as much as she could. But he only picked up her brooch from where it lay on top of her heavy wool cloak and then stood beside the ledge in the straw, studying the white enameled brooch and its three golden-brown feathers.

"You asked me if ever a golden eagle came down to me, the way the wrens and sparrows often do," Keavy said. "Such a bird did come to me on a spring day some eight years ago. I have never forgotten that day."

Aengus ran his finger over the three feathers in the brooch. "Did you find these feathers in the forest, and pick them up in remembrance of that spring day?"

"I did not. I . . . the eagle . . ." She paused. "I have never spoken of this to anyone. I am not sure I wish to do so now."

"Ah, I see. It is to remain a secret between you and this magical creature that appeared to you one very special day." He smiled and closed the distance between them with a single step. "Yet it may not be a secret after all. It seems to me that you did not find these feathers at all. I believe that the eagle came down to rest on a low branch of a birch tree near the river, only a little higher than your green and shining eyes . . . and that when you approached, unafraid, to stand before him and speak kindly, he reached out with one great wing and ran it down the softness of your cheek, in a way that no natural bird would ever do."

She could only stare at him in shock. "How could you know this? No one knows what happened that day. How could *you* know?"

He smiled. "You are wrong, Lady Keavy. *You* know what happened that day . . . and so does the eagle."

Keavy closed her eyes as Aengus reached out to trace the tip of one finger down the side of her face, as lightly and gently as the great bird had done so many years before. Even now it was difficult to tell whether the light touch at her cheek was that of a man's fingers or the feathers of a great bird . . . the feeling was the same, and it took her right back to that day.

Aengus withdrew his hand. Keavy opened her eyes. The king continued: "And before he left, this eagle made you a gift, for he wished you to remember him. He pulled from each of his own two wings, and from over his heart, three feathers, and dropped them to the grass for you to keep. He would be very happy to know that you did keep them and, indeed, have worn them near your heart ever since."

She dared to look up at him. "Who are you?" she whispered. "Do I dare believe that you are telling me the truth, and that you did not learn how I came to have these feathers through some other method?"

Aengus sat down again beside her on the ledge, turning a little to face her. "You know that I am Dun Gaoth's king," he began, and reached out to take the copper cup from her and then catch hold of her hand. She was too caught up in his words, in the anticipation of what he was about to say, to pull away, and so he sat with his hand covering hers on the soft, thick furs. "And because my family knew that one day I might be chosen as king—my uncle was king before me, and any man of his family could have been the one—I was given not only the training of a warrior, but some of the training of a druid as well."

Keavy nodded. She was well aware that the free men of the tribe could choose the next king from any man of the king's blood family—a son, an uncle, a cousin—and that kings were always trained in the ways of druids. "I do know these things. But . . . no king that I know has ever had the ability to . . . to . . ."

"To transform himself into a golden eagle?"

Her eyes widened, and she drew a deep breath. "There are poems that speak of some druids having this ability," she said at last. "They could take the shapes of creatures of the forest, of a deer or wolf or boar, or of a salmon in the river or a seal or dolphin in the sea. But most often those who had such power would choose to be a bird—a falcon, or a raven, or an eagle."

Aengus smiled, and he gently pressed his strong fingers around her hand. Keavy knew she ought to pull her hand away but could not bring herself to move.

"You are exactly right, Lady Keavy. The creature of choice was nearly always a bird, as it was for me. And not just any bird, but the most magnificent of birds—the eagle."

"But how?" she whispered. "How did you come to learn this thing?"

He smiled a little, and shook his head. "Some of the oldest stories tell of other men of my family, just a few of them, who had the ability to assume the shape of an animal or bird when they chose. I thought this to be the most wonderful idea I had ever heard, and dared to wonder whether I, too, might be able to do such a thing.

"There remained at Dun Gaoth, in those days, an aged druid who had helped my grandfather learn to change his form. He took me out on the cliffs and into the forests for many days and had me stay alone with only the great birds for company, until I nearly felt that I was one of them . . . and then this druid taught me the ancient words, the ancient spells, that would complete the transformation. And so, one spring morning as the sun rose, I stood on the edge of a cliff, stretched out my arms, and spoke those ancient words . . . and I found that I no longer had arms, but wings.

"The winds lifted me up and carried me high above the earth, and I found that I could see the scurrying of the smallest mouse in the fields and the tiniest movement of the flowers against the grass . . . and from that time on, I could, whenever I could clear my mind and let go my will and speak the ancient words, take the very form of an eagle.

"I did not do this often. It was tiring and difficult to make the change, even after I had learned it well, and I could not maintain the form forever—perhaps half a day, at most. I quickly learned to return to earth as soon as I felt my body growing heavy." He looked at Keavy again, and smiled. "I saw so many wonderful things as I flew above the world . . . but nothing so wonderful as the young maiden with the long and shining hair who caught my eagle eye so many years ago."

He lifted his hand from hers and reached out

toward her again, and this time he stroked one long and shining braid. "I would like very much to see that beautiful sight again . . . see that river of gold and silver hair."

Keavy turned to face him. Her heart began to beat very fast and she was instantly on her guard once again. But to her amazement the king merely lifted the end of her braid, worked free the golden sphere at the end and set it aside on the furs, then untied the neat strip of white linen that held her hair together. Before she could bring herself to speak or move, he began to unbraid her tresses.

It was the most innocent of gestures, yet intensely personal at the same time—and so unexpected that she found herself continuing to sit very still beside him, wondering what he might do next.

His voice broke the quiet of the house. "I am so glad to see you, Lady Keavy, no matter what the circumstances. I often wondered what might have become of you, and hoped that I might see you again."

She caught her breath at his words but stayed where she was. "How do I know that it was really you that day, who came to me in the form of the golden eagle? It is a fine story you tell, King Aengus, and I know such stories well, but I myself have never seen any man actually do such a thing. Nor do I know anyone who has. Tell me, please. Why should I believe that you were the man who took the shape of the eagle that spring day?"

Aengus laughed a little, even as he went right on with his slow and careful unbraiding of her hair. "I should have been surprised if a woman of your wisdom had not asked me such a question. But let me ask this of you: You said you had never told the story of the eagle and how you came to have those three feathers. If that is true, how is it that I know exactly what happened that day, just as if I had been there?"

She shook her head slightly. "You could have made a good guess, after seeing the feathers I wear in my brooch. Perhaps you were trained in the druids' ways of composing poetry and stories as well. Perhaps luck was with you on the story you told this night."

"It was not luck, Lady Keavy. I was there, and I knew you the moment I saw you here tonight. And I am happier than I can say—happier than I have been in a very long time—to see you again at last."

Half of her hair now fell freely down her back. The tension eased at the side of her head as her hair was released, and with infinite lightness King Aengus ran his fingers through the long, rippling fall and spread it out across her shoulder. Without a word he reached for the second braid, removed the golden sphere and the linen strip from it with equal care, and began to separate the tightly braided plaits of hair.

"King Aengus," Keavy said, still facing straight ahead, "when the eagle came to me and behaved in a way no natural creature ever would, I knew I would never forget such a thing—and I have not. It affected me very deeply, so much that I think it is why I have never wanted to go so far as to make a contract of marriage with any other. I knew, somehow, that this was not really a bird at all, but something far more—something meant only for me, something very special, something worth waiting for until the day when I would see it again."

He finished unbraiding her hair. It lay loose and streaming down her back, and as he stroked its softly shining surface Keavy turned to him.

"Please, Aengus—understand how important this is to me. If you are not simply making up a story, if you are not merely trying to impress yet another woman—then prove to me that you are what you say. Show me, here, now, that you can indeed transform into an eagle, and then I will know, truly, why I have waited so long to find my husband—because I was waiting for the magnificent man who was an eagle that day, a man who was so special to me that I was willing to wait forever for him."

She reached up and caught hold of his strong, warm hand. "Please, Aengus. Show me that you are indeed the eagle who came to me that day."

His fingers tightened on her hand, and he tried to smile at her. "Beautiful Keavy," he said, "I would give my entire kingdom at this moment, I think, if I could prove this thing to you. The truth is, though . . . I cannot."

"You cannot," she repeated, holding his gaze.

He looked away from her. "The day you saw me in the birch tree was one of the last times I made the transformation. My life . . . changed not long after that day, and nothing was ever the same for me."

"So I must simply take your word that the strange and wonderful bird I saw was really you in the shape of an eagle."

King Aengus could only shake his head. "The last time I made the attempt to become the eagle—and it was not long after I saw you, no more than a few full moons—I failed. Nothing happened at all. I have not had the courage to try since."

"Not once?" she asked, leaning close to look into his eyes.

"Not once. Your heart must fly first, before you can hope to have wings . . . and my heart has not flown for a very long time."

"Why does your heart no longer fly?" she asked, reaching out to touch his arm. But he only smiled tightly and looked away, and he seemed to be thinking of something far removed and very far away.

Before she could move, Aengus turned back to her and took hold of the hand she had placed on his arm. "I think you do know who and what I am, even as I knew you. Listen to your heart, Keavy. What does it tell you?"

Her fingers were caught between his hand and his arm, but she found she had no desire to withdraw. "I know only that I would like nothing more in life than to believe you," she said. "I do not know how you know what happened that day with the eagle, though it would seem to prove that you are what you say you are."

He nodded, gently pressing her fingers with his hand, holding her hand close to his arm. "I understand. You would like more proof. Someday I may be able to transform myself again—but I can say to you only that I am sorry I cannot do it now."

She realized that his face was very close to hers, and he and she were looking right into each other's eyes. She saw only his intense amber irises, and just for a moment she saw once again the bright, piercing stare of the eagle—and then Aengus's gaze became soft and dark once again, and he reached to touch her hair.

Keavy stood and tried to step past him, but the king was on his feet and caught her arms almost before she could move. Now that they stood face-to-face he towered over her, his chest and shoulders so wide that she could not see past at all. She was aware only of the great strength radiating out from this man, this king, who held her fast with far more than the power in his hands.

She had thought she would be afraid. She had thought she could never go through with this. But as she looked up again into his eyes, she saw, with a flash of memory, the piercing gaze of the eagle. When he released one of her arms and stroked her cheek, her hair, with one finger, she saw and felt again the eagle's golden-brown feather stroking her in just the same way.

"Will you go, or will you stay?" he asked, his voice a whisper. "I will not ask again."

She looked up at him, feeling his closeness, feeling him leaning down over her, enfolding her in his strength and urgency and sheer male power the way an eagle might enfold her with its wings. She became aware that their breath came together, ragged and quick, and she did not doubt that at this moment their hearts also beat as one.

You came here to make a marriage.

Keavy caught her breath and forced herself away from him.

"Lady Keavy," Aengus said. "We have talked, and we have eaten, and we have shared a cup of good wine, and we have learned that we may well already know each other. But we cannot forget the reason you are here."

He sat down again on the side of the ledge and reached out to take a tight hold of her hand. "You were brought to the home of the king so that your marriage might be lawfully consummated. If you still wish to leave, you must go now and take the consequences that your leaving will bring. But if you stay, you must understand that your marriage will be consummated, for it is my duty to do so, and I promise you this: if you do not go now, it will, indeed, happen on this night."

Chapter Eight

Something had changed inside the stone house, here in the dark shadows of the sleeping ledge behind the sheltering screens. The tension began to rise. Keavy could feel it from Aengus, feel the gathering strength in this man who had so calmly talked with her and unbraided her hair only a short time before. Keavy drew back from him and pulled her hand away—but before she could stand he was on his feet and standing right in front of her, leaning down so that his face was only a breath away from hers.

"This is the oldest and most respected of customs," he whispered. "You came here to make a marriage, and a marriage it will be if you stay here."

She must act now. There would be no escape, or she would only find herself in a similar situation later on. She must get this over with. In the faintest of whispers, she gave him her answer. "I will . . . stay."

Quickly she sat down on the ledge and swung her feet up onto it. She reached for the niche in the wall where the single lamp still burned, and blew it out.

Now all was darkness, save for the soft glow of the hearth on the other side of the screens. All she could hear was Aengus's breathing and the pounding of her heart in her ears. But he did not move, he was waiting for her. And so, in the darkness, Keavy unlaced her folded leather boots, slipped them off her feet, and let them fall to the straw below.

Covered by darkness, protected by night, Keavy made herself act quickly before she lost her resolve. Knowing the king was still almost near enough to touch, she rose up on her knees in the furs and untied the thick brown leather belt at her waist, pulled it free, and dropped it to the ground near his feet. Next came the heavy red wool dress, which she wrestled off over her head, and then she carefully pulled her long length of hair back through it. Last of all—with only a little hesitation—went the red linen undergown worn beneath the woolen one.

She began to tremble, both from anxiety and from the cold air of the spring night, but made herself stretch out in the darkness on the furs as near to the wall as she could get. She closed her eyes, trying but failing to still the violent shaking of her legs.

Keavy listened closely to hear what he would do next. She expected to hear him start pulling off his boots and tunic and trews, but the only sound she heard, apart from her own pounding heart and ragged breathing, was Aengus's low and gentle laughter.

Humiliation flooded through Keavy. Her eyes flew open. She had no doubt he could see her a little in the soft glow of the hearth beyond the screens and he must have been amused at what he saw. "You are laughing at me?" she asked, her voice shaking noticeably. "I assure you, I find nothing to laugh at in this situation. I am sorry if you—"

She was silenced by a long length of clean linen being thrown over her, covering her body from head to toe and even settling over her face. It was joined by the welcome weight and warmth of a fur robe . . . and then Aengus sat down close beside her.

Keavy pulled the linen and the furs close, very grateful now for their presence, and shrank even closer to the wall. And as she lay huddled there, she heard the king chuckle again.

She pushed the furs away from her face. Aengus sat there looking down on her, backlit in the faint glow of the fire, laughing gently and shaking his head. "We may both be here out of duty, not out of love or choice—but I have never believed that this duty must be carried out in a cold or uncaring manner."

As she stared up at him, blinking, King Aengus pulled his linen tunic off over his head. Keavy could not help but pull the covers up over her face again. In the darkness she heard the sounds of him untying and pulling off his folded leather boots and stripping away his trews.

In the shadowy light of the fire she could see the ripple of muscle, the cut of his broad chest, the smooth glow of his skin . . . and the gleam of the golden torque Aengus wore around his neck; the king's torque capped with the heads of eagles. No longer did he bear any resemblance to the tired, mud-covered man she had seen earlier this night.

Keavy began to shake again. What had she gotten herself into? How had she let this happen? Perhaps it was not too late; perhaps she could still get away . . .

But before she could move he had sat down once again beside her and leaned down to stroke her hair. "I thought you might feel more at ease with something to cover you," he said. "And a bit warmer, too."

He seemed to smile in the darkness, but Keavy's trembling would not stop. "I am sorry. Idon't know what to do," she whispered. "I have never . . . No man has ever—"

He ran his finger over her lips to quiet her. "Do not worry. You need not do anything at all. I will take care of you." And before she had time to do more than catch her breath, he lifted the fur and linen and slid beneath them.

A wild combination of fear and anticipation rushed through Keavy's veins as he stretched out his body—warm as the sun, and possessing just as much power—close beside her own, pressing his entire length against her. His hair fell feather-soft against her face and throat as he leaned over and slid one arm around her waist to hold her close. For a long moment tension filled him, and he pressed his legs and body hard against her own . . . and to her amazement, she realized that he was trembling, too.

He raised himself up on one elbow and looked down at her, so close that all she could see was the gleam of his eyes in the darkness. Then she closed her eyes as he leaned down to kiss her gently on the forehead, right where her hair met her hot skin, then moved down the side of her face and neck, kissing her gently all the way down. His mouth hot and soft and the soft slick hair of his beard and mustache slid smoothly against her skin, brushing over it the same way the feathers of the eagle had done.

And then Keavy found that her own body was undergoing a transformation unlike anything she had ever known before. The world faded away, it seemed to her, and there was nothing in existence save herself and this man who now held her in his power—a power that sent heat and life pouring through every vein to every part of her body, especially to the most hidden places that no man had ever seen or touched.

Still kissing her cheek, her neck, her lips, he raised his hand to the curve of her breasts, tracing them so gently and lightly that she began to arch her back and press against his hand, suddenly coming alive at his strange but increasingly desired touch. All the while he kept his body pressed close and warm against her, raising himself up even farther so that half his weight lay over her, locking the two of them together and letting her know, without words, that he intended to make good on both his promises: that he would take care of her, and that this marriage would, indeed, be consummated.

Now he moved down to kiss her curving, aching breasts, and as he did he slid his hand over her belly toward her thighs. The heat flooded through her there, and she could not help but rise to meet his touch.

As though from very far away she was aware of great tension within him, but it seemed like nothing compared to her own—compared to these new and strange sensations that poured through her like the heat of the sun and left her entire body hot and soft and yielding.

He chose exactly the right moment to bring the rest of his weight atop her and hold her firmly in his arms: before she could lose her desire, before she could think of what was happening, before she could question whether she should allow this. Keavy was aware only of Aengus's great chest and shoulders holding her down as he kissed her, and of an even greater heat and a welcome strength between her legs as he pushed forward and took what was his without question.

A brief sharpness she felt, but he continued to move, continued to take and to thrust and to hold her in his powerful arms until at last she gasped and threw her hands up over his back to cling to him. A strength and a power she had never known existed carried her away on a tide of heat and desire.

It seemed to Keavy that she had been asleep for a long time and dreaming the most otherworldly and unbelievable dream; but even before she could open her eyes, she became aware of the great weight that lay across her body and the warmth that enveloped her. As she looked up, blinking, she saw the straw roof of a house, faint in the low light of the hearth, and saw that she lay on a sleeping ledge on soft thick furs—and that an enormous and powerfully built man lay across her body like a great wolf might lie across its prey.

Now she remembered all else that happened on this night—the heat, the strangeness, the newness, the closeness, even the fleeting pain—and was somehow relieved to find Aengus was still there. It would have seemed cold, frightening, even insulting, if he had simply gotten up and left and showed no further thought for her once his duty was done.

Her quickened breathing must have awakened him, for King Aengus lifted his head and blinked his eyes, and then eased his weight off her, though he still lay close. Keavy was startled at the sudden draft of cold air that struck her where he had been lying, and she was grateful when he immediately pulled the linen and furs up and tucked them in close around her.

She tried to smile at him. "I am glad you are still here," she said. "I suppose I thought you would simply be gone once . . . after we . . ."

He smiled back at her. "It is a delicate time. Not a time to be leaving any woman alone. It is the least I can do for you." He tucked the covers close around her again, and then he sat up on the ledge and swung his legs down over the side. "I will take you back to your own house now. It is still dark; the morning is not yet close. You can awaken in your husband's house when the sun finally rises."

He reached down to the straw to get his trews and tunic, but she stopped him with a slender hand on his thick wrist. He turned to look at her, puzzled. "What is it?"

By way of answer she closed her fingers around his wrist and drew him back to her. "I cannot leave yet. I am not ready."

He smiled kindly. "Your duty is done, and so is mine. You must return to the house of your husband. It will seem very strange if you do not. I will walk with you there, if you wish. You will not be alone."

She shook her head and raised herself up on one elbow. "Please. Do not send me away to lie alone in the cold and the dark in the house of a stranger. Please . . . not now. Not yet."

He sat very still as understanding dawned on him. "You are certain? I must tell you, there is a reason why the bride must leave once the king has done what he must."

"Why? Why must she leave?"

"Because no bond must ever form between them," he whispered. "And nothing draws a man and a woman together more strongly than the act of love. The Ancients knew this well, and so that is why—"

"There was already a bond between us. It was formed many years ago." Keavy lay back down on the furs. "I feel that it has only been renewed, not created."

"You are sure of me, now? I may never be able to prove it to you. I may never be able to transform myself again."

"I am sure that I could never feel this way about any man, save the one I was destined for—the one I have waited for ever since I met the golden eagle in the forest. Please . . . do not send me away."

As she looked up at him, his soft gaze changed to a piercing stare. He slowly leaned forward until his lips reached her own, and this time the two of them kissed each other without fear, and without trembling, and without any sense of duty whatsoever.

Daylight shone down bright and warm through the hole in the straw roof of King Aengus's home, for the sun was high overhead and the day was well under way. Keavy, sitting alone on the edge of the sleeping ledge, hastily pulled on her red linen undergown and heavy red wool gown and then put on her belt and boots. She picked up the two delicate golden spheres she had worn on the ends of her braids, gathered her hair, and threw it back over her shoulder, giving it a twist to try to hold it in place. Finally she took her enameled bronze brooch with its eagle feathers and pinned it directly to her red gowns. Her heavy brown-and-purple cloak stayed where it was, lying in a heap on the straw.

She walked out from behind the screen to find Aengus sitting on a cushion beside the hearth. Seanan worked there at preparing the morning meal. The king was dressed in the same clothes he had worn the night before when she had been brought to his house, and it was with something of a jolt that she again saw him dressed in the simple linen tunic, dark green woolen trews, and soft brown leather boots and belt.

"Good morning," Aengus greeted her, and touched the worn leather cushion beside him. "Will you sit with me? Seanan has made oat porridge for us, boiled with milk and butter and honey and few dried apples. It is a favorite of mine. Oh, and there is roast mutton, too, heating in the coals." He smiled up at her, his hazel eyes gleaming. "I am sure you must be as hungry as I."

A mild blush crept up Keavy's cheeks. She folded her hands in front of her and glanced at Seanan where he worked at the hearth, and was dismayed to see the servant was staring at her with his eyes wide. Then he quickly looked away and did his best not to notice she was there.

The porridge smelled wonderful, filling the house with the scent of hot butter and oats. Keavy suddenly felt as though she had not eaten in days and could not help but return Aengus's smile. "I suppose I *am* a little hungry," she admitted, and sat down close beside him on the cushion.

Seanan came over to hand each of them a wooden bowl of thick hot porridge and then immediately returned to the hearth. But Keavy caught sight of his wide eyes and scandalized look, and when she glanced over her shoulder she saw that he was frankly staring at both of them. "What is wrong?" she whispered, leaning over to Aengus. "Am I not supposed to be here?"

Aengus scraped the last of the sweetened oat porridge out of his bowl and ate it. Seanan returned just in time to take the empty dish and exchange it for a plate heaped with strips of mutton left over from the wedding feast. The king was eating like a man who'd been starved for days, and for that Keavy had to smile just a little.

"Well, you see," Aengus began, chewing and swallowing an enormous mouthful of hot roast mutton dripping with juices. "It is not normally the custom for a new bride to actually stay the entire first night with the king. In all other cases I have escorted her back to the house of her husband immediately—as I offered to do for you last night."

"I see," she said with a small nod, feeling rather uncomfortable and quite daring all at once. "I remember now that you did say that to me. But I could not . . . I just . . ."

He smiled kindly at her. "It was not quite the right time for you to leave."

"I suppose there will be consequences from my staying here all night."

The king only shrugged and went on eating. "I suppose there could be. But I do not believe it will be anything serious."

"Can you . . . tell me what I might expect?"

"Gossip, I should think. But that will happen anyway. If you are asking me how your husband might feel, I do not know. That is for you and him to determine." She raised her chin at the mention of her husband, but Aengus merely went on eating. "It is not a concern of mine."

Suddenly feeling insulted, she sat back and set her bowl of porridge down in the straw. "I see that I should never have stayed. I did not realize what would happen. I told you I knew nothing of this custom before I came here. I should indeed have gone last night, as soon as . . ." She started to gather her skirts so she could get up. "I will go right away, since it was not proper for me to stay in the first place."

But he caught her wrist before she could stand. "Please, Keavy. Stay here with me, at least long enough to eat."

"But you said it is not the custom—"

"The custom be cursed. I would like very much for you to stay with me now."

She held very still, looking down at his serious

face and gleaming hazel eyes, and then slowly sat back down. "Thank you," she said. "Perhaps I will stay, just for a short time."

Keavy settled on the cushion again and lifted her bowl from the straw, smiling into Aengus's eyes and trying to ignore the feeling of disapproval coming from the other side of the hearth.

The meal went by in comfortable silence, and before long Keavy forgot Seanan's presence as the older man worked quietly in another part of the house. As she devoured her porridge, she stole glances at Aengus and studied him in the light of the midmorning sun that poured in through the small, high windows of the house and through the hole in the top of the straw roof.

She saw a man who seemed older than his years, but younger than she had thought when first she had seen him the night before. He was indeed tall and broad-shouldered and powerfully strong, but seemed unaware of his great strength, as though some inner weariness kept his broad shoulders a little weary, and some unresolved burden weighed on his mind.

His face commanded her attention. She noted how his hazel eyes remained gentle and soft when he was at ease, but changed instantly to piercing sharpness whenever something caught his attention. His skin showed the marks of years of wind and rain and cold, and more recently the sun, but was smooth and taut—and hot with life, Keavy remembered, her face warming to a deep shade of pink.

His nose was straight and slender, and his mouth difficult to see, for it was hidden beneath the hair of a long mustache and neatly trimmed beard, both of which were the same rich brown color as his hair. Yet Keavy knew very well how soft and tender that mouth was, soft as a cloud and warm as the brightest sun of midsummer . . . and when he looked up at her, studying her as she was studying him, they both smiled at each other. The meal was over all too soon.

At some unseen signal Seanan came around and took the plates and cups from them, and then Aengus got slowly to his feet. He offered his hand down to Keavy and drew her up to stand before him. "I am sorry, but I must take you back to your husband's house. Though it was my wish—and yours as well, I know—that you stay this long, I do not want you to suffer any more ill feeling or humiliation than you must for having broken this custom somewhat . . . though I was the one who urged you to do so."

She tried to smile at him, though a feeling of loss was beginning to descend upon her. "Last night everyone urged me to keep this custom of yours, and now that I have, you chide me for wanting to keep it all too well," she said as lightly as she could. "I . . . I . . ."

Keavy looked up into his eyes and found she could not speak, for her throat had closed and her eyes began to burn; and she saw that he, too, was looking back at her with an expression of sympathy and loss.

"Will I not see you again?" she whispered as a tear fell on her cheek. "Was last night nothing but duty for you?"

He moved forward and held her in his arms, resting his bearded cheek gently against the side of her face. "The first time, perhaps, was duty, I will admit . . . but the second time was not. The second time was born of your desire that it should happen, and I will tell you—for I know the question is in your mind, even if you would never ask it—that whenever a bride was brought to me, what happened occurred out of duty alone. Never did any of them reach for me out of desire on that night."

Keavy could only close her eyes and listen to the beating of his heart, and feel Aengus's arms around her for what might well be the last time.

At last she drew back and turned to go; but he placed his fingers beneath her chin, raised her face to his, and kissed her softly on the lips.

"King Aengus," she whispered, her burning eyes still closed. "It seems cruelty indeed to make me leave now, after a night such as we have had and after a kiss such as this."

She looked up at him then, and saw his stricken expression. "I . . . am sorry," he said. "I wished only to give you a proper farewell. I am truly sorry, Lady Keavy. We should never have . . ." He paused. "I fear I made a great mistake last night."

Then he straightened, and without another word placed his hand on her back to guide her to the door. Aengus pushed it open and Keavy blinked in the bright sunlight—and then she caught her breath at the sight that awaited them both.

Chapter Nine

The grassy yard in front of the king's house was filled with a waiting, staring crowd of people. It seemed that every last man and woman of Dun Gaoth had gathered there to wait: nobles and servants, warriors and craftsmen, tall, silent druids, some standing, some sitting. And at the front of the crowd, nearest the front step of the house, stood Keavy's parents, and Coilean's, and the sullen, staring Coilean himself.

"Is this part of the custom, too?" Keavy whispered, leaning close to the king.

Aengus smiled tightly and then looked out at the waiting crowd. The people who had been sitting on the grass began to get stiffly to their feet, as if they had been waiting for some time. And every one of them stared at Aengus and Keavy with expressions ranging from puzzlement, as on the faces of Keavy's parents, to insult, as on the faces of Coilean's parents, to sullen anger, which was clear on Coilean's face.

"Good day to you all," Aengus said, waving his hand toward them. "It is kind of you to come greet me this day, and walk with me as I escort this lady back to her husband."

Keavy glanced from one side of the crowd to the other. They remained silent and staring and gave a distinctly hostile impression. It was clear that she and Aengus had overstepped the boundary here. He had said that no other bride ever stayed the entire night with him, and that he would always take her back to her husband's house well before sunrise.

But she had not gone back. Of her own choice, she had stayed with Aengus long past sunrise, had stayed so long that the sun had moved high overhead and beyond. . . .

None of the people said a word in answer to their king. Keavy realized that those in the back looked almost amused, as though they had gathered to hear lively music or a humorous poem, and nudged and whispered to each other as they watched and waited to see what would happen next. But those nearer the front—especially Coilean and his parents—continued to glare at her and Aengus both.

She felt very disquieted at seeing the look on Coilean's face. Never in her life had she met a more passive and sullen young man than Coilean—but now something had finally seemed to engage him enough to bring out a sense of anger and indignation.

As Keavy watched, Coilean's father nudged him

hard in the ribs, and Coilean actually clenched his fists. Then he walked straight across the open lawn in front of the house, up onto the front step, and grabbed Keavy by the wrist. "It is time to go to our home, my wife," he said, entirely ignoring the king. He turned to walk back across the yard, pulling her after him so firmly that he nearly caused her to stumble down the step, caught by surprise as she was by the man's actually taking charge of something.

She managed to glance back over her shoulder at Aengus. Surely he would do something to help her. He would not let someone like Coilean drag her through the yard in front of everyone! But though she saw him tense and shoot a cold glare at Coilean, he remained where he was, and she knew in an instant what she must do.

He was the king. He could not interfere with this matter—but Keavy herself most certainly could.

Coilean managed to drag her past his glowering parents, her wrist still caught in his surprisingly strong grip—but at last she dug in her heels, forced him to stop, and wrenched her arm free.

He turned to stare coldly at her, but Keavy drew herself up as tall as she could, which meant she was nearly a head taller than he. "Why have you done this?" she demanded. "Why do you humiliate me by dragging me across the grounds like a wayward sheep?"

"Humiliate!" he cried. "You do not know the meaning of humiliation! My wife has spent the entire First Night and over half of the following day alone with the king! You have made me look a fool!"

In spite of her anger, Keavy burst out laughing. "Coilean, you need no help from me for such a thing . . . nor I from you."

The crowd burst out laughing, turning to one another and shouting and slapping each other on the shoulders. Keavy knew that most of them were anticipating the entertainment of a battle between a newly married man and the wife who, it seemed, had dallied too long with the king. She had no wish to serve as their entertainment and knew that this should be discussed in private, though she was almost too angry to care after Coilean's treatment of her.

"I am sorry," she said a little more quietly, trying to keep her anger under control. "I know I made you a promise, but now I find that I simply cannot do this thing. Things are different now. Show me to your house and we will talk."

Her glared at her, but said no more; then finally he turned and stalked away across the grounds. She followed him to one of the houses, greatly relieved to see that the crowd stayed where it was even though everyone stretched their necks and strained to listen. Coilean walked inside his small house and she quickly followed him, pulling the door closed after her.

Keavy glanced around the inside of the little dwelling, from the creaking door to the cold, dirty hearth to the rickety wooden shelves half falling down under the weight of rusted iron tools and dented, crusted cauldrons. She placed her hand over her heart at the sight of a tumbled stack of polished wooden boxes and new leather bags on the floor beside one of the sleeping ledges, for these were her own belongings brought from Dun Mor. They looked quite out of place among the wreck that was this house.

"I thought you lived in the home of your parents," she asked, trying to keep from touching anything.

"I did. When they knew that I was to be married—or *thought I* was—they arranged for me to stay here. Five other men, two of them married, also live here."

"I see," Keavy said faintly, and folded her arms close across her chest as she continued to look around at some of the worst squalor she had ever seen.

She shivered. This awful place was where she would have slept the previous night—her wedding night—and all the nights to come for another three months if she kept to her bargain.

"Our marriage was never a real one," she began. "It was merely an agreement between the two of us to please our parents. I went through with the legalities, as required, just as you did. Why should it matter to you if I stayed with the king for a time? It was not my idea to go to him in the first place!"

He folded his arms across his chest and looked away from her, red with anger. "The arrangement of our marriage is known only to us, not to anyone else. Certainly not to our families, not to the druids, and not to the king!"

Keavy swallowed, and tried to smile at him. "In three full moons I will be gone from your life and cause you no further trouble."

"But three full moons is a long time from now! Half the people of Dun Gaoth have been following me all this day, pointing and staring and whispering and laughing, and asking me where my wife is!"

Keavy pulled herself up even taller, if that were possible, and stared him down with the coldest look she could muster. "I would remind you, Coilean of Dun Gaoth, that I was the one who was forced to spend the first night of my marriage with your king! No one told me of this custom. No one asked me if I wished to do this thing. I was merely handed over to him like a fine young heifer led before the bull. And you dare to grab my arm and drag me across the yard like a slave or a criminal and then snivel that *you* are humiliated by nothing more than the gossip and stares of those with naught to do but watch their neighbors? I did not expect you to behave towards me as a loving husband—but I did expect you to at least be polite."

She fairly shook with anger, both at her own predicament and at Coilean's reaction. "If I had not stayed with the king last night, our marriage—the one we had decided was our only salvation—would have been immediately declared invalid.

How humiliated would you have been then, Coilean, when your family found out you still had yet to make a marriage? Let me tell you: it would not be half of what I felt last night when I learned I would be expected to stay the night in the bed of a man I did not even know."

She thought he might apologize, but he only waved his hand impatiently. "It is not the fault of anyone here if you did not know the custom. You agreed to marry a man of Dun Gaoth, and that is how a marriage is made here. I am talking about what happened after the consummation occurred—which, I presume, it did?"

Keavy raised her chin and gave him a cold stare. "I have nothing more to say to you, Coilean of Dun Gaoth—except that I am not your wife and never will be." She walked out of the dark and dirty little house then and let the door bang shut behind her.

Walking with long, determined strides, Keavy returned to the house of the king. As she had expected, the crowd was still there, and they began to laugh again at the sight of Coilean hurrying to catch up to his very tall and most unmanageable bride.

"Once the king has done his duty, he is supposed to bring the bride back to the house of her husband!" the boy cried, almost spitting with anger and frustration. "He does not sleep the entire night with her! He is not her husband! The lawful husband would be laughed at everywhere he went if such a thing were ever allowed to happen!"

From among the crowd, especially near the back, came another roar of laughter. "Too late!" someone called, but then they all fell silent again as Coilean stepped closer to Keavy and began to speak more quietly, clearly hoping to reason with her.

"Please. Listen to me. Come back to our home, as you promised you would. You are my wife. We can speak of all this again, if we must, after three full moons have passed. Come now!"

But she only glared back at him as the crowd fell silent.

Coilean's eyes narrowed. He glanced over his shoulder at the staring people and reached for Keavy's wrist again. "Now, wife. We will go home now."

But she jerked her arm away before he could touch her. "I already told you—I am not your wife, Coilean of Dun Gaoth," she called in a clear, calm voice. She could hear the gasps from the crowd, but kept her gaze fixed on her erstwhile husband. "I am sorry, but I simply cannot do this. At the first opportunity, you treated me with cruelty instead of respect. And even if you had not . . ." She paused. "There is no love at all between us and never has been. I know now that I could not keep up such a ruse for all that time. I am sorry, Coilean," she said again. "I know we had an agreement, but that agreement is no more. This is something I simply cannot do."

A strange look, like some combination of shock and frustration and fear, crossed over Coilean's face. "You cannot break this agreement! You cannot!"

"I can. And I have." Her gaze flicked to Aengus, and she saw that he stared at her with an expression somewhere between amusement and disbelief. "It is done," Keavy said to the king. "We have no marriage. I will go directly from here to live among the servants, and there I will stay, if they will have me."

Coilean's eyes were huge. His mouth hung open as he struggled to find words. Then, before saying anything, he followed Keavy's gaze until he was looking directly at the king.

For a moment the two men stared each other down: the powerful king and the small young bard. Finally Coilean turned back to Keavy. "I see," he said, his voice shaking. "I see what has happened here. And so does everyone else. This has naught to do with how I have treated you. The king has stolen what is rightfully mine!"

Keavy looked at him, shocked at his words. "What do you mean, rightfully yours?" she whispered, bending her head down close to his so that the others would not hear. "We agreed to a marriage in name only! You have no interest in me, nor I in you! We both knew this from the start!"

"That agreement means nothing to anyone save you and I." His voice was a hissing whisper. "But everyone in Dun Gaoth *does* know that we were married yesterday. You went to the house of the king for the First Night, as the law requires. But you did not return to your husband when you could, before dawn, as is expected. You stayed until midday next with the king, and it is clear from the way you look at him that he did not force you to do so!"

"Coilean—"

"The king has stolen my wife! And every man and woman in the fortress knows this! If I no longer have a marriage, it is all because of the king!"

Well, Coilean was bolder than she'd given him credit for if he would publicly accuse the king like this. Keavy sighed as she listened to the low murmuring of the crowd. "I know you are not angry at the thought of losing me. I suppose I can understand that this may be an embarrassment for you—"

"Embarrassment! It is humiliation of the worst sort! You could not possibly understand."

She set her jaw. "Well, I will not debate that with you again. Perhaps there is something else here that concerns you more."

He looked sideways at her, frowning deeply, but said nothing.

"Maille."

He looked away. "I cannot allow her to be sent away. I cannot. I was willing to do anything to prevent that—but you have decided otherwise." He turned back to her again and gritted his teeth. "You and the king."

Keavy cocked her head and looked closely at him. "There is something you seem to have forgotten, Coilean."

He looked back at her again, glowering. "What have I forgotten?"

She folded her arms across her chest. "Consider this. Suppose we had carried out our marriage for the span of three full moons, as we agreed, and then each gone our own way, and you married your beloved Maille. She will have to spend her First Night with the king, too, will she not—as all brides do in this place?"

To her surprise he did not react, but merely shook his head. "Maille will not. The law of the First Night applies only to women from outside the kingdom of Dun Gaoth."

Keavy paused. "So, this law of yours only applies to outsiders," she said. "And Maille has lived her whole life at this fortress? She was born here, to one of the serving women?"

Coilean shrugged. "She has lived here for perhaps three years."

"Three years? She was not born here?"

"She was not."

"Where is her kingdom?"

"She has no kingdom."

"Then where—"

He sighed, looking up at her with growing impatience. "Maille was born among the rock men. They have no kingdom, no land—they just live where they can in the forest and on the hills. She and her mother begged for a place here among our servants, and it became their home. She is as much a woman of Dun Gaoth as anyone born here, whether servant or noble."

But Keavy only laughed and shook her head. "Coilean, Coilean . . . have you spoken to the druids about this?"

"I have no need to speak to them. Maille is—"

"Maille is an outsider, every bit as much as I was. She was not born here. When she marries, she will be subject to the law of the First Night just as I was." Keavy shook her head. "I can understand that you would not care that I had to endure such a ritual—but surely you must care that Maille will do the same."

"She will not! She will—"

"Ask them!" Keavy whirled around, her long loose hair flying back behind her. "Ask the druids! They will tell you that a woman born outside Dun Gaoth, whose family was never a part of this place, will be taken to the king on the first night of her marriage—not to her husband! Ask them!"

Keavy looked sharply at one of the druids who stood near her parents. His eyes flicked from her to Coilean and back again, and then slowly, without saying a word, he nodded.

Keavy turned back to Coilean. He made no sound, made no move; he only stood stock-still, his face flushing red, and clenched and unclenched his fists.

"Not Maille," he whispered at last. "Never Maille." Shaking with anger, he turned away from the silent crowd and shot a cold, hard glare at King Aengus.

The crowd began to murmur again, as surprised and disturbed as Keavy by the murderous glare that the usually meek and self-effacing Coilean had dared to turn on the king. Aengus kept very still, looking at Coilean with a steady, solemn gaze. Keavy expected Coilean to turn away from the king's unrelenting stare, but he seemed only to grow more enraged as he stood there.

"Go to your home, Coilean," Aengus called, still watching him. "Your wife will return to you when she is ready."

Keavy drew herself up and walked a few steps toward the king. "I said I will not," she said. "It is true that I agreed to marry Coilean, but that was before . . . It was at a time when . . ." She paused, gazing steadily at him. "I said I am no longer his wife, and I meant it. I am no man's wife, and I shall remain so until the day I myself choose to marry. No one will ever decide such a thing for me again."

She kept her gaze on Aengus, away from the murmuring, buzzing crowd, and saw that the king was beginning to smile but doing his best to hide it. And she, too, found it difficult to hide her own relief and happiness at seeing that he just might be pleased at the thought that she was no longer married.

"Keavy!"

But there were others, she was forced to remember, even as she continued to gaze at Aengus, who would not feel the same way.

Slowly she turned from the king and looked out over the crowd, where her father and her mother pushed and elbowed their way to the front and stood glaring at her, their anger and confusion plain to see on their faces.

"Keavy!" her father shouted again. "What is the meaning of this? Why do you humiliate us in this way?"

"I see we are back to humiliation again," she said. "Strange how everyone here believes they have been humiliated and gives no thought to what I was expected to do—not even you, my own parents."

"You did as the law and custom required!" snapped her father. "There is no humiliation in that. But there is terrible shame in turning your back on your own husband the morning after your wedding!"

"Coilean is not my husband. He never was, and he never will be." Keavy kept her voice as quiet and controlled as she could. "It is over. I cannot make this marriage. I will go from here and live among the servants of Dun Gaoth, and work just as they do."

"Oh, Keavy, I thought you had come to your senses at last!" cried her mother. "You have been so stubborn for so long, until finally you accepted this fine match we made for you! Surely you do not mean to reject your marriage after you have made it!"

"I have made nothing. I—"

Her mother leaned down close to Keavy with a deep frown on her face. "I will have to give back the *coibche*!" she said in a hiss. "You do understand that, do you not? All of the beautiful golden plates and cups and finger rings and armbands will be gone, back with Coilean and his family, never to be seen again! How could you let this happen?"

Keavy could only look at her and sigh. "I am sorry, Mother. I know how much the *coibche* meant to you. But I cannot marry a man I do not love, not for any amount of gold."

"But marry you will, and you had best find a reason you can live with!" roared her father. Before she could move, he reached out and caught her by the arm and began pulling her after him as he stalked off toward the tunnel that led through Dun Gaoth's thick stone walls. "If you will not stay here with this husband, you will come back to Dun Mor, and we will find you one that you will stay with, if we have to marry you off to every last man in the kingdom!"

Chapter Ten

Keavy tried to pull away, but it was no use. This was not weak Coilean who had her arm in his iron grip; it was her very angry and very determined father, Egan. "Let me go!" she cried, her anger and frustration rising. "Let me go! I will not go back. I will not—"

She nearly ran into him as he abruptly stopped. Pushing her long, streaming hair out of her face with her free hand and peering over her father's arm, she saw the pale and angry faces of Dallan and Sorcha, Coilean's mother and father, as they stood shoulder-to-shoulder like a wall between her father and the tunnel leading out of the fortress.

"This woman is our son's wife! You will take her nowhere!" insisted Dallan.

"They must be allowed to work things out!" shouted Sorcha. "Surely you understand that it is only their first night! They simply need more time!"

"I am sorry. I have no intention of working things out with your son," Keavy said, trying to ignore the fact that her father still held her arm in his grasp as though she were a wayward child. "This marriage is no more."

"Coilean!" shouted Dallan over the heads of the crowd. "Coilean! Come here! *Now!*"

Head down, peering up at his angry father from beneath deeply furrowed brows, Coilean made his way through the staring, waiting crowd. Keavy wished they would all just go back to their homes and to the hall and to the armory, and see to their weaving and stitching and sword making and *fidchell* playing. But there seemed little chance of that. These people were clearly enjoying the entire scene and had no intention of going anywhere until the little story had played itself out—and it showed no signs of being over anytime soon.

Dallan took his glowering son by the arm and held him so he faced the similarly restrained Keavy. "You must explain this, Coilean!" his father said. "Your wife is saying that she rejects your marriage!"

"A marriage that took place only yesterday!" added Sorcha. "How do you explain this?"

"We too should like to hear this explanation," said Egan through gritted teeth.

"That we would," agreed Keavy's frowning mother.

"As do we!" shouted someone in the crowd; and as the rest of the gathering laughed out loud all four of the parents—and Coilean and Keavy—turned to glare at them.

The group fell silent as Dallan turned back to his son. "Explain this. I will not ask again."

Coilean peered up at his father with a grim scowl. "You saw it, just as everyone else did. The king has stolen my wife. He kept her long past First Night and now she refuses to stay with me! This is not my fault. The king is to blame!"

A sudden silence fell over the crowd. Even Keavy caught her breath. Not many men would dare to talk of the king in such a way, and any who did would no doubt pay dearly for his insolence. She half expected a few of the king's men to drag Coilean out at sword point. Even now, she could see the stunned look on Aengus's face and the growing annoyance of the warriors around him. One of them moved his hand to the hilt of his sword. . . .

And then the crowd began to laugh. There were snorts of derision and low-voiced insults at first, and then ripples of laughter began to spread, until practically every last man and woman of Dun Gaoth was shouting with laughter at the sight of a pathetic, sullen youth like Coilean blaming King Aengus—or anyone else—for not being able to keep his wife. Even Aengus ducked his head and seemed to be biting his lip to keep from laughing out loud right along with the rest of them.

But this was the last thing Coilean's father wanted to hear. His face flushed red as he stepped back from his son, and he flung away his arm. "You were told this was your last chance!" he shouted. The crowd quieted down to listen, and Coilean looked sullenly away. "But you could not stay married for even one night, not even to a woman like this!"

Keavy glanced at them for a moment and then lifted her chin to look at Aengus, but he simply stood impassively watching. This was one story that would have to play itself out without interference. She looked away and saw that Coilean's father went on glaring coldly at his son. "We can only believe that you have tricked us—that you had no intention of staying married to Keavy at all!"

There was a tug on her arm. "And we can only believe the same of you, Keavy," her father said. "You have both tricked us. Your contract stated that you were to stay together for at least three full moons—and yet, on the very first morning after the wedding, the bride has left her husband and the husband is blaming the king!"

Keavy's father was just as furious as Coilean's. The laughter that erupted among the crowd did nothing to improve his temper. He, too, flung away Keavy's arm in a gesture of disgust and frustration. "You, daughter, have broken the bargain. That means you will come back to Dun Mor with us immediately so we can find you a husband you will stay with! I thought we taught you better than to break a lawful promise made to your lawful husband!"

"And you, my son, have also broken the bargain. That means the servant girl will be sent away at once. This will teach you to bargain unfairly!" Dallan said to Coilean.

Keavy clenched her own fists. "I will *not* go with you! I will not be sold away again!"

Coilean looked at his father with real anguish. "You will not send Maille away! I will not allow it!"

"Do you think that we will let you, whose family has the blood of kings, marry a girl from the poorest and commonest of people?" Dallan asked Coilean.

"You no longer have any choice in the matter," Egan told Keavy.

"And neither do you." Dallan, too, grabbed hold of his wayward offspring.

Keavy's father began pulling her toward the tunnel in the wall. "You will come home with us now, and there will be no more arguments about it!"

"I will go nowhere with anyone!" Keavy shouted, and she grabbed hold of the first arm she saw going past her—which turned out to be Coilean's. The two of them actually held on to each other as their parents tried to wrestle them away, bracing against the pulling arms and tugging hands and managing to hold their ground, at least for the moment.

But at the sight of the two families struggling to pull apart their newly married children, the crowd burst into a frenzy of excitement. They shouted encouragement to one family or the other, crowding around whichever one they favored, offering help and taking wagers on the outcome.

But when a few began piling on and trying to force Keavy away from her father while some tried to help him drag her toward the gates, Keavy heard a thundering shout.

"Stop this! Stop this *now*!"

The pulling, tugging hands suddenly released her. Keavy nearly fell, but she managed to stay on her feet. Pushing her long, tangled hair away from her face, trying not to trip on her trailing, heavy red gown, she drew herself up tall and looked at King Aengus, who had shouted his people down and ordered them to let her go.

He walked straight toward her, ignoring the people in the crowd who hastily got out of his way, and looked into her eyes as though there were no one else anywhere near. She could see concern for her there in those bright hazel eyes, but also a touch of amusement. He came to stand before her, made her a slight bow, and offered her his hand as the silent crowd looked on.

Drawing a deep breath, and summoning all the dignity she could manage while standing at the center of a staring crowd with her hair streaming down tangled and disheveled past her knees, she placed her hand atop the king's and nodded to him in return.

Aengus looked out over the crowd, his face serious. "Listen to me, for I will not say this to you again. This lady, Keavy of Dun Mor, is a free woman, and she shall not be made to go anywhere she does not wish to go. Is this understood?"

He fixed them all with his fierce gaze, looking from face to face until he was satisfied that no one would argue with his decision—including Keavy's frustrated, glaring, but entirely silent parents.

"And I further say to you all that the contract of marriage between Coilean of Dun Gaoth and Keavy of Dun Mor, recited yesterday, is hereby broken and void. It shall be as though this contract were never made." He looked up at his druids. "Are you in agreement?"

The three druids turned and looked at each other, bending down to engage in conversation. After a moment they looked up at the king again. "Was this marriage not consummated?" the first asked.

Aengus frowned. "It was not. The wife has never gone to the house of her husband, and swears she never will."

"I swear it too!" Coilean added, and the crowd laughed again until many of them were slapping each other on the back and all but rolling on the ground.

"Yet . . . Yet," the druid shouted, trying to be heard over the raucous crowd, "the bride did go to the house of the king for the First Night! Surely the marriage was consummated then!"

"That is not sufficient!" Aengus retorted, looking around at the druids and the crowd. "If a wife refuses her husband—"

"Or a husband refuses his wife!" called someone hidden in the back of the crowd.

Aengus bit his lip momentarily, but went on in a stern and practiced voice. "If a wife refuses her husband, there can be no marriage." He looked at the druids again, awaiting their response.

"Perhaps not," the druid begin, looking pointedly at Keavy and Aengus—then seeing the king's expression, he quickly finished, "This marriage is no more."

The crowd let out a cheer. A few of them began handing over bronze ornaments, small pieces of gold, and even a fine dagger—the losers of the bets, Keavy guessed.

Aengus turned to Coilean's parents and stared hard at them. But, like Keavy's mother and father, they kept their silence.

"Now, I have heard this lady say quite clearly, as have all of you, that she most definitely does not wish to return to Dun Mor. Since she has no husband here any longer, and no family, I will offer her a place in the king's house as my guest for as long as she might like to stay. What say you to this, Lady Keavy?"

She turned to him, catching her breath again, her fingers still held in his strong, warm hand. He was asking her to stay in the house of the king, stay with him in his own dwelling.

"I . . . accept," she said faintly. Then she smiled at him and spoke so that all could hear. "I accept!"

Glancing out over the crowd, she caught sight of Coilean and saw the very real fear and anguish on his face. Quickly she turned to Aengus and placed her hand on his arm. "I would ask a favor of you."

He smiled. "So soon? You have just become my guest, and already you are asking for favors?" She grinned back at him. "Tell me, then. What is it that I may do for you?"

"There is a servant here at Dun Gaoth—a young woman with the name of Maille. If I may, I would like to have her come and stay with me in your house."

He nodded. "I will have her sent to you this day."

"And . . . I would like you to say that she will not be sent away. Not as long as she serves me and does her work well."

Aengus turned to face the gathering. "Hear me now," he said. "The young servant girl known as Maille will stay with the Lady Keavy and serve her in my house. And there she will stay unless and until I say otherwise. Is this understood?"

"It is. It is understood," murmured the crowd. And Keavy saw Coilean nod slowly and unclench his pale fists.

She felt a little better now. Coilean was hardly an admirable man, but he did seem to have a genuine love for Maille, and Keavy knew he had accepted their marriage at least in part to prevent the servant girl from being exiled. It was no fault of Maille's that Keavy had backed out of the marriage, and she did not want an innocent to suffer.

She wondered, though, with a sigh as she watched Coilean drop to the ground and sit exhausted and sullen on the muddy grass, just how much suffering the poor girl would actually be spared.

Aengus turned to the gathering once again. "This night, when the sun sets, there will be a feast held just outside the walls, beneath the trees along the lake. Perhaps it will ease the feelings of all concerned to eat and drink together, to sit beneath the stars and listen to the most beautiful harps and the loudest of drums and the finest of poems."

The people of the crowd turned to nod and murmur to one another, clearly pleased by the idea. A few of them started to drift away toward their houses, but then the voice of Keavy's father broke in.

"We will not be staying for this feast or any other, King Aengus," he said loudly, his face red with anger. "You are holding our daughter hostage! We, her blood family, demand that she be released at once!"

"She is anything but a hostage. She is a free woman, as I said, and free to go wherever she wishes." Aengus turned to Keavy. "This may well be your last chance," he warned, in a low voice. "Do you wish to go back to Dun Mor?"

Keavy looked at her angry, glowering parents again, and shook her head. "I wish to stay," she whispered. "Perhaps someday I can go home again, but it will not be today. They will only trade me away again in their anger and embarrassment. Please . . . allow me to stay here, at least for a time."

Aengus looked out at Keavy's parents. "Your child is now a guest of Dun Gaoth," he said. "She is under my protection and will remain so for as long as she wishes."

"We shall see about that, King Aengus!" Egan cried, taking his wife by the arm. "We shall see if you change your mind when we bring the army of Dun Mor to your gates to rescue our imprisoned daughter, who is being kept from her husband and her family! Ready your warriors, King Aengus! You will soon have need of them!"

And with that, Keavy's father stalked out through the tunnel with his wife hurrying along after, followed by their servants leading pack ponies and hastily trying to catch up.

"A good day to you, too," Aengus replied under his breath as he watched them go. "I do hope you enjoyed your visit here."

He glanced at Keavy, his eyes bright with a little mischief, and she could not help smiling back at him. "I thank you for your hospitality," she said.

"Do not thank me. You honor me with your presence. Your parents' tempers will cool on the half day's journey back, and miss you greatly once they are there without you . . . but I shall be the one to miss you once you are safely home again."

"Safely home again! That time cannot come soon enough for us!"

Aengus and Keavy looked up to see Dallan glaring up at them as he hauled his son to his feet. "This I promise—as soon as this woman is gone, that servant girl will be gone, too. No son of mine will spend his life as the husband of a servant!"

He and his wife led Coilean away. Keavy could only imagine what the rest of his day would be like. The remainder of the crowd, seeing that the entertainment was over for now, began to drift away, until Aengus and Keavy were left alone with only his druids and a few of his men.

He turned to her. "I must go to the hall for a time, and attend to the things that await a king each day," he said, glancing up at the waiting druids. "But first I will escort you back to my home. Will you go with me, and accept my hospitality as king of Dun Gaoth?"

Keavy smiled, feeling as though some great weight had been lifted from her shoulders. "I will accept," she told him, and together they walked across the grassy yard of the fortress.

When they reached the door of his house, Aengus made a slight bow and then released her hand. "I will return for you in time to walk to the feast. Make yourself comfortable in my house. I will have all of your possessions brought to you here. Seanan will help you with anything you require."

"Thank you," she said. "Thank you for allowing me to stay."

"You are most welcome here. Good day to you, Lady Keavy."

"Good day to you, King Aengus," she whispered.

Eyes shining, the man turned and walked away, soon joined by his ever-present group of armed warriors. In a moment they had all disappeared among the many houses.

Chapter Eleven

Keavy drew a deep breath, and then carefully pushed open the door to the house that was, it seemed, to be her home for a time.

The door creaked and groaned mightily on badly rusted hinges. She had not noticed this before, in all the excitement and anxiety and noise. She pushed it closed again, cringing at the awful sound, and stepped inside the house.

The feelings that had engulfed her the night before all came rushing back—the fear, the anger, the curiosity, the wonder, the strangeness, and most of all the bond that had been formed between her and Aengus, whether it should have been formed or not.

Last night this dark and shadowed dwelling had been a place of mystery and fear—but now, she was relieved to see, it was only a house. It was the largest of all those at Dun Gaoth, but rather worn and plain, considering it was the home of the king. She could see, now, that the iron tongs and pokers above the hearth were edged with rust, that the bronze cauldrons hanging over the fire were dented and dull, that even the straw on the floor was old and flat and dusty and gray.

Suddenly the door creaked open again. Keavy turned to see Seanan struggling to step inside under the weight of a large wooden box, followed by two women. One was aged and gray-haired, while the other appeared quite young, but the younger's face was hidden by an enormous stack of folded furs and woolen fabrics that she struggled to carry and was just about to drop.

"Let me help you with that," Keavy said, hurrying over to the door—but just as she spoke, the whole stack of furs and fabrics went tumbling to the floor.

"Oh, I'm sorry. I'm so sorry!" the servant girl gasped, dropping to her knees in the straw and lunging after the fallen furs. "I've only just arrived, and already I will be sent away! I'm so sorry, oh, so sorry—"

Keavy crouched down in front of the distraught girl. "Maille! Look up at me. *Please*," she said, smiling and reaching out to touch the girl's face.

"How did you know my name?" The servant's dark brown eyes were huge in her very young face. Her skin flushed red, after having first turned white as milk, and her thick dark hair hung down her back in a loose and disheveled braid. Before Keavy could answer, the girl scrambled to gather up the furs and fabrics and started to get to her feet—but Keavy stopped her with a gentle hand on her arm.

"I asked for Maille, the young servant girl, and that must be who you are. Aren't you?"

Maille stared back at Keavy wide-eyed, then nodded slightly. "I am," she said. "I am honored to serve you, my lady. I thank you for asking for me."

Keavy sat back, even as Maille hugged the furs close to her chest. "Do you know why I asked for you?"

Maille started to answer, but then glanced up at Seanan and the gray-haired woman. "Because . . . because you are very kind, my lady." With great haste she picked up all that she had dropped, got to her feet, and moved out of the way to the far side of the hearth.

"We have brought your things here for you, Lady Keavy," Seanan said, still holding the heavy wooden box. The older woman went past him to take a few things to the hearth. "There is more just outside. Where would you like us to put them?"

"Oh . . . well . . ." Keavy turned away from them, both studying the house and hiding the faint blush she knew was creeping over her face and neck.

At the very back of the dwelling, right in the center, stood the painted leather screens in front of the king's sleeping ledge. Keavy's blush deepened. It was only now that she noticed how faded and flaking the paint was on the pictures of the eagles and the trees, how worn the leather had become, how the lacings that held it to the wooden frames were broken in spots and only crudely knotted together in others.

She could not see what the sleeping ledge behind the screens looked like and she was not about to go and look. Quickly she peeked behind the equally worn leather screen a few steps down the wall from the king's ledge, and saw another sleeping ledge. This one was covered with simple lengths of coarse dark wool and held only a single leather cushion, old and badly frayed. No doubt this was where Seanan took his rest. She had already seen how valued he was by the king, who had, it seemed, rewarded him with his own private sleeping ledge. Most servants slept wherever they could in the straw, or even in the cowsheds and sheepfolds.

Nearest the door and well away from the king's place was the last ledge, also behind an old and sagging screen. It appeared to be unused, for it was bare right down to its rough clay surface, except for bits of straw and a thick layer of dust. There was nothing at the foot of it save what appeared to be a stack of the worst of the cushions, frayed and worn and with old moss and straw spilling out through split seams. Some had been down there so long that a white coating of mildew had begun to form on them.

Keavy sighed, but then she turned back to the little group of servants. "This will be fine for me. I can see that it is not being used."

"Not any longer." Seanan's eyes met Keavy's for a moment; then he nodded and carried the heavy box to the ledge. The gray-haired woman remained standing still, staring at Keavy and at the empty sleeping ledge, and Keavy began to feel something like a chill in the warm air of the house.

"Good day to you," she said politely. "My name is Keavy, of Dun Mor. Might I know your name?"

The woman seemed startled, somehow, and forced herself to look away from the sleeping ledge and up at the one who addressed her. "Elva," she said quietly. "My name is Elva. I am here to serve you, as the king requested. I was the servant here for some years, servant to the . . . Before . . ."

She clearly had been about to say more, but seemed unable. "I thank you, Elva," Keavy said, and with a nod—and some relief—turned back to the matter at hand.

Keavy dragged the screens aside and moved the moldy cushions out of the way with her foot as Seanan set down the box at the end of the ledge. "The rest will follow," he said, and went outside again.

Keavy stepped back as Maille set down the great stack of furs and wools on top of the ledge, and began to spread them out across the bare surface and arrange them for best comfort and warmth. Again she turned to see Elva standing and watching her, her expression solemn and still, holding another of the heavy wooden boxes. "Oh, please . . . just set it down anywhere. I will see to—"

"Thank you, Lady Keavy." Elva set down the box on top of the one Seanan had left, and only glanced quickly at the sleeping ledge that Keavy had just claimed. She then hurried away again and went out through the door after Seanan.

Keavy sighed and turned back to the ledge. Well, this was a strange situation here in the king's house, she had to admit; not everyone was going to be as friendly as Maille or as polite as Seanan. She would simply have to make the best of things for a time. It was all that any of them could do.

Maille had done a fine job of making the sleeping ledge look comfortable. She picked up the old torn cushions and looked at them one by one, shaking her head. "I am sorry . . . these are not much good, I am afraid. I'll turn them as best I can, and—"

But Keavy picked up one of the cushions and looked at it closely. The leather was nearly rotted through from dampness, it had lain on the floor for so long. She set it aside with a sad smile. "We can do better than this, Maille. The king's house can do much better—and I'm just the one to make it happen."

A short time later, all the screens had been pulled out to enclose a space in front of Keavy's sleeping ledge. Keavy herself, her long hair twisted and pinned atop her head with long wooden pins, sat soaking in a narrow bronze tub filled with steaming water scented with apple blossom.

The tub was dented and in poor repair. The bronze showed a definite green tinge, and Keavy suspected it was leaking in several places. But it would do for now, and the hot water did help to ease the tensions of the day—not to mention those of the evening before.

After soaking for a time, Keavy picked up her small, neatly hemmed square of heavy linen and the small piece of soap that rested on it. She was aware that Maille watched her closely as she rubbed the soap on the wet linen, worked up a thin lather, and began scrubbing herself all over with it.

"Maille, did you get the little dish of ground oats from Elva?"

"I did, Lady Keavy, but I have never heard of such a thing before! Whatever do you mean to do with ground oats in your bath?"

Keavy smiled at her. "You have been a kitchen servant, have you not?"

"I have. I am so sorry; I know nothing of how to serve a highborn lady as a body servant. I did not even know it was possible to get the scent of apple blossoms into water, or that oatmeal had any place in washing!"

"Well, the apple blossom scent was distilled from last year's flowers and worked into the cream I use on my hair and on my skin. It also works wonderfully well in the bath to keep the soap from being too harsh. And as for the oatmeal . . ."

Keavy reached up and pulled the long wooden pins from her hair, letting it fall streaming down her back. Then all at once she slid beneath the water so that her hair was completely soaked, and came back up again to see a wide-eyed Maille.

"Now, then. I need your help. Just take a little of the wet soap lather, and a little of the cream, and work it all through the hair along with the oatmeal. Keep pouring water on it to keep it soft and wet. There, now—just scrub away with your fingers, and let the cream and the soap and the oatmeal lather work their way down the long part of the hair. Ah . . . perfect!"

"Why, so it is! I suppose the soap and the oatmeal work to clean the hair, while the cream keeps it soft. How lovely! No wonder your hair is so beautiful!"

"Thank you, Maille. And all that is left now is to rinse." As before, Keavy slid beneath the water, then scrubbed away the last of the soap and the oatmeal from her hair. "Done!" she said, sitting up to wipe the water from her eyes.

With a sigh of contentment, she lay back to relax one more time in the water while it was still warm. "Maille—if you would, please lay out a gown for me. Whichever one you like is what I will wear tonight."

"Oh, I will, I will." There was the sound of a wooden lid opening and then a great rustling of woolen and linen fabrics. "So beautiful, so beautiful," Maille murmured. "I almost fear to touch them. Oh, please, tell me, lady, wherever did you get them?"

Keavy opened one eye. Maille had laid out three gowns on the clean furs of the sleeping ledge and stood with her fingers hovering over a soft wool gown the color of pink violets. "I made them."

"You made them?" Maille looked back at the gowns. "The wool is light as air, the weave smooth and perfect, the color as delicate as the sky at dawn! I have never seen anyone who wore anything as fine as this, much less anyone who could make them! And this work . . . oh, this work . . ." She shook her head emphatically. "It looks like magic to me. Did the Fair Folk make these designs for you, and work such tiny stitches? Or did they teach you the magic to do such things?"

Keavy laughed. "I have never met any of the Fair Folk. My mother taught me the simple skills of spinning and weaving and stitching, and I merely added one more element: time spent in learning how to do these things in the very best manner that I could. That is what you see."

But Maille only shook her head once more. "It is not just skill and patience that I see when I look at these things. I see also the love you have for them. That is what gives them such beauty."

Keavy blinked and looked up at Maille. "They told me you were only a servant girl, born among the rock men who barely scrape by. How is it that you have such a thoughtful and elegant way of speaking?"

Maille turned a deep shade of pink all the way from her neck to the roots of her dark hair. "Oh, lady, there is nothing at all elegant about my way of speaking, though it is kind of you to say so. It's just that . . . just that I've always loved beautiful things, though I know nothing of how to make them myself. I love beautiful gowns and wonderful music and the sweet words of the poets, and it has been wonderful to live here at Dun Gaoth and be surrounded by such things."

Keavy could only smile at her, both surprised and pleased. No wonder she had been attracted to Coilean. He was supposed to be a musician, and might be a fair poet, though she had not heard him say enough words at one time to know if he had any skill with them or not. Maille was sweet-tempered and intelligent, and would probably be quite pretty if—

"It looks like I may be here for a while," Keavy said, "and already I see what I might do to both pass the time and earn my place here. Would you like to help me?"

"Help you?" Maille's eyes opened even wider, if that were possible. "I will do whatever I can, lady, but what could I ever do to help you?"

"You can help by letting *me* help *you*." And at Maille's baffled expression, Keavy just laughed aloud and slid down deeper in the water.

This was going to be something she would enjoy.

* * *

A short time later Keavy sat at one end of her newly covered sleeping ledge wrapped in a warm fur cloak, while Maille sat behind her at the other end of the ledge with a wooden comb in one hand and a small stone jar of scented white cream in the other—and her lap full of Keavy's long, damp, silver-blond hair.

"I am sorry, lady," Maille said, her voice full of hesitation. "I have never done this before. I should use . . . which one first?"

Keavy smiled and glanced over her shoulder. "First, divide the hair into two sections, parted down the center as best you can. Then touch your fingers to the cream, rub them together, and draw them gently through the hair."

Clearly doubtful, Maille gave the scented cream the lightest of touches and then drew her hands carefully along the long damp tresses. Keavy instructed, "Now take the comb and use it, starting at the ends and moving up. Do not go from the top down! Use a little more cream if you need it. There—is it working?"

"Oh, it is, it is!" Maille said softly. "So much easier than the way I have always combed my own hair. I must pull and tear it, and it hurts, so I do not comb it at all if I can avoid it. I just leave it in the braid." She sighed.

"Then you will have to use some of this, and I will show you how to properly comb and braid your hair. For today you can practice on me."

"I would be glad to practice on your hair, but mine will never look like yours! My hair is as coarse and thick as the wool of a sheep in the field, and I am lucky to get it into any sort of braid at all!"

"Oh, I will teach you," Keavy said with a laugh. "Now—once the hair is smooth and untangled, simply make two braids, one on each side, beginning at the neck. Make them tight and smooth, and then I will show you how to finish them."

Maille went to work. "Now, braiding is something I have learned to do, however poorly, though never with hair that was so very, very long. And now I can see why it has grown so long! Mine has always broken off in my battles with the comb, and never gotten much past my shoulders. I would love to have hair as beautiful as yours."

"You will. I promise it. But for now, while you are braiding, perhaps you will tell me how you came to meet Coilean."

She could sense Maille's blush without having to look. "Oh. It was not long after my mother and I came to live here, only a day or two after we arrived. I was walking across the grounds with a few of the other women, on our way down to the stream to bring the day's water. And as I walked toward the tunnel with the buckets thrown over my shoulder, I heard a sound—one I had never heard before."

"And what was that?"

Maille slid her feet to the floor, still holding the braid, and stepped back so she could continue braiding Keavy's long length of hair. "It was the sound of birds singing . . . or so I thought. It seemed to be coming from inside the hall, and I simply could not resist peering inside, though I knew that I should not. I had work to do, and—"

"I am sure no one would punish you for simple curiosity about your new home. What did you see?"

Maille stepped back again, working her way down the braid. "Something I had never seen before. It was a frame of wood with strings of bronze, and it sang whenever it was touched—the most magical thing I could ever have imagined."

"And who was playing this harp?"

Her hands grew still. "It was a young man with a gentle face. It was Coilean."

"Coilean." Keavy glanced back over her shoulder, and the gentle tugging resumed as Maille went on braiding. "And you liked him?"

Maille giggled. "I did, lady. I did! He smiled at me, and played the harp just for me, until the others hurried me along to go and fetch the water. But I didn't forget, and it seemed that he didn't either, for almost every time I went out I would see him."

"Ah, every time," Keavy murmured, trying very hard to keep the amusement out of her voice.

"He would play for me, or he would recite one of his poems." Maille sighed. "So wonderful! Since then I have heard other men play their harps and recite their poems, but none of them sounded anything like Coilean."

"I am sure they did not," Keavy agreed, putting her hand to her mouth.

"I was so happy every time I saw him," Maille went on. "But then . . ."

Her hands stopped again. Keavy turned to her. "Then his parents learned that he loved a servant girl, and they dragged him off to marry a woman he barely knew."

"And . . . and threatened to send me away from Dun Gaoth if he did not." Maille's eyes filled with tears, and she dropped the braid she had been working on.

Keavy reached for her hand and squeezed it. "No one is going to be sent away. And you know as well as I that he had no wish to marry me. He did it to protect you, Maille. That was his only reason."

"I know all that," she answered. "But now that there is no marriage, his family still wants to send me away. And if he were married to you, we still could not be together—oh, it's all just so impossible!"

Keavy reached for her, and hugged the girl for just a moment. "It seems impossible for all of us," Keavy said, "but I promise you we will find a way to work it out. I promise you we will find a way."

Chapter Twelve

Keavy sat on a cushion near the round stone hearth and anxiously watched the door, well aware of the lengthening shadows outside. "Lady, we should go. The feast will be ready soon," Maille called. "Everyone is gathering."

"But the king has not yet returned. Since I am a guest in his house, should I not wait for him?" Keavy tried to keep her voice steady and cool, but her mind was racing. *He asked me to wait for him—he said that he would walk with me to the feast. Has he changed his mind?*

"It is true that you are a guest, Lady Keavy," Elva said, from where she worked on the other side of the hearth. "But a guest only. Not—"

Keavy glanced at her. Elva raised her chin, her face stern, clearly disapproving of the whole idea of the king keeping a wayward bride in his house as a guest. Keavy sighed and got up from the cushion. "I suppose we should be going," she agreed quietly. "Maille, will you get my cloak for me, please?"

Maille was already holding the long wide swath of pale green and creamy white wool. She smiled as she looked at Keavy's gown, and shook her head. "It is even more beautiful now that you are wearing it. I did not know that wool could be as light as air, or made to hold such a delicate color, or that such embroidery could be done by any but the Fair Folk."

"Thank you. And I agree with you, for this gown is one of my favorites. This is the sort of thing that I prefer to wear, not the hideous . . . not the things I wore yesterday."

The gown was indeed one of her treasures. She herself had never seen such a rare and delicate shade of pink on any fabric. The dyers had done their work well that day, carefully distilling the color from blackberries and dandelion roots that Keavy had gathered. The hems of the sleeves and the curving neckline were covered with wide bands of embroidery done in bright green and dark brown and soft cream in an interlocking pattern of the leaves and branches and blossoms of an apple tree. A belt of delicate gold links rested on her hips, and soft boots of dark brown leather completed the outfit.

"It looks like an apple grove under a spring dawn," Maille said softly. "I didn't know that clothes could look this way."

"It's not so difficult to do such things, really,"

Keavy said. "All it takes is the basic skill—and a love for what you are doing."

"Well, I know I would love to look as beautiful as you," Maille said, and then laughed. "I'm just not sure I could ever do such work."

"You will if you truly want to," Keavy said, and started for the door. "But for now, come with me. We'll leave the king to his home." With a glance at Elva, whose face remained solemn and disapproving, Keavy stepped outside the house with Maille close behind her. They closed the heavy wooden door and started across the nearly deserted grounds.

"I'm afraid we will be late," Maille said. "Everyone else must already have left."

"Not so late as the king. I suppose you were right—we should have gone at the same time as the others. But I thought it only proper that we should wait for the king."

"Of course, lady," Maille said, her dark eyes sparkling; and together they walked through the narrow tunnel through the stone walls of Dun Gaoth and started on their way across the open, grass-covered hills toward the stand of tall birch trees along the shore of the lake.

A few other people were ahead of them, hurrying so as not to be any later than they already were. Far in the distance, near the trees, the servants were lighting a line of torches even though the sun was still above the horizon. On the grass in front of the silver-barked birch trees lay the same line of large wooden squares that had rested on the straw of the hall the night before, but which tonight lay in two long neat rows on the lush green grass beneath the torches.

Most of the people were already standing behind the furs and cushions and fleeces thrown down, waiting for their invitation to be seated. All of them turned to look at Keavy as she and Maille walked across the last stretch of grass—Coilean and his parents among them—and so did Aengus, the king, standing with his druids at the center of the row nearest the trees, facing the distant stone fortress and looking straight at her with a gleam in his eyes.

Keavy halted for a moment, startled and suddenly uncomfortable as all of the other people, standing behind the places along the waiting wooden squares, quickly followed Aengus's gaze and turned to stare at her.

"How is it that the king has arrived before us?" she whispered. "I thought that he was going to . . . I thought—"

"I don't know, lady, but he has arrived, and now we are very late!" Maille gathered up the green-and-cream cloak and thrust it at Keavy, and then hurried off to join the other servants where they worked at the firepit and boards set up on a wide expanse of straw a little distance from the gathering.

Keavy drew herself up tall, throwing back her shoulders and raising her chin as she stared back at the king. She was well aware of his gaze taking in her long braids, gleaming gold belt, and delicate, flowing pink gown. Then, before anyone could speak, she turned and walked far around the rows of people until she reached the gathering of busy servants working to prepare the food. Aengus watched her, but made no move to follow or give her any greeting at all.

"Shouldn't you take your place with the others?" Maille asked anxiously, hurrying past Keavy with a large tray heaped with freshly baked wheaten flatbread. "They all seem to be waiting for you. Even the king is waiting!"

"So he is," Keavy acknowledged, moving around to the far side of the straw and putting as many servants between herself and the guests as she could. She repeated, "How did he get here so quickly? We waited, out of courtesy to him, until it was nearly too late!"

"I don't know, lady. Perhaps he simply came here directly from his business at the hall. Perhaps—"

"He did no such thing," Keavy said, trying to look back at him without having it look as though she were looking back at him. "He must have readied himself at some other house without returning to his own."

"Oh . . . well, perhaps his business kept him—"

"Or perhaps he simply did not wish to be seen walking with me to this gathering." Keavy's mouth tightened, and she looked away. "He is putting me in my place. He is telling me, and everyone gathered here, that I am naught but a guest in his house, nothing more than . . ."

She paused, becoming aware that almost all the servants had stopped to stare at her, confusion plain on their faces. "Well, lady," Maille ventured, "isn't that what you are?"

Keavy clasped her hands together. "Of course. Of course I am," she said, smiling at them even as the warmth began to creep up over her face and neck. "I am a guest in the king's house and I am grateful for his hospitality. He has done far more for me than I ever expected he would."

She turned away and lowered her head to hide her blushing cheeks, pretending to look at the large wooden plates of steamed clover greens and boiled dandelion roots and the wooden bowls of pale spring butter along the outer edge of the straw. "Now, what can I do to help all of you?"

"You can come and sit beside me at the feast, Lady Keavy."

She turned at the sound of that deep pleasant voice—a voice that had already become very familiar to her. The speaker stood in the shadows near the edge of the straw, in a shadowed spot just beneath the silvery birches.

"King Aengus," Keavy answered, keeping very still. "Why would you wish me to do such a thing? I am no one of consequence to you. I am merely a guest in your house, one of many that you must have had over these many years that you have been king. I am grateful that you have allowed me to stay there. But that is all I am to you."

He smiled gently at her, and even as he stood in the shadows beneath the pale leaves she could see the sparkle in his eye. "It is our custom that any visiting guest be invited to sit with the king and share his plate. Of course you would be extended the same courtesy. I hope you will accept it."

She raised her chin. "I would not wish to be invited merely out of your sense of duty. That would mean that I am no different to you from any other guest."

"I assure you, Lady Keavy . . . the custom may have had its origin in duty, but I ask you now out of my own wish. Will you come and sit beside me at this feast?"

Her face flushing even more, well aware that everyone at the entire gathering must be aware of what he said, Keavy nonetheless nodded her head. "I will accept your kind invitation to sit with you this evening, King Aengus."

She saw him smile through the gathering darkness. Without a word, he stepped forward and offered his hand.

He did look a bit more like a king today, Keavy had to admit. His trews and boots and iron-ringed belt were of good brown leather; his tunic was a fine plaid of blue and brown and white; his soft golden-brown hair and beard and mustache were all clean and neatly combed. He wore his king's torque just as he had yesterday night when she had been taken to him. Seeing that heavy gold around his neck, seeing those fierce and gleaming eagle's heads, was a forceful reminder of—

He reached down and took her hand, and

stepped back so she could go ahead of him. Together they walked across the grass even as everyone looked up to stare at their king and this outsider he walked with, though it seemed that at least some of his subjects actually smiled as they turned to each other in whispered conversation.

As Keavy walked with her hand placed lightly on King Aengus's there was a familiar whirring sound at her shoulder. She merely glanced at the wren that had landed there and kept on walking, but Aengus stopped short.

"Why, what is this?" He blinked in surprise, but then a delighted smile broke through. "This little wren seems to like you very much."

Keavy shrugged and went on walking. "You may recall, King Aengus, that I mentioned this thing to you when . . . when we first met. It happened often to me at home, and I am glad to know that it still happens here in this place that is so strange to me."

"Perhaps the bird believes it has found a blossoming apple tree, surrounded by a field of pink clover beside a shining silver stream," Aengus said. He stopped and turned to her. "For that is what I might have thought upon seeing you wear this gown with your shining braids falling down across it."

Keavy blushed again, and turned to keep on walking. "I thank you, King Aengus," she said, just as another wren came down to alight on her arm.

Aengus could only smile and shake his head. "Perhaps we should cover you with a nice dark cloak before every bird in Eire comes to sit on your arm."

"Too late." Keavy laughed as a third wren came down to perch on her other shoulder. She and the king sat down together at the center of the row nearest the trees, facing the distant stone fortress. The birds fluttered their wings as Keavy made herself comfortable on a leather cushion, but made no move to leave her.

Aengus chuckled as he looked at Keavy and the bright-eyed birds who kept their precarious perches on her shoulders and her wrist. "I do not recall inviting three extra guests to my feast," he said, still grinning. "But they are welcome to stay, if they are friends of yours."

"They are indeed my friends. Perhaps my only friends at this place," she teased.

"That is not so, Lady Keavy." He reached for her fingers, but the little wren sitting on her arm cheeped angrily, raised its wings, and made as if to peck him. He withdrew his hand. "I see that I must be cautious when your friends are about. Will they at least allow me to speak with you?"

"I am sure they will," she replied, "even as they are allowing it now. But I cannot imagine you would wish for anything more than ordinary conversation with me."

His eyes grew soft. "And why would you believe that?"

She reached for her bronze cup once a servant filled it with blackberry wine. "I waited for a time—for as long as I could—before leaving with Maille to come to this feast."

"There was no need for you to wait for me. You should have gone as soon as you wished."

"I thought it only courteous to wait. I believed you said . . ." She stopped, and took another sip of her wine.

His eyes brightened in understanding. "Ah. I see now! You waited for my return so that you and I might walk to this gathering together."

Keavy looked away, her face warming again. "I thought it only courteous to wait for my host, who invited me to walk with him. But I see now that you had no wish to be seen arriving here with me."

Aengus reached for his cup. "That is not true. I had things to attend to among the warriors, and before I knew it the sun was nearly gone. I simply left and came straight here, thinking you would have already arrived."

"And so you were spared having to be seen walking with me, as though I were . . . more than just a duty."

He looked down, and his voice was quiet. "You are my honored guest this night, Lady Keavy. That is why I have asked you to sit beside me."

She raised her chin. "And you also made it clear that such an invitation is extended to any and all who might be a guest of the king, is it not?"

"It is . . . but surely you did not expect more than this. Did you?"

His voice remained soft. He was trying to be

kind, but she found that his politeness only made her feel worse. "I do not know what I expected," she said, looking down at her hands. "I only know that I made a great mistake last night."

Aengus turned and smiled pleasantly at a few of the people across from him, lifting his cup. He raised his hand to signal one of the servants. "Begin the music, please," he called "and serve the food as well." In moments the lively sounds of the harp and drum and wooden flute floated over the gathering and gained everyone's attention, even as the servants brought out the first large wooden plates of flatbread and butter.

As the guests turned their attention to the music and the food, Aengus turned back to Keavy. "Tell me, please," he said quietly. "Why do you feel you have made a mistake?"

Keavy looked down at the wooden plate of hot bread and cold butter that a servant set down between them, but she made no move to try the food. "I told you last night that I knew nothing of your custom of the First Night and had no intention of going along with such a thing. And yet, before the night was over, I did accept it—I accepted it more than once."

Aengus ran his finger over the rim of his bronze cup, but remained quiet. He never took his eyes from her. "You did your duty as law and custom required . . . even as I did. You have no reason to—"

She gave him a quick glance. "I did nothing out of duty. That is what you must understand. It may have been duty for you, but it was not for me."

He paused, and she saw a faint gleam in his eyes. Whether it was from amusement or apprehension, she did not know. "Well, lady . . . I do not know what other reason you could have had for, ah, staying with me last night. Surely you are not in the habit of staying the night in the beds of men you have only just met, especially when you have just married another."

Keavy jerked her head up, sending one of the wrens on her shoulder flying off into the gathering dusk, and then smiled politely at the diners across from her who had been startled by her sudden movement. As calmly as she could, she took another sip of wine, and then set down the cup. "You are quite right, King Aengus. I have never done such a thing and never would. I believe that last night I was . . . I was . . ."

"Persuaded, perhaps, by kind words and pleasing appearances?"

"Under a spell," she whispered, staring down at her cup.

"A spell." She thought he would laugh again, but he did not. "A spell? How could this be?"

"I do not know. It could only have been a combination of things, for even I know that this is how magic is made. Magic is never just one thing, but many, all coming together at just the right time."

He nodded slowly. "That is my understanding of magic, too."

She turned to him. "Then you do know something of this. You are a king, you have been trained by the druids, you told me yourself you had once been able to take the form of an—"

He stopped her by placing a quick but gentle finger across her lips, causing the wren on her arm to squawk and hop up into the air to fly away. "Please do not speak of such things here, Lady Keavy. As I told you, it has been a very long time since the days when I had such powers."

"Yet I do feel that there must have been some magic on me last night," she insisted. "I was under great pressure to yield to this custom, it is true . . . but I also felt so strongly that I had, indeed, found that great golden eagle that came down to me so many years ago and who left me a gift of his feathers."

"Pressure to yield, and long-remembered magic," Aengus said lightly. "Was there nothing else to persuade you?"

Slowly and deliberately, she turned to face him. "King Aengus," she began in a tight whisper, "if those things were not enough, it would mean that I found the simple presence of a strong and handsome man enough to convince me to give myself to a stranger. Do you truly think so little of me?"

His eyes widened a bit, and his face grew serious. "Oh," he said, and seemed to be deep in thought. She thought he would apologize and was considering whether to accept it or not—when he suddenly grinned, looking extremely pleased with himself. "Then you find me strong and handsome."

The third wren, the last one sitting on Keavy's

shoulder, took off into the darkness of the forest.

Keavy looked away, toying with her cup of wine as her indignation rose. "Perhaps you are right. Perhaps it was just the lateness, the darkness, the strangeness of it all, that would convince me to go along as easily as I did . . . not to mention the poor feast and endless cups of blackberry wine." Her fingers tightened on her cup, and her eyes began to burn with tears. "No magic at all . . . just a lonely, frightened woman given to the king and made to think she had no choice."

Still staring down at the cup of wine and the plate of bread, Keavy heard him sigh. "You did have a choice. You did not wish to go back home only to be bargained away again, and so you honored the lawful marriage you had made."

"But—"

"I say to you, Lady Keavy, that you must not think of this anymore. You did what was proper and expected for one in your position, and now it is done, and you need think no more about it."

"But it is *not* done," she whispered. "I have made a great mistake, not so much by following a lawful marriage custom, but by allowing myself to form a bond with a man who cares nothing for me. *That* is why I should have resisted, even if it meant being sent home to risk another unwanted match." She shook her head and almost laughed. "A greater mistake I could not hope to make."

Aengus set down his cup and folded his hands on his knee. "Lady Keavy." His voice was soft as any man's might be. "It is not that I care nothing for you. This experience is still so close and new for you. You need not tell yourself such things now. Wait a nineday . . . wait a fortnight . . . wait until the next full moon. Let this thing take its place in your past, as it should, and it will not trouble you then."

She looked him full in the eyes, seeing pity and concern for her there but little else. "This thing will always trouble me. Of that I am certain. It is not the sort of thing that I will ever forget. Not in a nineday, not in ninety years."

He was silent for a time, but then smiled. "I will give you a little time, Lady Keavy, and we will see what effect it has on you. I think you may be surprised, once you allow yourself a bit of time to adjust."

She wanted to answer but could not find the words. Aengus reached out and briefly covered her fingers with his hand, patting her gently. "Come now. There is no reason why you should not enjoy this beautiful night, with good food and lively conversation and beautiful surroundings."

He withdrew his hand and moved the wooden plate a little closer to Keavy. "Here. Try a bit of this good bread and butter to begin your evening. Wheat bread is a favorite of mine. I always—"

He stopped as there was a sudden flutter of wings around Keavy, and all three of the wrens returned to sit on her shoulders and her wrist. "Well, beautiful Keavy," he said, "I am sure you have heard the old tales of how a goddess of healing and of harmony is often to be found in the company of wild birds who choose her company freely."

She managed a small smile. "I am anything but a goddess, King Aengus."

He shook his head. "You are as beautiful as any goddess could ever wish to be . . . and I have no doubt that you will, one day, find the man whom you can truly love."

Keavy reached for her plate and broke off a few bits of bread, offering it to the wrens. They took it eagerly and hopped along her shoulders and her arm, clearly hoping for more. She glanced up at Aengus and met his hazel eyes. "I have found that man. But it never occurred to me that once I found him, my love would not be returned. I should have known that there would be another, even if she remained forever in his past. I see that I am only a foolish young girl after all."

"Lady Keavy." His voice was very quiet. "I would like nothing better than to return your love . . . but I dare not do such a thing to you. I—I am not the sort of husband you deserve, for you deserve far better. I only hope that someday you will understand."

He tried to place his hand over hers, but she quickly returned her attention to feeding the birds. She was determined not to look into those shining hazel eyes ever again.

Chapter Thirteen

The feast went on, and Keavy tried to relax and enjoy it as best she could. She tried to tell herself that Aengus was right. What was done was done and there was nothing she could do to change that now. And neither could she change the fact that he did not, could not, return her love, as she had so foolishly believed. It seemed that for Aengus, no woman could ever replace his dead queen.

She would simply have to do her best to avoid him, so that she could let time do its work and she could begin to forget . . . but for tonight she was trapped at his side, since to get up and leave in front of all Aengus's people would be the worst sort of insult.

She told herself it was only for one evening.

The servants brought the next course around, which for the king was a prime cut of venison. Again Aengus offered her the plate first. "Ah, quite good, don't you think?" he asked, turning the plate to present her with the choicest part. "Nothing like good wild meat straight from the forest. Tame beef and mutton are just not the same."

She took a small piece of the venison, touched it to the scant juices on the plate, and tasted it. After a moment she shook her head. "I am sorry to tell you, but I find it of passable quality—at best. It is too dry and too plain. I do not wish to boast, King Aengus, but I can make better myself, and have done so many times."

"Have you, now! You are indeed a lady of many accomplishments. Perhaps, if you wish, you could show my servants how to make it, and then we could all enjoy it properly."

"I would not be unwilling to do such a thing," she answered, reaching for another small bit of the meat, "but I am not sure that I should. In fact, it is becoming clearer to me every moment that I should not be here at all."

He sat back a little, looking at her from the corner of his eye. "Have you changed your mind? Do you now want to return home? If this is truly what you wish, I will see that you are escorted there at dawn tomorrow. I hope that you will not leave Dun Gaoth—but neither can I make you stay. If going home is truly your wish, you shall have it."

She started to speak, but hesitated, and sipped her wine instead. "You know as well as I that I cannot go back now. I must give my parents time to calm their tempers and forget the insult I have given them—but then I will, indeed, return to Dun Mor and do what I must to save myself from being bargained into marriage ever again."

Aengus took a large strip of venison from the plate. "I am glad to know you will not be leaving yet."

"But I should be leaving. I should be leaving your house. I should stay with some of the other women, or among the servants, and pass my time teaching them things I know that they might enjoy, such as how to prepare venison in seasoned drippings . . . or even making decent cushions for the king's house."

He smiled tightly. "I must apologize for the state of the cushions in my home. Perhaps this is, as you say, a very good reason for you to stay there even longer. If anyone could make a home a beautiful place, I believe it is you, Lady Keavy."

She set down the cup and shook her head. "I should not be there at all. How can you expect me to stay there, when—"

"I will tell you again, my lady, that you have nothing to feel embarrassed about."

"When I know," she continued, "that I will never be anything more to you than one of a long line of brides, no more than a polite but unseen guest in your house."

"It would not do for you to leave my house and live with someone else here, especially not the servants. It would be a terrible insult to the king and his home. You are a lady of such manners yourself that I am sure you understand."

"Again, I am glad to know that the wishes and feelings of everyone else are far more important than my own," she murmured. "But I do know well that rejecting a king's offer of hospitality is not something that I—or anyone else—can do."

"Then what may I do to make you more comfortable while you are here?"

She did not look up at him. "You can allow me to sit elsewhere the next time there is a feast. You can look up at the sky or down at the grass or marvel at the wind in the trees the next time you happen to see me walking across the grounds of the dun. And you can leave me to myself while I am in your house and you are there, and tell yourself that I am no different from any other guest who might stay with you. *That* is what you can do for me, King Aengus."

"I am sorry it must be this way," he said, so softly that she could scarcely hear him. "But this is not something that can ever be changed."

"I understand. I am a woman who would like to find a man to love and to marry, and you are a man who has no wish to ever again take a wife. And now I understand very well why you have no need for one. No man would, in your position."

It was his turn to gaze down at his plate and cup. "I might be persuaded to take a wife again someday," he said cautiously, "if ever I were to meet the right woman."

Keavy laughed, and he looked at her in surprise. "Every man says such a thing. Every one of them. And it is usually a very long time, if ever, before this 'right woman' can be found. I can only ask you, King Aengus, why you have need of any wife at all, when there will be an endless parade of beautiful young brides brought to you so long as you have the strength to service them?"

"Lady Keavy . . . I truly am sorry. I have no wish to hurt you, but neither will I mislead you."

She sat back then and looked at him, smiling as politely and as coolly as she could even while seeing a look of something like pain in his hazel eyes. "I know. I do believe that. And I must thank you for your honesty. Most men would be only too glad to tell a woman in my position whatever she wanted to hear and then take full advantage of the situation for as long as he possibly could. I am glad to know, at least, that you are not that sort of man."

"You are right, I am not. But sometimes, I will admit, I wish I were."

Just then the servants came around with the third course, which was roots of clover and dandelion boiled in meat drippings and covered with steamed clover leaves. Aengus sat back and signaled again to one of the servants. "Tell the bards we should like to hear them now."

Keavy drew a deep breath, then turned her attention to the food. She lifted a serving of greens onto her dish with the bronze knife resting on the plate and mixed a little of the rather dry venison in with the clover and roots. It was a bit tastier that way, she found.

She told herself that it was time, now, to simply

move on. Before long she would be able to go home and start a new life. She should be glad that she was not actually married to Coilean, glad that she had found the strength to stand on her own for once. Three full moons might seem like a short time to most people, but it would have been worse than a lifetime if Keavy had actually been the wife of Coilean—even in name only.

She saw him now, sitting several places down with his parents across the slabs of wood, staring morosely at the food on his untouched plate. He would occasionally shift his eyes toward the servants, where they worked far past the end of the rows, no doubt looking for Maille; but as Keavy watched him, he slowly began to sit up a little straighter, and then turned to look toward the bards, who had begun to play and sing.

Everyone else was looking at the bards, too, and beginning to smile and laugh. One played the harp while the other sang, but he was not just reciting any poem. This was a satire, meant to ridicule its subject and allow everyone to enjoy a great laugh at his expense. And as Keavy listened to the lively music and rhythmic words, she heard what the bards were saying:

What does a woman need? A husband, to make her a bride.
Where shall the bride find a husband? At Dun Gaoth.
What does a husband need? A husband needs a member.

Where shall the bride find a member? At the king's house!

The heat of embarrassment began to flood over her, even as she had to force herself to keep from laughing. It was clear whom they were talking about. She stole a glance at Coilean, who sat hunched over with his head low, glowering up in furious silence at the bard reciting the song.

When the sun rises
Where will the bride be found?
Not in her husband's bed!
She chose to keep the member
And let her husband keep his own!

Everyone erupted in raucous, jeering laughter. Even Aengus was grinning. The bard bowed low to the crowd and sat down again, and the music began once more.

Keavy let out her breath. At least it was over now. Such songs were common, practically expected. Surely no one would think too much of this one.

But it appeared the damage was done. Coilean could only hide his burning face in shame and take a long drink of wine while trying to pretend he had not heard. The crowd laughed even harder as his furtive actions caught their collective eye.

Aengus could only shake his head. "He will be hearing about this for quite some time to come, I am afraid," he said, still chuckling. "Perhaps he will learn a bit of humility at long last."

Keavy watched as Coilean continued to stare at his plate, even while both of his parents glared fiercely at him. "It is not his fault," she said, feeling sorry for him in spite of herself.

"Not his fault?" Aengus laughed again. "Of all the men at Dun Gaoth, not one would disagree if I said that Coilean was the weakest of them all. Everyone here knows it—except, it has always seemed, for Coilean himself."

"He is not the one who refused to keep his lawful marriage. He is not the one who broke a promise to many people simply to do as he wished." Keavy looked down. "Perhaps he was not so selfish as I."

"Perhaps if he had even half your strength, he would not have allowed himself to be pushed into a marriage he did not want."

"But he did so in order to protect—"

"And he would never have had to do such a thing if he had been man enough to defend Maille some other way."

Keavy stared up at him . . . and then bit her lip to keep from nodding.

"Look, there, at his parents," Aengus said, looking down at his cup and signaling the servants to fill it again. "They, too, are suffering from the weakness of their son—and from his inability to break away from his old poor habits and do what must be done, uncomfortable though it might be for him for a time."

Apparently Coilean's parents were beginning to

feel the same way. As the music played and the others began to go back to their conversation and laughter and food and wine, Coilean's parents turned to their sulking, humiliated son.

"Perhaps *you* can sit here and listen while a satire is made about you, but I assure you, we cannot!" his mother said in a hiss.

"You can also be sure that you will never marry anyone—not even the lowest slave or most wretched servant—until every last man in the kingdom is finished laughing at you," his father said in a growl through clenched teeth. "And that will not be for a very long time!"

Slowly and deliberately, the two of them got to their feet. They nodded politely to the king, who nodded back, and then they both hurried away as quickly as they could over the open rolling hills toward the torchlit fortress of Dun Gaoth.

As soon as they were gone, Coilean got quickly to his feet and stalked off with his head down, his fists clenched, and his skin paler than ever. He looked at no one, not even the king, but just scuttled away like an insect. He headed far around the boards and into the deep darkness of the trees along the lake.

Keavy sighed. "Of all of us, I believe this will be hardest for him."

"I believe you are right about that. He should have done what you found the strength to do: stand up for himself and admit when he had made a mistake. But instead he clung stubbornly to his old ways, and now he will be suffering for it for a long time to come."

"I am not so strong," Keavy whispered.

Aengus looked into her eyes, and raised his cup to her. "You were strong enough to set your life to rights—yours and Coilean's both—when it had clearly begun to follow the wrong path. Now he is free to make his own way, however clumsily he does it; and you, beautiful Keavy, are free and unmarried, and an honored guest of the king."

He lowered his cup and leaned toward her, and she thought he would offer her a chance to drink—but instead he continued to move closer until his face was right in front of hers, and his breath was warm on her cheek, and his lips were soft on her own.

All of the birds with her quickly flew away, but Keavy scarcely noticed against the pounding of her heart and the roaring in her ears. She blinked, feeling dizzy, as Aengus calmly sat back and nodded politely to the other guests, lifting his cup and saluting the musicians and then reaching for a few greens to go with his venison.

Slowly Keavy turned back toward the boards, and tried to both catch her breath and arrange her features in something like normalcy . . . but it was not easy. Instead she placed her hand on his wrist and pressed it until he turned to look at her again.

"Why did you do this?" she whispered, her voice trembling. "How could you do this, after what I have told you?"

He looked down, but then glanced away, suddenly seeming unsure of himself. "Why . . . Because I—"

"Because you are in the habit of kissing attractive women whenever you wish. Because you are the king and no woman can refuse you."

"Because you are the most beautiful woman I believe I have ever seen. Because I could not let this evening come to an end without making certain that you knew this."

She shook her head. "There are many other ways to offer a lady a compliment. Do you not see the cruelty in allowing me to think you have affection for me, when you have plainly indicated you are not a man who wants to take another wife?"

"I have no wish to be cruel to you, Lady Keavy."

"Then do not treat me with anything but the most distant courtesy. If you wish me to stay at arm's length, since we could never have a future, then you must leave me there. Do not draw me close if you do not want me there for more than just one night."

He hesitated, looking down at her with something like pain in his eyes, and then nodded. "I understand. And I am sorry."

She set down her cup, gathered her flowing pink skirts, and got to her feet. "I know that you think of me as just another woman. I have no choice but to accept this as a fact. But you must carry this always in the deepest part of your heart:

I will never think of you as just another man. Good night to you, King Aengus."

Somehow Keavy made her way across the grass-covered hills, keeping her eyes on the fortress walls. Heavy clouds moved quickly across the sky and kept obscuring the moon and stars, but little light was needed to see the bright white stones of the enormous ring that was Dun Gaoth. It was not long before Keavy was walking past the guards and through the low, damp tunnel that led inside the fortress, and then crossing the quiet grounds to the house of the king.

The fire burned low within the hearth. All was silent and still, for the servants were still working at the feast. Keavy closed the creaking door behind her and quickly crossed the straw-covered floor to slip behind the leather screen guarding her sleeping ledge, as though she were afraid someone would see her even in the dark and empty house.

In the near-total darkness, Keavy ran her hands over the worn furs covering the wide ledge, and over the only two cushions she'd been able to salvage from the rotting stack on the floor. There was so much that needed to be done here . . . so much that she could do for this place, that she could do for Aengus . . . but none of it would happen now. Any fleeting hope she'd entertained of having a future here—a future with Aengus—was gone.

She was a woman who believed she had found

the man she was meant for, and indeed had given herself to him in that belief. But he was a man who had no desire, and no reason, ever to marry.

Keavy unhooked her belt of gold links and placed it at the far end of the ledge. In a moment her beautifully embroidered pink gown lay atop the belt, leaving her dressed only in her long cream-colored linen undergown. She sat down on her ledge, threw her green-and-white cloak around her shoulders, and began to unbraid her hair, carefully working the golden spheres free from the ends and then quickly undoing each long plait with practiced fingers.

At last she pulled the fur coverings up over her and lay down with her head on the cushions, suddenly feeling chilled in the cold, damp spring night. Keavy closed her eyes and tried her best to sleep—she should surely be tired after a day like this one—but found that all she could do was listen for the sound of the door being opened.

Just when she had begun to despair that anyone would return to this house tonight—when she was certain that he must have decided to stay at the house of one of his men, or, she thought, feeling a sudden stab in her heart, at the house of some other woman—the heavy wooden door creaked open on its aged iron hinges.

Keavy caught her breath, but made herself keep still. In the darkness she heard Aengus's low words to his men and to Seanan, the creaking of the door as he closed it again, and the sound of his footsteps in the straw as he made his way around the central hearth.

The footsteps halted just outside her screen.

She hardly dared to breathe. He was here. He had come back to her. In just a moment he would set aside her screen and sit down to face her on the edge of the ledge, leaning over her and smiling in the darkness, reaching for her and—

The footsteps moved on again.

She could only listen as he walked across the house until he reached his own sleeping ledge at the very back. There was the soft, distant rustling of the tall leather screen being moved aside in the straw, and moved back; then the house was quiet once again.

Keavy closed her eyes to keep them from burning, to keep the tears from starting. What had she expected? she asked herself fiercely. Had she thought he would return to her bed the way a husband returned to a beloved bride? She was *not* his bride and she was not his beloved, and she had best remember that and get used to it, and not ever forget it for a single moment—not ever again.

Chapter Fourteen

The next morning, just as the first soft gray light filtered into the house, Keavy rose and dressed herself as quickly as she could, putting on a plain blue linen gown and soft brown leather belt. Peering out from behind the screen, she saw only Maille, who was just getting up from her makeshift bed in the straw.

"Maille, would you help me, please?" Keavy sat down again on the ledge, retreating behind the screen, and found her comb and a long wooden pin in the box of cosmetics on the floor nearby.

"Just comb it out, and help me make one single braid. I'll pin it up after that. But you must work quickly. There's not much time."

"What is the hurry, Lady Keavy?" Maille asked, brushing bits of straw from her plain wool dress. She hastily sat down on the ledge and began to separate Keavy's hair into three long plaits. "Are you going somewhere today?" Suddenly she stopped, almost dropping the plaits of hair. "Oh, you're not leaving, are you? You're not going away?"

Keavy glanced back and smiled. "I'm not going away just yet. It would be even worse for me if I leave now. My parents are so angry, and their pride so hurt, I think they would trade me away to the first group of outlaws who came along."

Maille sighed, and straightened Keavy's hair again. "I am so glad to know you aren't leaving. If you leave, it would mean that . . . it would mean—"

"I know. It would mean that you might well be sent away to some other fortress, or even to some distant farm family, and not see Coilean again—not for a very long time."

"Well, it would. And of course I am afraid of that. But Lady Keavy, even if I would never be sent away, I would miss you very much if you were gone."

"And I would miss you as well."

She paused. "Maille . . . I am so sorry that Coilean had a rough time of it at the feast last night. Those who make satires can be very cruel."

Maille sighed. "They can, they can! I have never heard such talk, yet it only makes me love him all the more to think he would endure such cruelty so that we might someday be together."

Keavy could not help but smile. "I suppose that is a fine way of looking at it."

"So . . . will you please tell me why you are in such a hurry this morning?"

Keavy took a deep breath, and carefully

reached down to the floor to get her boots. Maille continued to braid her hair. "I seem to have little choice but to stay at Dun Gaoth. I would move out of the king's house if I could, but it would be nothing but an insult to him after everyone heard him extend me the hospitality of his house. I will just have to make the best of this situation—but for that, I need your help."

"My help?"

"Yours. I want to be out and working at some task—spinning, combing, weaving, stitching—before the king awakens each day. We can take a bit of food with us and be at work among the women in the hall before the sun is even risen."

"That we can. But Lady, how can you hope to—"

Keavy turned to look at her. "I cannot hope. That is why we must leave early, before he sees us. And we must do so on this morning and on every other morning, so long as I am here."

They did slip away that morning before the king could see them, and as Keavy had wished they spent the day in the hall in the company of the other women of Dun Gaoth. The time passed pleasantly enough as they all worked at weaving good wool fabrics and stitching them together for tunics, gowns, and cloaks. Keavy made herself concentrate on the work and on the conversation, and especially on teaching Maille to weave cloth smoothly and evenly and to sew with neat, tight stitches.

Such activities helped to keep Keavy from constantly glancing around the hall to see if the king might enter with his men, and allowed her to turn away and lose herself in her work whenever he did come in to hear a legal complaint from one of his people or to discuss some matter with his druids or sit with a few companions for a game of *fidchell.* Yet it seemed that whenever King Aengus was anywhere in the great hall she could feel his eyes upon her, whether he was speaking or sitting or even turned away from her.

Surely it was just her imagination.

She managed to get through the first day without too much difficulty, without thinking of him every waking moment, without allowing their eyes to meet even once . . . and at the end of the day she and Maille sat and ate with the servants and returned to the king's house well after dark, and Keavy lay down to sleep without her path ever crossing his. She knew that it could be no other way, not if she were to stay anywhere at Dun Gaoth, much less in his own house; but as she closed her eyes, she could not help but think how impossible this was going to be.

Three days went by, with Keavy rising before dawn each morning and dressing plainly and simply and pinning up her single braid and keeping herself as busy as possible—and avoiding the king at every turn. And then, on the fourth day, while she sat among the women of the hall cutting out new leather for cushions, Maille came hurrying in to see her.

"Lady Keavy! Oh, lady!" the girl cried, falling to her knees in the straw beside her and burying her face in her hands. "He has taken up with all of them. All of them!" She began sobbing, all but curled up on the floor.

Keavy glanced at the other women, all of whom looked as baffled as she felt, and set aside the pieces of leather and her small, sharp knife. Quickly she got hold of Maille's quivering shoulders. "Come now. Come, stand up, walk outside with me now, and tell me what has happened. I'm sure all will be well. Come now."

With some difficulty Keavy got the sobbing girl to her feet and steered her outside, away from the curious stares and whispered questions of the other women, and stood with her in a quiet spot beside the long, high wall of the great hall.

"Now, tell me, Maille," Keavy said, gently smoothing back the servant's wild, thick hair. "What has happened? Whatever are you talking about?"

"It is just as I said. He's taken up with all of them! All the women of Dun Gaoth!"

Keavy frowned. "You are talking about Coilean?"

"I am, I am! How could he do this?"

"If this is true, you will not be the only one asking that question," Keavy murmured. "Now . . . you are telling me that Coilean has 'taken up with' some other woman instead of you?"

"He has. He has! *Many* other women!"

"How could that be?"

"Why . . . he . . . I don't know. But he is—They are all there with him!"

Keavy sighed. "Show me," she said.

After looking up at Keavy and blinking, and quickly wiping her eyes on a corner of her cloak, Maille started off across the grounds. She wended her way between the houses, often pausing to peer around a corner as though afraid she would be seen. Finally she looked past one more house and then instantly flattened herself against the wall. "There!" she said in a hiss. "In front of his own house! He's there—and so are they!"

Keavy started to look past the side of the building, but Maille caught her arm. "Careful! Don't let him see!" Keavy nodded patiently, unable to imagine what Coilean could possibly be doing that demanded this much secrecy, and cautiously took a look around the corner.

Coilean sat on a fleece thrown down on the grass near the door of his house, playing very softly on his small lap harp. He was entirely alone.

"Maille, whatever do you mean? He is just sitting out practicing his harp. There's no one with him. No one at all."

But Maille shook her head emphatically. "Just watch! It will happen again!"

Curious now, Keavy peered around the building again. And as she did, a pair of young women happened to walk past Coilean's house, each one carrying a large basket piled high with wool. They were clearly on their way to the hall to work with the other women.

Coilean played a bit more strongly on his harp and stared up at the two women. His face remained grim. As Keavy watched, the two stopped and turned to him, staring down at Coilean as though they had never seen him before.

"Why, what beautiful music!" said the first.

"I have heard nothing like it before," said the second. "May we see?"

Coilean smiled faintly as they approached, though his eyes were narrow and cold. "Of course," he said politely. "Let me show you my harp. It is very special."

The women came close and bent down to examine Coilean's harp, even as he continued to play. They seemed to be looking closely at some objects dangling from the top of its willow-wood frame, lifting them up for a closer look.

"Why, that's very nice, Coilean," said the first woman, straightening up again.

"Good day to you now," the other said, and the two of them walked away again to continue on their way to the hall.

"Do you see what I mean?" Maille asked, dissolving into tears once more.

"Well . . . all I saw was two women politely greeting him and then going on their way again. But now that I think of it, I suppose such attention from any woman at all would be unusual for Coilean. Most of the time, I should think, they pay him no notice at all. I know I would not, if I hadn't—"

"But now he is trying to attract them! He must have done something! I think . . . I think he is trying to use a spell of some kind!"

"A spell?" Keavy looked at Coilean again. Yet another young woman had stopped to greet the bard and run her fingers over his harp, where normally she would simply have walked on past without so much as a glance. "Well, something has certainly caught their attention. I'd best go see what it is."

After a brief smile at Maille, Keavy folded her hands and walked across the grounds to Coilean. He kept his head bent down over his harp, playing steadily, and she saw him smile just a little as her tall shadow fell across him. "Good day to you, my lady," he said. "May I show you my harp? It is very special to me."

"I have seen your harp, Coilean." His head jerked up and his playing stopped at the sound of her voice. "I am just curious as to why so many other women here are suddenly interested in it."

"Are *you* not interested in it, Lady Keavy?" he asked, staring straight into her eyes with his cold gaze and beginning to play once more. "Would you not like to take a closer look?"

Keavy studied him, entirely baffled by his behavior. His playing was mediocre at best, not beautiful or enticing; his expression was cold and determined, not warm and welcoming. Even the harp itself was rather plain and quite unexceptional—but for the very strange assortment of small objects tied to the top of the frame.

As Coilean continued to play his simple tune and stare at her, Keavy leaned down for a closer look. Dangling from the harp, and moving in time to Coilean's rather uneven plucking of its bronze strings, was a collection of attractive objects: a slender gold chain; a shining, polished bit of white quartz; a strip of very fine green linen, embroidered with a pattern of interwoven lines in bright shades of blue and cream with a little gold wire serving as a border. There was also a tiny wooden cup with a few drops of honey inside, and a flower—a yellow primrose—swinging from the frame.

"Why have you fastened these things to your harp?"

He peered up at her again. "Do you not like them? I have found that most women like them very much."

"Of course . . ." Keavy straightened again, and shook her head as she gazed down at him. "These are all pretty little things that women would find attractive."

"So they are. Do *you* not find them attractive?"

Keavy turned and waved her arm. "Maille! Come here!" And Coilean's playing ceased as Maille came hurrying over, anxious and tearful once again.

"Oh, Coilean! What is this? Why are you doing this? Why—"

"Hush now, Maille, and listen. Coilean, please

do explain to both of us what you have done."

He looked away, sullen as ever. "I do not want Maille to hear this. It does not concern her."

"Oh, but I think it does," Keavy argued. "It concerns all three of us. And two of us are still waiting for the explanation."

Coilean seemed to grow smaller and paler beneath the withering stares of the two women. "One of the druids helped me," he mumbled.

"Helped you?" Keavy said. "Helped you to do what?"

"Helped me . . . to use a little magic."

"Magic."

"To . . . to turn the attention of a woman away from one man and toward me."

"Oh, Coilean," Maille wailed. "You did not need to do such a thing! You know I have no eye for any man but you!"

She started to go to him, but Keavy stopped her. "What woman's attention were you trying to turn?"

He scowled, and looked away again. "Yours."

Keavy nodded, even as Maille's mouth fell open in shock. "You were trying to turn my attention from King Aengus to you."

He made no answer. Maille burst into tears once more.

"And would you please explain to Maille why you wished to do this?"

Again the cold, sullen stare. "You saw what happened in front of everyone on the day after our marriage. You heard the satire of the bards at the feast. And that is only the beginning of the ridicule that awaits me!

"I have been humiliated beyond the endurance of any man! I had to do something! And if I could make you return to me just for the sake of appearances, as our marriage was always intended to be nothing more than that, I would have my lawful wife back—a wife who had clearly chosen me over the king. I would no longer be humiliated and shamed before the entire population of Dun Gaoth!"

Maille sniffled. "But all those women—I saw you with them!"

Keavy ran her fingers over the objects still dangling from Coilean's harp—the gold chain, the sparkling quartz, the honey, the primrose, and the beautiful linen embroidery. "These are all things that any woman might like," she remarked. "But they are especially things that I myself would like. I believe that Coilean tried to use a bit of magic in order to lure me to his side—but as often happens with magic, the spell has had an unplanned effect. It seems he has managed to lure every other woman in the fortress *except* me, however briefly."

Coilean scowled again, clenching his fists in frustration. "You are certain you are not the least bit attracted?"

Keavy began to laugh. "Listen to me, both of you. Coilean, put away the harp. Magic is not a tool you should ever think of using. I think we can find a better way to solve this problem."

A short time later, all three of them sat on fleeces and cushions tossed down on the soft green grass. Coilean's harp was safely hidden away inside the house. And as before, any woman who happened to walk by paid Coilean no attention at all.

Keavy sat facing Coilean and Maille. She reached out and took each of them by the hand. "We are an unlikely threesome," she began, "brought together by the strangest of reasons, and each of us is in love with someone we cannot have. But I do know this: we will accomplish more if we try to work together than we will if we continue to struggle against one another.

"Maille—you must trust me to help you become the lady you wish to be, so that you might have a chance to marry the man you love." Maille's eyes shone, and she nodded vigorously.

"And Coilean—is it truly your wish to marry Maille, no matter how difficult the path that leads to marriage?"

He glanced at the young woman, and Keavy saw his face soften as she had never seen it before. "I *do* wish it," he said, and though his voice was quiet Keavy had no doubt he was sincere.

"Then you must give up playing with magic and think of bigger things, such as how this custom of the First Night might be ended so that your true wife will not have to endure it."

Maille nodded and then gazed at Coilean with bright eyes, clearly very happy at the thought of being a fine lady with a husband. But Coilean only frowned. "Do you want to see this custom ended for Maille's sake? Or is it because you hope to someday marry King Aengus and be a queen, and you do not wish to have your husband carrying out a ritual like First Night?"

He stared hard at her. Keavy caught her breath, and was about to give him an equally cold reply—but instead she looked away and tried to smile.

"You are right, Coilean. My feelings for him have surprised me, and I know they will not change. I can only hope that perhaps someday he will feel the same."

"He has sworn never to marry again," Coilean said, still watching her. Maille kept her silence, staring with enormous eyes.

"So he has. And if he keeps with that oath, I may well end up never marrying either, since I cannot imagine ever giving myself to another. Yet if there is a way to change his heart, I will find it."

"Then you would be married to a man called upon to sleep with other women as part of his duty."

Keavy drew a deep breath. "I am not ashamed to tell you that having my husband leave my side for a First Night ritual would be painful beyond endurance for me. I cannot imagine that any woman could be happy to live with such a custom, either as a bride or as the wife of the king. I am certain that you and Maille both must feel the same."

Coilean shrugged, but his face remained cold with anger. "How can *I* hope to stop it? It is a very old law. There is nothing I can do alone to change it."

Keavy shook her head. "Perhaps not. But perhaps together we can find a way. And in the meantime, I will start by setting Maille in a new direction, just as I promised I would on the day that I arrived."

Over the next fortnight, as the moon waned, Keavy did her best to think of nothing but helping Maille and Coilean, and to make as many improvements as she could to Aengus's house. She was eager to do as much as she could not only to help two people who very much needed it, and to repay Aengus's courtesy in allowing her to stay in his house, but to keep her from thinking of him any more than she already did.

She had thought that avoiding him and trying not to think of him would ease him from her mind and allow her to forget she had ever known King Aengus . . . but it had not helped at all. If anything, the unexpected glimpses of him across the dun, and the fleeting moments of eye contact in the hall, and, most of all, the nights in his house when she could all but hear him breathing as he slept alone on his distant ledge, kept him in her mind just as much as if he had walked beside her all day long.

Yet she did not know what else to do. She told herself that the next full moon would be the soonest she could think of returning to Dun Mor.

She would simply have to hold on as best she could until she could go home.

Rather to her surprise, Seanan and Elva began to accept her presence without protest, and treated her almost as the mistress of the house. Seanan seemed quietly pleased when she mended all the leather screens in the house, and gave her a small smile when she promised to touch up their patterns as soon as she could get some proper paint. And the formally polite Elva allowed her to bring in ten newly made cushions, made from good new leather and filled with the best straw to be had. Elva herself threw the old rotted and mildewed cushions one at a time into the fire, though as always she remained aloof and spoke only when necessary.

Keavy was not sure what she could do to help Coilean. He continued to show nothing but cold anger and contempt toward her, blaming her for his entire situation. Somehow he was going to have to find the strength and determination on his own to fight for what he said he wanted, which was the freedom to marry Maille in spite of his family's disapproval. She knew that until he found the courage to stand up to them, nothing much would change for him.

But one person she could help was Maille. With each day that passed, the young servant girl leaned something new from Keavy about making fine furnishings for a home or sewing the most exquisite of clothes. And soon her long, thick hair, formerly wild as a pony's mane, was clean and smoothed into soft, shiny braids. And though Maille, much shorter and rounder than Keavy, could not wear any of Keavy's gowns, she was soon at work on making a new one for herself and even creating some simple embroidery for its neckline and sleeves.

It was not much—but if Keavy could help raise Maille's status from the lowest servant to that of a lady's handmaiden and then up to that of a respected craftswoman, the girl would have a much better chance of finally seeming acceptable to Coilean's highborn family, and the two of them could marry, as they clearly wanted.

Also, Keavy had to admit, it would ease her own conscience if she could see Coilean and Maille living happily together. It simply was not right for anyone to go about marrying someone they did not love—no matter how good they believed their reasons to be at the time.

Chapter Fifteen

Somehow, the fortnight passed. Late one afternoon Keavy stood up from her cushion in the dusty, sunlit hall and stretched her arms wide. The other women looked up from their work and smiled. "Are you finished so soon, Keavy?" one of them asked. "I still have half a basket of wool left to spin."

"It seems I am finished for today," Keavy said, holding up a wooden rod thickly wound with smooth, fine, dark woolen thread. "Perhaps this will make a fine shade of blue, once it has been bleached and given to the dyers. But for now . . ." She closed her eyes and breathed deep of the soft, warm breeze blowing in through the open doors of the hall, a wind sweet with the smell of fresh new grass and blossoming primrose.

She set down the spindle. "Maille, I have been sitting for much too long. I am going out to walk along the trees by the lake. I will be back well before dark, I promise."

"Oh, do be careful, lady!" Maille warned. "You are not so familiar with this place as those who have lived here far longer."

Keavy smiled. "I will not go out of sight of the fortress. I've just been closed up within walls for too long—and this day is just too beautiful."

"All right then, Lady Keavy—but I will wait and watch for you!"

"Just take my thread back to the house for me, Maille. I promise you, I will not be long."

She had not seen the king all day. She did not know what had kept him and did not want to know. She had managed to find a measure of peace, as if she had locked him away in her heart where he could not hurt her again, and so long as she could keep him there—and did not have to see him or hear him or be in his presence—she would be safe from him. The smallest contact only made her long to have him all her own, and that was impossible.

He was a king, and he did not want to marry. Keavy knew she was only one face among many to him. Better to be alone out here on the gently rolling hills, with the birds and the grass and the bright yellow primrose and dandelions, than in the company of a man who did not have it in him ever to put her first in his life.

As she approached the tall silver birch trees lining the lake, lifting the hems of her gold-and-green-plaid skirts and walking with long strides across the soft, thick grass, Keavy became aware of hoofbeats somewhere far behind her.

She looked over her shoulder, then slowed and stopped, letting go of her skirts. Riding up to the entrance of Dun Gaoth were four men—King Aengus and three of his warriors—and they were plainly looking right at her.

There was no place to hide. She was out here on these wide-open hills, and they had no doubt seen her long before she had heard them. Running for the trees would do no good at all. There was nothing to do but wait as the three warrior men dismounted at the fortress and Aengus turned his horse and cantered toward her.

"Good day to you, Lady Keavy," he called, pulling up a short distance away. "Why do you walk alone outside the walls? Is something wrong?"

"Nothing is wrong," she said, turning and continuing sedately on her way. "I simply wanted to enjoy a bit of wind and sun for a time before nightfall."

"Ah, I see. It is indeed a beautiful day." She could feel his eyes on her as he turned the horse and began walking alongside her. "I can understand why you would not want to stay within the hall."

Suddenly he swung down from the horse, turned it around, and sent it trotting back to the others waiting outside the walls of the dun. "I should like very much to join you on your walk, Lady Keavy, if I may."

She stopped and faced him, folding her hands together, and tried to steady her quickened breathing and calm her racing heart. She glanced around at the wide open space where they stood, and at the men waiting near the fortress walls.

"Are you not worried for what people will say, when they see you walking out with me?"

He smiled gently, and then he reached out and took her folded hands between his own. "I am far more worried that I will have to spend another day, another sunset, another heartbeat, seeing you only from across my hall, hearing your voice only from a distance, breathing in the scent of you in my house at night while you sleep far away from me."

Keavy drew in her breath and stepped back from him, sliding her hands free. Her face flamed hot. "I did not know of these feelings of yours. I thought you wished to keep me only as the king's guest. I thought you wanted me only at arm's length . . . and I had come to believe that even arm's length was too close."

Slowly he shook his head, and his hazel eyes were soft in the late-afternoon sun. "I thought I could do this thing . . . but never has any king been more wrong about anything."

"But I must return home," she said, her mind in a whirl. "There is no place for me here. I am only a guest in your house—a guest who arrived under the most unusual of circumstances, and who remains there in an equally strange predicament. You have said . . . you have said that you are a man who does not want another wife. You have said there can be no future for us."

He seemed not to have heard. "Lady Keavy . . . it is true that I can make you no promises this day. Yet it seems to me that our knowing each other has been upside down from the start. We began with each other at the place where most couples end."

Keavy blushed and looked away, and heard him laugh a little. He continued, saying, "And that was no fault of yours. Tell me, Lady Keavy, do you wish to stay here with me for a time and see how you truly like me? Will you walk with me, and sit beside me at the feasts, and allow me to take your hand and touch your face from time to time?"

She could only gaze at him, blinking, as she searched for words.

"You may sleep alone on your ledge for as long as you wish," he assured her.

Keavy closed her eyes. "I am only one woman, King Aengus. Do you truly believe I am worth the trouble your attention to me will cause, both at Dun Mor and here among your own people?"

He reached for her hands again, pressing them together between his own and lifting them up to touch his lips. "I believe you are worth any risk," he whispered, "except that of losing you. Please come with me now, and let me walk with you back to Dun Gaoth . . . and in the morning I will take you on a ride through the most beautiful parts of my kingdom so that you might enjoy the sun and wind to your heart's content."

Keavy could only smile at him, her heart still beating fast, and she placed her hand upon his arm and walked beside him all the way back to the fortress.

That evening passed more slowly than any Keavy had ever known. All night she half expected Aengus to appear at the screen surrounding her sleeping ledge, but he was true to his word and kept to his own. She was both relieved and disappointed, for she was not sure what she might have done—or not done—had he appeared beside her bed that night.

At long last, the first faint gray light began to filter through the small, high windows of the house. Keavy got up, unable to lie still a moment longer, and began to wash and dress.

Soon she was ready, wearing a wide-skirted gown of green and cream and bright blue heavy wool plaid, with boots and a belt of plain but good brown leather and a cloak of cream-colored wool. As always, Keavy's bronze and white enameled brooch with the three feathers from the eagle fastened her cloak securely at her shoulder.

Peering past the tall leather screen, Keavy saw that Maille still slept in the straw, though she was beginning to stir. There was no sign of anyone else in the house and no sign of any movement behind Aengus's screen. Keavy tiptoed past the girl, reached the door, and pulled it silently open—she'd had all the hinges properly greased—and slipped outside.

Just the sight of the delicate spring sunrise lifted her spirits, almost as much as the realization that Aengus wanted her to be in his company today . . . that yesterday out on the hills, he had seemed drawn to her almost as much as she was drawn to—

Behind her, a door closed. She turned around.

Aengus stood watching her, feet apart and legs braced, his hands on his hips and a wide grin on his face. His wide blue cloak moved gently in the early-morning breeze, making a smooth fall from his broad shoulders over his gold linen tunic to his knees. "I am so glad you are ready to go, Lady Keavy. Come with me and we'll see about getting you a horse."

She could only smile back at him, feeling as light and airy as any of the birds that flew through the bright dawn skies. For at least one day they would be together. If nothing else, she would always have this one day with Aengus—one day to go with the one night she would never forget.

From the entrance of Dun Gaoth trotted some twenty riders: the king and thirteen of his men, five servants with a pack of nine small hunting hounds, and one lady whose little gray mare stayed close beside the king's tall, pale golden mount. The riders quickly covered the open rolling hills and reached the stand of birch trees at the edge of the lake, and began to follow the shore around to the other side, where the heavy forest began.

Aengus and the men kept an anxious eye out for game, but Keavy found that it mattered not at all to her whether the hounds found anything or not. She was so happy to be out on this beautiful day, jogging along on the gentle gray mare with a sparkling lake beside them and a cool, dark, shadowy forest beckoning ahead, that she would have been perfectly content simply to ride through the country enjoying the beauty of this perfect spring day and had no need to hunt anything at all.

They rode beyond the lake and into the welcoming forest for a time. The dogs cast back and forth but found nothing, and Keavy simply rode along enjoying the sight of the tall sheltering oaks and listening to the many birds calling high in their branches.

The dogs eventually led them near the edge of the forest at one point, and for a little while the group rode along the crest of a bare and rocky hill. Keavy looked down into the valley below and was startled to see that a large number of people—perhaps two hundred, perhaps more—had apparently made a camp there.

"Who are they?" she asked.

Aengus glanced down into the valley. "The rock men," he answered. "The poorest of all who live in Eire. Some are criminals driven out of their own tribes. Some are farmers who came upon hard times. And some are merely the unfortunates who never found a place anywhere else, not even as servants."

Keavy stared down at them. All of the rock men wore only the plainest and coarsest clothes of dark and undyed wool. They had created make-shift tents of animal hides on the bare and stony ground and built little cooking fires here and there. Women tended to the fires and to their children and to their few head of sheep. Men came and went from the campsite to the forest, a few lucky ones carrying a small trapped animal or perhaps a handful of clover or watercress.

"These must be Maille's people. She spoke of coming to Dun Gaoth with her mother, and having been born among the rock men." Keavy looked up at Aengus. "Can you not help them?"

"I *am* helping them," he answered. "They live undisturbed in my kingdom. They may hunt and gather as they can. A few, like Maille, even find a place in my fortress. I have not tried to drive them out as others—like Dun Mor—have done. In return, they may someday be called upon to help me fight an invader. But so far, nothing of the sort has been necessary."

"I wish we could do more," Keavy said, looking down at them again.

Aengus glanced at her. "There is not room for them all within the walls of Dun Gaoth," he said. "We take in who we can, as we did with Maille and her mother. In my kingdom they are free to make their own way as best they can, as is any other man or woman in Eire."

Keavy nodded, though she continued to watch the ragged people down below. "I understand, King Aengus. I will not forget this."

Soon their path took them back into the forest

again. After a time they came to a pleasant grassy clearing, and Aengus gave the order to call in the dogs and stop for a midday meal. Keavy found she was grateful to slide down from her mare and hand its reins to one of the servants. She moved a little stiffly after nearly a whole morning of riding—she would be sore tomorrow!—and walked over to sit beside Aengus on the green wool cloak thrown down for them on the soft grass of the clearing.

One of the servants brought fresh cold water in wooden cups. Another quickly arrived with a single plate heaped high with thick slices of roast venison, dried apples boiled in milk, chunks of hard white cheese, and wheat bread with butter, and placed it between her and Aengus. Keavy closed her eyes and let the cool spring breeze blow her hair back from her face—those few strands that had come loose from her long, neat braids during the ride—and then she smiled up at the king as he offered her the plate.

"On a day like this, I think I could be happy to do nothing else but ride over the country and then sit down to eat such delicious things here in this beautiful forest."

Aengus looked at her, his eyes bright. "So it is only venison and cheese and pretty scenery that attracts you? The company and conversation hold no delight for you at all?"

She smiled shyly and reached for a slice of the venison. "The company is fair enough."

"Fair enough to coax you out again?"

"Quite possibly—especially if there will be more of this meat. It is much better than the last time, as I recall."

"Better, is it? I should hope so. I set the servants to work with the strictest orders to make a better dish of meat than what was had at the feast. If it is truly to your liking, then I shall see that there is all you could want, and more." He, too, reached for some of the bread and meat. "Yet I must tell you something that is not quite so pleasant."

Her eyes flicked to his. "And what might that be, King Aengus?"

He took a quick bite of the buttered bread. "A messenger came to me yesterday. A messenger from Dun Mor."

Keavy set down her venison and turned to him. "From Dun Mor? What message did he bring?"

"The message . . . that those at Dun Mor are feeling ever more insulted by our refusal to return you to your home."

She frowned. "All there are well aware that I do not want to go back—certainly not anytime soon. I believe my parents are the ones to say such things to pressure me into returning to them, just so they can sell me away again." She looked off into the distance, her lips pressed into a tight line. "What does Dun Mor propose to do?"

Aengus shook his head, his face more somber now. "They are talking of war. Not just an ordinary battle, over in an afternoon, where all are satisfied to go home and drink barley beer and brag at the end of the day. This would be very different. This would be a true war."

Keavy began to feel cold inside, but managed to laugh. "War? Over me? Over nothing more than a wayward woman who has refused a husband, one she felt was not right for her?"

"Over a contracted bride who was, apparently, stolen by the king and kept away from her lawful husband—and who is allegedly being held against her will by that same king and not allowed to go back to her husband at Dun Gaoth *or* to her family at Dun Mor."

"But that is ridiculous!"

"Of course it is. But there is another thing here, which you may not know. Dun Mor also covets a beautiful valley that lies between both kingdoms. No place else has such fine apple trees, or colder, clearer water in the streams, or produces so much honey in the hives. This might just give them the excuse they need to gain some allies and bring about a total war against Dun Gaoth."

"Surely they would not," Keavy whispered. "I know them. Dun Mor was my home. I know the king; I know many of his men!"

"You know them when they speak to a beautiful young woman. You do not know them when they have been deeply insulted—or believe they have. Or when it *suits* them to believe they have. You do not know them when they want a certain piece of land and feel sure they have found a way to get it."

"I simply cannot believe it would ever come to this. I cannot imagine such a thing."

Aengus smiled and covered one of her hands with his own. "Then I will not ask you to imagine it. Fighting is the business of warriors and kings, not of a young woman who is no doubt feeling very much alone in the world."

Keavy nodded, looking down at the green wool cloak she sat on, her eyes momentarily burning with tears. Then she thought of something else. "Perhaps I am not the only one who feels alone in the world."

His hand stopped halfway to his plate. Slowly he withdrew it and sat back from her. Peering up at him, Keavy saw him smile gently at her. "You may be right . . . though I am not sure I have ever thought of it that way."

"I would like very much to know," she ventured, "why a man like King Aengus of Dun Gaoth is, indeed, alone in the world."

He looked down again. "I am surrounded by friends and companions and druids and loyal men. Indeed, sometimes I *wish* I could be alone," he answered lightly, staring at Keavy; but she merely looked steadily at him and waited, and in a moment he smiled and went on.

"I am sure you have the same question that so many others have: why does the king not take a new wife?" He gazed out into the deep oak forest, where the leaves rippled in the breeze and the birds continued to come close to hop and call and peer down at these intruders in their domain.

"You are aware that I did have a wife, and that Queen Deirdre died just over one year ago. You probably do not know that Elva—the lady who serves you in my house—was her mother."

Keavy sat up straight. "The mother of the queen is now a servant in her own daughter's house? How can this be?"

Aengus held up one hand. "Elva had no other family. She lived with and cared for her daughter, always. I tried, as gently as I could, to find her a place among other high-born women so that she would not be alone; but it was clear she had no wish to go anywhere else. She wanted only to remain in the last place her daughter called home, and I had no heart to make her go."

"And that is why she is so suspicious of me," Keavy said under her breath. "It is almost as though she believes I am trying to take Deirdre's place."

"You chose Deirdre's sleeping ledge for your own."

Keavy closed her eyes. "Then I will never sleep there again. As soon as we return I will move all my things and sleep in the straw beside Maille. I will—"

"You need not move, Lady Keavy. Elva does not begrudge you a place to sleep. Her daughter rests in the Otherworld now, and has no need of a bed in anyone's house."

Keavy was silent for a moment, but then she pressed on before determination left her. "I'm sure you must know my next question. Why did the wife of the king need her own sleeping ledge?"

Aengus stared at her for a moment. Keavy instantly thought she had been too bold and had offended him—but then he got to his feet and reached out for her. "Walk with me, if you will," he said, and when Keavy took his hand he raised her up. Together they started toward the forest, away from the servants and the horses and the dogs and the warriors of Dun Gaoth.

Chapter Sixteen

At last Aengus stopped and turned to face Keavy, though he continued to gaze out over her shoulder into the shadowed forest. "There are many at the dun who think that if the king has no wish to marry again, it is because he loved his now-dead wife too much and cannot bear to replace her. But the truth of it is . . . Deirdre and I never loved each other at all."

Keavy kept herself very still. She looked up at Aengus and waited for him to go on, even as her heart began to pound.

"It was an arranged marriage, of course. The king needed a wife and so he got one. All was settled between our families before we ever even saw each other. And when we did . . ."

He paused, and a strange expression came over his face. It was one of puzzlement, but it was not unkind. "We liked each other well enough. I found her plain but honorable, and as far as what she thought of me . . . well, I never really knew, for she never spoke of it."

He turned to Keavy and looked straight into her eyes. "There was never any love of the heart between us . . . and after that first night, no physical love, either. We worked together as partners when it was required of us, and we were polite to each other, but that is all. When she died, I had all of my gold put away to show respect for a queen who had died far too young—but that was the only reason. I swear it to you, Lady Keavy, on this gold torque of kingship I wear around my neck, the only gold I wear. There was nothing more between us than that."

She nodded, seeing the sincerity in his eyes and feeling it in her heart. "I do believe you," she said, "and yet . . ."

And yet I do not understand how any young woman married to a man such as you could turn her back on him the morning after their wedding! What sort of woman could Deirdre have been? Why did she no longer want you to touch her?

"And yet you wonder why the king did not take another wife—or even two or three, as some do—since he must have been under a great deal of pressure to do so."

Keavy blinked, and then smiled politely. "I was indeed wondering," she murmured.

He reached out and brushed a strand of hair away from her face. "It is hard for a man who is a king to know whether a woman desires him for himself, or simply because he can make her a queen. I became accustomed to my life the way it was—to living apart from the queen, with all the privileges and responsibilities that came with being a king, and saw no reason to change it. I have been and still am a king and I have no wish to change this . . . and neither do I have any wish ever to find myself married to a woman who comes to me out of duty and nothing more."

His queen must have hurt him very badly, Keavy thought. But as she looked up into his dark hazel eyes she could not help but think there was something more that he was not telling her, and she wondered if she would ever know the whole story.

Before long the riders were again making their way through the forest, the hounds casting about for any sign of game. Birds of all sorts called and sang from high within the trees, and occasionally a wren or sparrow would flutter close by Keavy or even land briefly on her shoulder. But Keavy's attention was caught by a swift darting motion among the trees.

"She's here," Aengus said, and pulled his horse to a stop. "Do you see her?"

"I do." Keavy halted her gray mare alongside Aengus and looked far off into the trees, up among the highest branches. "I see both of them."

"Both?"

"Both. Two females. They are too large to be males." Keavy's glance flicked from tree to tree as the rest of the riders halted their horses and swung them around. The hounds scurried about their feet. "One there—and the other there, far away, watching us."

Aengus smiled as he followed her gaze. "So there are. Two of them watching you, though I have never seen such a thing before. Save for their mates, I have never known them to tolerate their own kind within their territories."

The breeze whispered at them through the forest. Distant birds continued to call and sing as the hunting party gazed up into the trees at the pair of sharp-eyed goshawks.

"The finest hunters in the wood," Aengus said softly. "I have learned to watch for them. Wherever they are, we can be sure the game is there, too—though I always counted myself fortunate to see just *one.* Never have I seen two at the same time!"

He grinned as he looked over at Keavy. "Any wrens that might be drawn to you this day had best beware." Then the king's eyebrow lifted as another thought occurred to him, and he looked even more closely at Keavy. "Or perhaps there is another reason why the hawks gather so near us. They are drawn to your presence, just as the larks and the wrens are drawn to you."

"The hawks are magnificent," Keavy said. "Often I would see them near Dun Mor." She smiled. "I love them, too, just as I love the little wrens, but I am grateful that the hawks never tried to light on my arm. I was always content to visit with them from a distance."

"I am glad about that, for your sake," Aengus said with a little laugh. "Though I often wish we could tame some of their power and keenness and train it for ourselves. No quarry would ever escape us then!"

Keavy laughed. The hounds continued along the tree line and the riders turned their horses to follow them. "Do you think you could capture such birds and keep them tethered like dogs, and have them hunt for you and politely give up their kill when you ask? I cannot imagine any such thing ever happening. They would no longer be hunters if they were ever to be tamed."

"Perhaps," Aengus said. "I do not suppose they would be willing to perch on my hand and then fly up to do my hunting for me. But even so . . . I have known of far more magical things to happen."

Their eyes met for a long moment; then Keavy could only smile to herself as she looked up into the trees again at the hawks. She blinked as both of them suddenly leaped into the air.

Then her horse flung its head up. So did the rest of her party's mounts, and Keavy realized that the hounds had gone tearing off into the forests with their noses to the ground, setting up a howl as they found a scent and went after it.

The hunters charged after them single-file. Keavy realized she was last, after Aengus. She clung to the wooden frame at the front of her sheepskin-covered saddle and clamped her long legs around her little mare's sides as the animal trotted fast into the forest to keep up with the others. "What . . . what is it?" she asked in a gasp, hoping Aengus would hear her. All she could see of him was his blue cloak flowing back over the rump of his pale golden horse.

"Hare!" Aengus called, over his shoulder. "Two—three of them! We'll get them in the next clearing, just ahead!"

Keavy could only hold on for dear life and trust that the mare would find her way—and then a blur of feathers shot past her. And another.

Far ahead of her she could see the two goshawks streaking through the forest, following the dogs toward their kill. But just as they approached the clearing, the hawks circled around and began to fly back through the forest, as though trying to be near Keavy once again.

She lost sight of the hawks as the hounds and horses burst out into the clearing. In a moment the hounds caught the frightened hares and two short shrieks pierced the forest. By the time Keavy's mare trotted up, the servants were beating the dogs away and recovering the bodies.

The two hawks appeared in the air overhead, circling over Keavy and the fresh kill below. The servants and the men hardly spared a glance for them, engrossed as they were in the excited dogs and blood-soaked rabbits and snorting, dancing horses.

Keavy halted her mare near the edge of the clearing, unwilling to go any closer to the unfamiliar confusion of the hunt. She kept her attention on the two female goshawks—and just as she looked up at them again, one screamed and dove straight down at the other, striking at her sister with sharp talons and knocking her out of the sky.

Keavy swung down from her mare, who skittered off to join the other horses, and the injured goshawk fell to the ground at Keavy's feet. The other bird screamed once again, and then flew away.

The injured hawk flapped and struggled for a moment in the grass and then sat still, her bright eyes darting from the men of the hunting party to the dogs and back to Keavy. One wing was stretched out wide, but the other was spotted with blood and badly misshapen, torn and broken by the other hawk's powerful talons.

Keavy could only crouch down a few steps away. "I'm sorry," she whispered. "I'm so sorry."

There were footsteps in the grass beside her. "I wondered how this might end, when I saw the two of them so near each other," Aengus remarked quietly. "Such creatures do not tolerate each other's presence. Perhaps one was looking for a mate and dared to come into the other's territory. It is spring, after all—I suppose such a thing could happen at such a time."

"Perhaps it could," Keavy said, "but I believe you had it right the first time. They were drawn here because of me. This is my fault. I should have tried to drive them off. I should have done something—"

"Dear Keavy," Aengus said gently. "Even you are

not so powerful as to control the hunters of the sky. Hawks go where they will."

The wounded bird made one last effort to fly, mightily working her good wing but unable to move the injured one. At last she sat still, her sharp beak curving open, and watched Keavy and Aengus with a frightened, golden-eyed stare.

"This my fault," Keavy said again. "I cannot leave her here."

"Cannot leave her? But what can you do for her? This is the way of nature, nothing more. We must ride away, and know that some other wild creature will soon make an end to her—or, if you think it kinder, I can have one of the servants finish her suffering now."

"We will do neither!" Slowly Keavy got to her feet. "I have caused this. It is for me to make it right. Please—ask your servants to bring me a wide piece of good leather and some strips to tie it with."

Aengus smiled, though he was clearly doubtful. "It is yours, my lady. But please be wary of the bird. Injured as she is, she is still a formidable foe."

"Thank you, King Aengus." She watched him go, and then turned her attention back to the hawk.

"I am so sorry, *seabhac*," she said. "If you will come with me, I will do whatever I can to help you."

Cautiously, but without hesitation, Keavy reached out to touch the injured creature. The hawk watched her closely but made no move to leap or strike as Keavy ran one finger ever so gently down the soft feathers of her back.

Aengus came back with the leather and cords. She heard him whistle softly under his breath. "I have seen magical things in my life, and count this as one of them. Do you mean to take her with us?"

"I do. I believe I can carry her; she seems very light for her size. Here, help me, please, if you will, and tie this leather around my arm."

Aengus took the wide, heavy strap and wrapped it around Keavy's left forearm, letting it extend out over her fist, then tied it firmly at each end with the leather cords. Prepared, Keavy crouched down and carefully held her arm low in front of the bird.

"Come, Seabhac," she said. "Come home with us now, where we can care for you and you will be safe."

The hunting company was silent as the hawk regarded Keavy with a fierce and frightened gaze. Then, from a great distance, Keavy heard them breathe in as one as the bird turned toward her, reached for her leather-clad arm with one talon, and stepped up to settle on Keavy's wrist.

Keavy stood as slowly as she could. The bird flapped her good wing and opened her beak again, but remained where she was. Her claws gripped tight but met only leather, and once Keavy was upright the bird settled and was still.

Keavy turned to Aengus and smiled. "If you will

help me up on my horse, I think Seabhac and I are ready to return to Dun Gaoth."

"A magical thing," Aengus repeated; and together they walked toward their horses with the great hawk riding on Keavy's arm as though she had done so all her life.

It was a long, slow ride back to Dun Gaoth. Keavy's arm soon grew weary from the weight of the hawk standing on it but she managed to find ways to support the bird as she rode. She gave the reins to one of the servants and allowed them to lead her mare, while she rested her arm on the front of the saddle or supported it from below with her other arm.

The latter seemed to distress the bird, however, as though she could not bear sitting almost on the horse's neck—or perhaps thought Keavy was going to take hold of her with both hands. She began flapping her one good wing, startling the horse. If she cried out it would certainly unnerve the poor, patient mare. Something would have to be done to soothe the frightened, injured creature.

Aengus stopped his horse. The others immediately halted as well. The hawk sat still, while Keavy's mare snorted and moved sideways, and Keavy was greatly worried at the sight of the injured bird, whose eyes were enormous and staring, but seemed to see nothing at all. The bird's beak was open and her breath came so fast that she hardly seemed to breathe at all.

Keavy stroked the feathers of the bird's back "I wonder if we will even be able to get her home," she said quietly. "It may be true that birds have an affinity for me, but she is still a wild creature, after all."

"Wild and injured," Aengus agreed. He slid from his horse, reached down to catch the end of his cloak, and—with some difficulty—tore off a long, wide strip of the lightweight blue woolen fabric. "Here," he said, walking around behind Keavy's horse. "Perhaps this will help to settle her."

Moving up behind the bird, he eased the wool up to her head and then dropped it over her eyes, quickly wrapping it loosely but securely around her head and neck and then tying off the ends.

The hawk sat still once the frightening sights of men and horses and dogs were shut out. Even her breathing seemed to slow a little.

Keavy smiled gratefully at Aengus. "Thank you," she said. "I wish I had been wise enough to think of it."

"There are times when it is better not to see what is around you," he said, looking solemnly at Keavy; and then he swung back up on his horse and they continued on their way.

Seabhac rode quietly with them all the way back to Dun Gaoth.

Darkness had fallen by the time they returned to the fortress. Keavy carried the hawk inside the house and placed her in the straw in a dark and shadowed section of the house, in the shadow and warmth of the hearth.

Both Seanan and Elva were wide-eyed at the sight of an injured goshawk being brought into their house and stayed as far away as possible; but they were clearly as fascinated by the beautiful, powerful bird as everyone else. They watched closely as Keavy unwrapped the strip of wool from the hawk's eyes and stepped back. The creature blinked and looked around with her sharp-eyed gaze, and opened her beak, but otherwise remained quiet.

Seanan brought over a heavy wooden bowl filled with water and gave it to Keavy. "Perhaps she will drink a little, if left to herself," he said. "How will you feed her?"

Keavy looked up at Aengus, who shook his head. "I do not think we should try to feed her tonight. She is distressed, and no doubt in pain, and probably would not try anything anyway. But tomorrow evening, perhaps, she would take an interest in a mouse."

Keavy placed the bowl of water near the bird. "Thank you for allowing her into your home."

He smiled. "I should thank her for allowing herself to be brought here. I hope she will like my house, even though she is from a place that is very different."

Keavy touched the hawk again, marveling at the softness and smoothness of the dark brown feathers. "I believe she will like it, King Aengus. I believe she will."

* * *

Keavy slept that night in the straw near Seabhac, for she could see that her presence seemed to calm the wild hawk. She spent as much of the following day as she could near the bird, unwrapping the wool fabric that covered Seabhac's eyes and leaving it off for as long as the bird remained quiet.

There was little to be done for the injured wing. With Seabhac's eyes covered, Keavy used a wet linen cloth to wash away the blood from the feathers and saw that the punctures appeared clean. Yet the tendons had been so badly damaged that the wing was all but unusable, and though Keavy was determined to try, she was not sure there was any way to heal such an injury. The bird would not die from her wounds, but would remain scarred—and quite possibly earthbound—for the remainder of her life.

Everyone in the house learned to speak quietly and not make any loud noises. Keavy was afraid to think of how the poor wild bird would react if someone should drop a bronze cauldron on the stone hearth.

But no one did drop a cauldron, or anything else. Keavy was most relieved that evening when Seabhac finally took a little water from the wooden bowl, and even more so when the bird examined the freshly killed mouse dropped near her in the straw and began tearing at it with her beak.

There was a quiet footstep behind Keavy. She

looked up to see Aengus watching Seabhac as the bird began to devour the mouse. "It is good to see her eat," the king whispered. "If she will eat, she will live, most likely."

"I do believe she will live," Keavy said. "But I fear she will never hunt again. Her wing will heal, but it is far too damaged to allow her to fly. You may well have another long-term guest in your house, if you are willing."

"I would be more than willing. Never did I think to have such a beautiful—such a magnificent—creature living in my house for *any* length of time." He started to walk toward the screen before his sleeping ledge, and then turned back. "Oh . . . and Seabhac is quite a beauty, too."

He disappeared behind the screen. Keavy laid her head down in the straw and smiled.

Chapter Seventeen

Not long after sunrise the next morning, Keavy stood outside the door of the king's house with Seabhac standing once again on her leather-wrapped arm. As she took off the hawk's woolen head cover, Aengus came out to join her.

"We will ask the craftsmen to make some sort of gauntlet for you—something that covers both your arm and your fist. If Seabhac were to take fright and leap from your arm to your hand, those killing talons could sink right through it."

"Her feet are her weapons," Keavy agreed. "That is how she would survive, if left to herself. But so far today she has been nothing but calm."

Indeed, on this early spring morning the hawk rode quietly on Keavy's protected arm, her eyes uncovered, blinking in the morning sunlight and taking in every motion and movement that happened around her.

Right away, it seemed, a few people had gathered, entranced by the sight of the great wild hawk standing calmly on Keavy's arm. They did not come too close, but stayed back and stared as more and more people gathered. Their great curiosity was evident, though no one was yet bold enough to say anything.

Aengus glanced at the crowd. "Beautiful, isn't she?" he asked. And to the amazement of the gathering, the king reached out and gently stroked the soft brown feathers of the hawk. She raised her wings a little at his touch, glancing around with her bright stare, but then quickly settled back and blinked her eyes in apparent contentment.

Aengus looked at the people again, his eyes shining. "Have you ever seen the like?"

"Never!" said one of the women, and the rest laughed. With the silence broken, the people began to ask many questions.

"How did you capture such a bird?"

"Is she truly tame?"

"How will you feed her?"

"Will you keep her, or set her free?"

Aengus and Keavy answered all the questions as best they could.

Keavy could not help but feel proud—and even relieved—to see the awe and wonder and respect on the faces of the people of Dun Gaoth as they watched her with the magnificent wild goshawk standing on her wrist.

Perhaps Seabhac was going to help Keavy's acceptance here more than she knew.

Keavy turned to Aengus and took a few careful

steps toward the house, mindful of Seabhac's increasing tension as the crowd continued to gather. "I think I should take her back inside now. She has done so well this morning, and I don't want to stress her too much and take a chance on upsetting her."

Aengus nodded. "Go ahead. She—and you—have given us all a magnificent sight today, one my people will all talk about for some time to come. I will see you this evening, Lady Keavy."

Keavy reached up to wrap the wool covering over the hawk's eyes—but before she could do so the bird started to raise her wings. Standing within arm's reach of her was Coilean.

"Be careful, please," Keavy said, moving Seabhac away from him. "She is very wary of anyone save King Aengus or myself."

"Oh, I am sure she is," he said coldly. "But I am not fooled by this."

"What are you talking about?"

He snorted. Seabhac hopped once on Keavy's arm and fixed her bright stare on Coilean. "I see that you have found yet another way to gain praise and attention for yourself, while I remain the butt of every joke told within these walls."

Keavy frowned, both at Coilean and at her increasingly restive hawk. "Coilean, this has nothing to do with you. We rescued this bird after another one struck her and ruined her wing. We could not leave her to die. We—"

"*We*—you mean *you*—have fooled everyone into thinking that this creature is wild, when clearly it is not, and you are simply tricking them into thinking you are so special that you can tame a wild hawk!"

Keavy laughed. "Where would anyone find a tame hawk?"

"I don't know! Perhaps you made a pet of a fledgling once, long ago at Dun Mor, and are using it now to play a trick on everyone here!"

She could only sigh. "I am sorry you choose to believe such a thing. I would like to help you, help you and Maille both, but as long as you—"

"I will show everyone what kind of trick you are playing," he said with a snarl. "I will show everyone just how 'wild' this pet bird of yours really is!" And to Keavy's horror he reached his right hand directly for Seabhac's feet, as though he meant to take her onto his own bare arm.

"Do not, do not!" Keavy gasped. Those fearsome talons could go right through his hand; they could tear his wrist to shreds! But before she could pull the bird away, Seabhac rose up, flapped wildly with her good wing, and struck Coilean's hand hard with her beak, leaving a bloody gash.

With a short cry he drew back, grabbing at his hand with a look of pain and anger and sudden fear in his eyes. "So you have taught the beast to attack as well!"

Keavy could only look at him in shock—and then she stole a glance at the gathered men and women and children who all erupted in laughter.

"Coilean thinks that a hawk can be tamed like a lapdog!"

"He does not believe it is a wild creature, suffering our presence only because it can no longer fly!"

"Everyone knows by now the Lady Keavy's affinity for birds. It is only natural that a wounded, hungry hawk might allow her to care for it!"

The laughter surrounded them again. Seabhac ruffled her feathers and glared at Coilean again, but remained quiet on Keavy's arm.

Quickly Keavy wrapped a woolen strip around the hawk's eyes and then carried her back to the quiet of the house. She left behind the furious, red-faced Coilean and the laughing, jovial crowd.

Later that morning, after Seabhac had been comfortably settled in the straw once again in King Aengus's house, Keavy stood beneath the armorer's shed trying to explain to the leather worker what she required.

"You have seen the wounded hawk I rescued in the forest," she began.

"That we have, Lady Keavy," said the older of the two men.

"A marvelous sight she is," said his grown son. "Marvelous—and fearsome."

She nodded. "You do understand. You've seen her feet, just as deadly as daggers. If I am to carry her and care for her, I must have protection from her talons, and that is why I have come here—to ask you to make me a long, heavy glove of the very best and thickest leather available. My arm and fingers are no match for her claws! Can you help me?"

The older man picked up a worn length of leather cord. "Hold out your arm," he said, and as Keavy did so he held the cord along its length and tied knots in it at her wrist and at the end of her fist. "It will be ready for you by nightfall. I hope you will be pleased."

"Oh, I have no doubt I will be very pleased," she said, lowering her arm. "I will come back at . . ." Her voice trailed off as something in the yard caught her eye. "What is this?"

She picked up the hem of her blue-and-gold skirts and hurried outside—where she saw five men riding past on horses and leading a pair of heavily laden pack ponies. The five were men whom she recognized from Dun Mor, and knew three to be servants and two warriors. They were all grim-faced and said almost nothing by way of greeting to the warrior men of Dun Gaoth who met them at the great hall. The two warriors, Desmond and Owen, allowed their riding horses to be led away, but ordered the three servants to wait just outside the doors with the pack ponies. Then the two warriors disappeared inside.

Keavy walked straight across the yard and followed them inside the dimly lit hall, standing just inside the door and hoping she could listen without being noticed. But she need not have worried. The attention of every warrior and every woman in the hall was on the two men from Dun Mor, who stood before King Aengus, who sat on a bench with his druids and warriors all around him.

". . . why King Ross has sent us," Desmond was saying. "The king of Dun Mor, and his warriors, and the family of this woman all insist that she be released and allowed to leave with us without delay."

"We have told you plainly, this woman is not a hostage," Aengus said. "She is not a prisoner."

"Yet she is hidden away at this fortress, kept from her lawful husband and from her family! We fear she is not receiving proper treatment here. We fear she does not have a proper house or decent clothes or even sufficient food to eat." He turned toward the door. Keavy stood very still, staying in the shadows, but he only called out, "Finnian! Bring it inside!"

As Keavy watched, the three servants brought in a stack of large leather bags and three big wooden boxes. The servants opened the boxes and emptied out the bags, and a low murmur spread through the crowd as they saw what Desmond and Owen had brought with them from Dun Mor.

Gowns. Cloaks. Boots. Belts. Earrings. Bracelets. Brooches. Dried meat. Bread. Dried fruit. Honey.

The murmur grew louder. Keavy put her hand up to her mouth.

One of the druids stepped forward, scowling fiercely at the visitors. "You have delivered the gravest of insults to King Aengus. You are saying that a guest of his does not even have clothes to wear or food to eat! Why have you come here and insulted his hospitality in this way?"

"Because no woman of Dun Mor will be kept from her husband or her family! If she is not with him, and yet does not come home to her family, it can only be because she is being prevented from doing so!"

The druid started to speak again, but Aengus raised a hand to silence him. "I assure you, the Lady Keavy has received only the best of treatment here, as befits a guest of her station in life. She is free to go with you if she wishes."

"Then where is she? Have you hidden her away? She is not anywhere to be seen!"

Aengus stood up, towering over the gathering. "Lady Keavy," he called, looking directly at her. "Would you come and stand beside me, please?"

Startled for a moment, for she thought she had slipped in unseen, Keavy drew a deep breath, folded her hands, and walked through the tense crowd of men to stand beside the king.

She turned around to face the men from Dun Mor, her long pale braids swinging past her knees. Aengus took her hand and raised it up. "As you can see, she is here, and she is safe, and she is well," he said. "Ask her anything you like. I'm sure she will be pleased to answer you."

"Lady Keavy," Desmond said, "we are here to take you home—or, at the very least, return you to your lawful husband. We do not understand why King Aengus is not allowing you to do either one."

Aengus lowered his hand, though Keavy continued to rest her fingers on his wrist. She said, "Desmond, I am no longer the wife of Coilean. I am a guest of King Aengus and Dun Gaoth. They have extended their hospitality to me and I have accepted. That is all."

"Yet you came here to marry another man. You did marry him. And now you say you want neither your husband nor your family. You want only to live as a guest among strangers?"

Aengus is not a stranger to me! she wanted to cry out. But instead she looked directly at Desmond and gave him a polite smile. "For a time, being a guest of the king is what I wish."

She took her fingers from Aengus's wrist and folded her hands together in front of her. "I have had many strange and unexpected things happen to me in a very short time . . . an arranged marriage, a long journey, a ritual that came as a great shock to me. Perhaps you can understand why—"

"We understand very well that a woman of Dun Mor was lawfully married to a man of Dun Gaoth, and that now she is being kept from both her husband and her home. That makes her no better than a prisoner. And it is clear to us that the one who has turned her head is none but King Aengus himself!"

Keavy took a step toward them. "You are wrong," she said quietly. "I have no husband. I am—"

"I will not force her to leave." The king's voice was low, but began to carry a dangerous edge. "You will return to Dun Mor at once. The Lady Keavy will return when she is ready to return—and not before."

Owen glared right back at him. "You understand that our king means to free this woman. He will not hesitate to use every strength and every man of Dun Mor if need be. Do you truly wish to meet the entire army of Dun Mor when they are determined not just to fight with you, but to destroy you?"

Aengus's eyes narrowed. "And I suppose I can count on meeting this great army of yours in the valley that you desire."

"We will meet you anywhere and anytime, King Aengus!" cried Owen. "This woman is one of ours and we will do whatever is necessary to free her!"

Aengus grinned at him. "It is a lovely valley, isn't it? Lush with grass and watered by the clearest brook in Eire. White with blossoming apple trees in the spring and covered with dropped fruit in the fall. Oh, and buzzing with bees making pot after pot of honey in their *skeps*. I, too, would do whatever was necessary to make it a part of my kingdom—if I did not already have it."

Both of the men turned a murderous glare on Aengus. A few of his own warriors stepped forward with their hands on the hilts of their swords, but Aengus waved them back. "I know you care nothing for Keavy or for Coilean—but their very short marriage does give you a fine excuse to fight us once again, and take a little more land if you should win. Good day to you, Desmond and Owen," he said. "I hope your journey back to Dun Mor is a pleasant one."

Desmond pointed his finger directly at Aengus, his face dark with fury. "You will not be laughing when we return for you with every last man of Dun Mor—and that is exactly what we mean to do!" He lowered his hand, turned around, and started for the door, followed closely by Owen.

"Oh, and thank you for the gifts," Aengus called after them. Keavy saw Desmond's fist clench, but the man continued on his way, and in a moment the two messengers were out the door.

Aengus was almost laughing, though the glance he gave Keavy held no real amusement. "It is just as I said. I have no doubt they have suffered embarrassment over your rejection of your husband, and I do not doubt that your family and everyone else at Dun Mor truly wants you back. But the real reason is the valley. That is why they are willing to go to war."

"I don't care what the reason is," Keavy said. Then she caught up the hem of her skirts and ran outside after Desmond and Owen.

They were both riding their horses, as were their three servants, and heading for the tunnel as fast as they could pull their slow but unladen pack ponies toward the fortress wall. "Owen!" Keavy cried. "Wait! I will speak to you!"

Owen swung his horse around and gave her a cold stare. "You have chosen to return home with us?"

Keavy sighed. "I have not. But I do want to speak to my family at Dun Mor—and to the king himself, if I may."

"Then you should go get your things while we saddle one of the ponies, for you will have to come home if you wish to speak to your family. Especially if you wish to speak to the king."

Keavy shook her head. "I will not return to Dun Mor. But I will meet with the king at another place."

Owen sat back on his horse. "The king will not meet with you here. You will have to return home for that. Desmond! Get a saddle for that pony. We'll send it back to them later."

"Wait, Desmond. There is no need for a saddle. I propose to meet with my family not here and not at Dun Mor—but at the valley King Aengus spoke of."

"The valley? Why there? Why not come home where you belong?"

"Because I do not want to be sold away to another man, simply because my parents have suffered a bit of wounded pride by pushing me into a marriage I did not want to begin with."

"Wounded pride! You don't seem to understand. Their daughter has publicly rejected the husband they most carefully selected and contracted for her! Both families have suffered great humiliation and far more than wounded pride.

You cannot think to simply walk away from it as though nothing at all had happened!"

Keavy closed her eyes. "I do understand. That is why I am willing to do what I can to ease the tension between these two kingdoms. The last thing I want is to see them come to war."

"Then come home!"

"I will be at the valley, alone, on the morning after next." Keavy looked the man straight in the eye. "If my family, or any of the warrior men, or the king himself wish to meet me there at that time—when I am alone and far from the walls of Dun Gaoth—they will know for certain that I remain at Dun Mor of my own free will, and that there is no need for anyone to talk of war over me."

"The morning after next," Owen said, "at the valley." He backed his horse away. "I will inform the king. And your family." With that, the group of them turned their mounts and trotted single-file through the tunnel, heading straight back to Dun Mor.

Chapter Eighteen

Two more nights went by, and Aengus got through them as he had all the other days and nights since Keavy had arrived at his fortress: by watching her from a distance, sharing a little time with her when he could, helping her with Seabhac, and staying as close to her as he dared without getting too close. Distance was vital here. He knew that if he got as close to her as he wished, he would never be able to pull himself away . . . and so he remained at that delicate point of balance where getting too close was torment and staying too far away was agony.

He got up and dressed himself. Stepping out from behind his tall leather screen, he found that as she nearly always did Keavy had already risen and left the house. Seabhac was well tended; her wounded wing had been cleaned and gently massaged, her straw was new, and she had fresh water.

Aengus took a moment to crouch down beside the hawk. She watched him with her bright gaze;

then, as he slowly reached his hand out to her, she turned to face him and stood very still as he stroked her smooth soft feathers.

This quiet moment with the fierce hawk drew his thoughts back to the days of his own transformations, to the days when he, too, had flown on feathered wings just such as these. If Seabhac could fly again, wounded as she was, then perhaps he could dare to hope that he, too, might fly again someday.

Ah, well, he would watch for the Lady Keavy all day, as he always did, and take comfort and pride in knowing that she had chosen to remain at this fortress when she could easily have gone back to Dun Mor with Owen and Desmond.

Here with him. Here in his house.

He walked outside. The morning was quiet, with just a few servants moving back and forth as they went about their tasks, and Aengus began to take a casual walk along the curving stone wall of the great fortress. He would be inside the hall for much of the day, listening with his druids to all those who had complaints against another and wanted justice, and this might well be the only time he would have to walk alone and search her out. And if he should just happen to see the Lady Keavy as he took his morning walk, it would do no harm to speak to her and look into her eyes and touch the softness of her cheek. Such things would get him through the days until . . . until . . .

Before he knew it, he had completed his circuit of the wall—but there had been no sign of Keavy.

The only birds he saw, little groups of sparrows and wrens, either flew overhead or perched on the houses. They did not hover and dart near any one spot, as they normally did when Keavy was there. Well, then, she must already be in the hall, hard at work weaving some fabric of incredible perfection and lightness or embroidering some sleeve or neckline with colorful work of fabulous detail.

But she was not in the hall.

Aengus walked out through the doors of the hall faster than he'd ever walked in his life. A few of his men, also out early as he was, noticed his anxiety and hurried to catch up with him.

"What is it, King Aengus?"

"Where is she?"

"Where is who?"

"The Lady Keavy! Where is she?"

"Lady . . . Keavy?" The men looked at each other. "Is she not in the hall, with all the other women?"

Aengus broke into a run and headed straight for the tunnel in the high stone wall. "Watchman!" he shouted. Quickly the man atop the wall turned around and looked down at him. "Have you seen the Lady Keavy this day?"

The man nodded. "Indeed I have, King Aengus," he called out. "She rode out alone just after sunrise."

"Rode out alone!" Aengus could only stare at him. "How could you let her ride out alone?"

The man's mouth fell open, and he began to

turn pale. "I . . . I am sorry, my king. I thought she was a guest here, free to come and go as she wished. She said she would go only a short way and would not be gone long—"

"Which way did she go?"

"Why, toward the south. Straight over the open hills."

"Over the hills," Aengus whispered. "Straight for the valley."

Though she left right at dawn, it took Keavy until the sun was high overhead, and then some, to travel on her small gray mare through heavy oak forests and up and down the rocky paths along the cliffs until at last she reached the beautiful valley between the two kingdoms. With a groan she slid down from her sheepskin-covered saddle, already stiff and sore from the nearly half-day-long ride. She led the mare to the stream to let her drink and patted its damp gray neck. "I do not usually ride so far. I am almost always one who walks," Keavy told her. "I only hope you are not so sore as I!"

As if in answer, the mare suddenly threw up her head and skittered backward a few steps, drops of clear water flying from her muzzle. Keavy kept a firm hold of her thick leather reins and got the mare stopped, and then looked across the stream to see what had startled her.

Walking through the widely spaced stand of tall and silvery birch trees lining the opposite bank were eight . . . ten . . . twelve riders, all of whom she recognized instantly as warrior men of Dun Mor. Owen and Desmond were both among them, but King Ross was not, and neither was her father.

This was a party of warriors, nothing more and nothing less.

"Good day to you, Lady Keavy," called Desmond. "I am glad to see you have kept your word about being here this day. Are you truly alone?" He and all the rest of the men continued straight toward her, their horses splashing through the cold clear water of the stream, until all twelve of them surrounded her. The gray mare raised her head and snorted, anxiously looking left and right at the many strange horses suddenly pressing in on her.

"I am alone, as you can well see," Keavy answered. "Where is my father? Did he not wish to come and see me? Please . . . is he well?"

"Quite well," answered Desmond. "And he does want very much to see you, but not here."

"He wants to see you at home, at Dun Mor, and no place else," added Owen.

Keavy drew herself up tall and looked them all straight in the eye. "I told you I would meet you here alone so that you—and, I had hoped, King Ross—might know, beyond any doubt, that I stay at Dun Gaoth of my own free will. Look around. Do you see any of King Aengus's men here, forcing me to stay? You do not. And so I hope that now you will understand that I stay because I wish to stay. I will return to Dun Mor only if and when the time is right for me to do so. This should remain a personal matter between me and my family."

Owen snorted. "Do you not understand, Lady Keavy, that this ceased to be a personal matter when you abandoned your lawful husband in favor of the king of Dun Gaoth? Many have been deeply insulted and lost face over your actions. They all want compensation of some sort for this—and if you and King Aengus refuse to give it to them, they will come and take it by force."

"My mother has already agreed to return the *coibche* to Coilean's family. And he is entirely free of me, free to move on and marry the girl he truly loves."

"Do you think that returning a few trinkets will make this right? You abandoned your husband because the king turned your head. If you had come home right away to your parents, perhaps all would have been forgotten—but it is far too late now!"

"I do not doubt that many were embarrassed and insulted," Keavy said, "but this is only a matter for gossip and satire, not for war! I am being used by men who only want an excuse to fight over this valley where we stand! King Aengus warned me of this!"

"Come home, or there will be war," Owen swore.

"I would make any wager there will be war in any case. None of you cares what happens to me! My father wants an aging daughter married off.

My mother wants grandchildren, to say nothing of the *coibche.* Coilean is weak and his family knows it, and they want someone else to blame for his problems. And you only want an excuse to fight over a piece of land! I am so glad I could be of service to you all!"

With a quick move, Desmond reached out and jerked the leather reins from Keavy's hand. "Get on your horse, Lady Keavy. You are coming home with us."

Aengus lashed his tired bay horse and struggled to keep it going over the steep, rough, rocky terrain. It was not his own horse, but simply the first one at hand; one of his men had already caught and saddled the long-legged gelding and was preparing to ride out before King Aengus had run up and taken the horse on "a matter of the greatest urgency." And so, before anyone else could follow, Aengus had taken the horse through the stone-lined tunnel and sent it galloping over the hills to the south.

Now the sun was high overhead, and he was nearly at the valley. He felt he was as tired as the sweat-lathered horse and was about to slow down . . . and then, from far away, he thought he heard a scream.

Instantly he dragged the horse to a halt. Far in the distance, from the direction of the valley, he heard the scream again.

It was Keavy. He was certain of her voice, and who else could it be? Someone must have arranged to meet her here, for he could not imagine any other reason why she would ride out alone so far away. Surely she did not mean to leave him and return to Dun Mor! She would only have had to say so, and though it would have caused him great pain he would have called out a group of his best men and had them escort her back.

But then another thought struck him. Perhaps she did not want to have to tell him how she really felt—that she had grown tired of being nothing more than the polite guest of a man who showed only a passing interest in her, a man who said he would never marry again, a man to whom she had already given herself but who treated her like a servant instead of as the woman he cherished more with each passing day.

He drove his horse on and galloped up the side of the highest hill, the one that overlooked the valley, hoping he might be able to spot Keavy from there and bring her home before it was too late.

The horse labored to get him up the hill. The way was strewn with boulders and stones and scattered trees, with ditches carved by the rain into the thin, poor, windblown soil. They had nearly reached the top when Aengus kicked the bay horse to get one last effort out of him—and as the animal lunged in response, he tripped across a ditch and dropped hard to his knees on the stony earth.

Aengus stuck to him, even as the tired animal

managed to stay upright and slowly regain his feet. Aengus slid down to look at him and tried to lead him forward, but the horse limped badly and had clearly strained his left front leg in the fall. There was no blood, no broken bone, but the creature was in pain and could go no farther.

Quickly Aengus tied a knot in the long leather reins so they would not trail underfoot, and he turned the horse around to face the north. "Go home now, poor fellow," he said, raising his arms to send the animal away from him. "They will care for you there. You can help me no more this day." He watched briefly as the exhausted horse began to make its limping way back to Dun Gaoth, and then Aengus turned and ran as fast as he could to the top of the hill.

Breathing fast, he cast his gaze over the tops of the hills and far on the other side of the valley—and there, racing between the scattered oaks, driven by twelve men toward Dun Mor to the south, was Keavy on her small gray mare.

"Keavy!" he shouted, but even as he did he knew it was futile. She was too far away to hear him, and without a horse he had no hope of catching her.

No hope . . .

There had once been a time when he could have caught up to her in the space of a few heartbeats, soaring on the winds and driving off her attackers with deadly talons. He must do this again—he must make it happen, he had no other way of saving her, no other way. . . .

As he had done years before, so many years that it seemed like something he had only imagined, he closed his eyes and stretched out his arms and turned his face to the sky. With all the strength of mind he possessed, Aengus tried to still his raging anxiety and anger and think only of lightness and flight, of great powerful wings climbing into the air. For an instant he felt nothing at all. It seemed as though he did indeed float weightless on the wind—and then the earth leaped up and struck him hard in the face and chest.

He pushed it away with his hands, spitting out dirt and gravel and slowly climbing back to his feet, just in time to see Keavy disappear into the distant forest surrounded by the men of Dun Mor.

Driven by anger, fueled by frustration, Aengus made the long walk home at a determined pace, stopping only briefly here and there for a little water. Most of all he stayed to the most traveled path leading from the valley to Dun Gaoth. His men would have to know that he had come this way, for the watchmen knew that Keavy had ridden south. And if—when—the poor injured horse reached Dun Gaoth without his rider, surely a group of the king's own men would immediately ride out to search for him and—

He looked up to see five riders with one riderless horse cantering up over the top of the next hill. "King Aengus!" shouted Parlan, kicking his horse into a gallop. "King Aengus! What has happened here?"

He watched as they all galloped up to him and pulled their mounts to a halt. "They've taken her," Aengus said, reaching for the reins of the riderless horse. "Twelve men of Dun Mor have somehow kidnapped her. She agreed to meet them, I am sure, but now they've forced her to return."

Parlan handed him a water skin. "You are sure of this?"

Aengus glanced at him as he drank. "I am sure," he said, drinking deep and then fastening the water skin to the wooden frame of his saddle. "I saw her from the top of the highest hill. But my horse had fallen and was lame, and I could not . . . I could not follow her."

Parlan looked down. "I am sorry; that is not what I meant. Did she . . . are you sure she did not go with them because she wished it?"

Aengus stared hard at him. "She did not. They disappeared into the forest to the south, and she cried out."

He drove his horse forward past his men and set it trotting on down the path. "I intend to get her back this night, before they can arrive at Dun Mor. Since they do not believe anyone saw them, they will likely be in no hurry and will feel safe on their own lands. If you want to come with me, come now, else go back to Dun Gaoth and take your rest. I thank you for bringing me the horse."

Without another word or a backward glance, Aengus galloped straight to the south. The other men followed closely just as the sun began to approach the western horizon.

Weariness descended with the darkness of the night, though King Aengus fought it off ferociously as his horse jogged along and the stars swung slowly through the black and cloudy sky. He found the food in the leather bags hanging from his saddle and devoured the bread and butter and beef, only to find that the first taste of the honey smeared within the rolled-up flatbread reminded him so much of Keavy and the delicate foods she loved that he felt something like pain—as if he needed any further reason to think of her.

They had crossed the valley and gone off the path so as not to meet any border patrols that might be out, for they were well into Dun Mor's own territory now. They swung back toward the path and climbed over one last hill and saw a small fire among the trees down below. The flickering flames and the glittering stars showed them a group of people gathered around the little campfire, as well as the silhouettes of horses tethered beneath the trees. The sounds of conversation and laughter floated up to them.

"Enjoying their casual evening beneath the stars, are they?" Aengus murmured. "All the better for us. Tie the horses and come with me, quiet as you can."

Aengus crept down the hill in the darkness. His five men followed him closely. They circled around and peered out through the bushes at the little gathering of twelve men and one woman.

Keavy stayed to herself, sitting on a fallen log beneath the trees and close to the spot where her gray mare was tied. Her head was bowed and her hands were clasped in front of her, and even from where he was Aengus could see her shining silvery-gold braids lying on her back. He was glad to note that the men paid no attention to her at all. He was not sure what he might have done if he had thought she was being treated with anything less than the utmost respect.

He gripped the hilt of his sword and glanced at his men. "Spread out. Encircle them. On my signal, we'll give them a surprise. Go now."

Owen stood a little apart from the others, telling them all some fabulous story. Aengus crept up until he was right behind Owen and then in an instant had his sword at the man's throat. "Let her go. She's coming with us. Tell your men to stay where they are."

All of the men leaped to their feet, dropping their cups and food and fumbling for swords or daggers, but each found himself suddenly facing armed and ready opponents.

"She's not going anywhere with you!" shouted Owen, and struggled to reach the sword at his belt—but Aengus wrenched him down on the ground and stood over him, just as the rest of his men kept the others at sword point before they could draw their weapons.

"Keavy! Run into the forest!" shouted Aengus.

"We will find you there! We have come to take you home!"

The men of Dun Mor glared at their captors. An ominous silence filled the air. And then Aengus heard Keavy say, in a clear but trembling voice, "I cannot go with you."

For the first time that day, something like fear touched Aengus at the sound of her voice. He shoved Owen back down with his foot. "Keavy! Run! Run now! You must go now! We have come here for you!"

"I cannot. You must let me go. I . . . I wish to return home!"

"There. You see?" said Owen, in a snarl from down on the ground. "We are her people and we are taking her home!" With that he shoved aside the sword at his throat and rolled to his feet, grinning at the stunned Aengus. "That's not what you expected her to say, is it?" he said. "Well, then. You'll have to fight for her, if you mean to take her. And then you *will* have a war on your hands!"

Owen swung his iron sword and Aengus blocked it with his own. He could hear the shouts and the grunts and the clanging of metal on metal as his own men fought Keavy's guard. But he could not spare a glance for her, for Owen pressed him hard and he was forced to parry again and again—and as he did, almost to his amazement, he found that his arms and legs surged with power and his pounding heart sent renewed energy surging through his veins.

He should have been exhausted at the end of

this long and terrible day. But the thought of Keavy being taken back to Dun Mor, where he might well never see her again, made him shout out loud and strike one last powerful blow—and as he did, he was rewarded by the sight of Owen's sword flying end over end into the black night sky and then crashing down into the trees.

Owen threw him a startled glance and tried to reach for his belt to get his dagger, but before he could draw it Aengus's clenched right fist had struck him so hard on the side of his jaw that he dropped to the ground and lay motionless.

Aengus turned to see that his own men again had their adversaries subdued. "Keavy!" he cried out; but there was no one beneath the trees. With a sinking heart he realized that the gray mare was gone, too. "*Keavy!*"

"She rode off," Parlan said, glancing over his shoulder. "We could not stop her, for we were busy with this lot. I am sorry! We should have done better."

"Wait here," Aengus said, and then he dashed back up the hill to the place where their horses were tied.

Chapter Nineteen

She would have gone south. Aengus was sure of it. For some misguided reason Keavy now believed she had to give herself up to Dun Mor, but she could not have gone far. The night was cloud-shrouded and moonless, and neither she nor her mare was accustomed to being out alone in the forest in the dark.

He held his silence, fearing she would only ride away if she heard his voice and knew he was coming for her; so he kept the horse to a soft, steady jog and wove in and out of the trees and rocks, keeping watch for a spot of light gray in the darkness.

And then he saw it. And heard, as well, a long, frightened whinny.

Not far ahead, a small gray mare was doing her best to stop and turn around and join the horse that was following her, much preferring the company of another of her kind to being alone in a dark and windy forest.

Aengus slid down from his mount. The frightened mare trotted up to stand close beside his horse and touch her nose to Aengus's arm. "Would that *you* were as glad to see me, Lady Keavy," he called, taking hold of the gray mare's reins.

Keavy stared down at him with her enormous pale green eyes. Her skin looked white as milk in the darkness, but her voice was steady. "I am glad to see you, King Aengus—but you must let me return home."

He shook his head, still gazing up at her. "I have never felt so baffled. I thought—I hoped—that you considered Dun Gaoth to be your home, at least for a time. I thought you wished to stay. I knew nothing of the fact that you had changed your mind. Tell me, please. How has this come to be?"

"It is very simple," she said. "I understand it now. I did not see until I spoke alone to Owen and Desmond, but now I see clearly. I have no other choice."

"So it was your choice to ride all the way out here to meet with Owen and Desmond?"

She nodded.

"Why did you not tell me of this? Did you give no thought to how I would be concerned for you when you simply vanished from my sight and the watchman said you had ridden off alone to the south?"

"You cannot afford to be concerned for me,

King Aengus. I am not willing to be the cause of your losing your kingdom."

He lifted an eyebrow and gave her a small smile. "I did not know you were so powerful a lady that you could give away a whole kingdom on your own. How is it that you can do this?"

She continued to gaze down at him from the back of the mare, though he saw the slight trembling in her hands where she held the reins. "I do not intend to let such a thing happen. In my ignorance, and arrogance, I thought that my family and the king and the people of Dun Mor truly wanted me back. Wanted me enough to go to war for me." She shook her head. "I see now that you were right. I was only a small part of the reason for their aggression—really no more than an excuse to try to take possession of a fine piece of land."

Aengus watched her carefully, and kept a firm hold on the reins. "I am certain that many at Dun Mor would fight to the death to bring their Lady Keavy home. However, I agree with you about this battle. I do believe it would be over that piece of land—and you would indeed be used as the excuse they need to go to war."

"I see that now."

"But if you see that, how can you still believe that war will be averted if you return to Dun Mor?"

"Because they will have no excuse once I am back at Dun Mor."

Aengus laughed a little, though he quieted at

seeing the distress in her face. "Dear Keavy . . . I know that you are no warrior, and not well versed in these things. But surely you can see that if one excuse is gone they will simply find another. And when they do find another, where will you be then?"

Keavy raised her chin. "I cannot know what the men of Dun Mor—or the men of Dun Gaoth—might or might not do. I can neither stop nor persuade them. I only know what *I* can do, and that is return to my family. Then, as you say, another excuse to start a war will have to be found. And I will know that no battle was fought—that no one was killed—because of me."

She looked straight at him as she spoke those words, and Aengus could see the fear in her eyes.

Fear for him?

He stepped forward and reached up to cover her hand with both of his own. "Yet you forget one thing," he whispered. "Did you truly think I could just stand aside and let you go?"

"You must," she said. But her voice trembled. "You have no choice. . . ."

He straightened, withdrawing his hand, and looked into her pale green eyes. "I am a king. All choices are mine to make, so long as I am prepared for their consequences—and I am. And I find that the one thing I am not prepared to do is let you go."

Keavy started to turn her mare away, but Aengus kept hold of its reins. "Do you truly want to return to Dun Mor, never to see me again? Can you look at me and say those words?"

She looked him straight in the eye, but her voice caught. "I . . . I want—"

He reached up for her with both arms and took hold of her waist, gently but firmly drawing her toward him and pulling her out of her saddle. He did not wait for her to formally change her mind but simply took charge the way he had learned to do with a woman who was willing to yield to him but uncertain of how she should display that willingness. It was the same way he had taken charge of her on the first night they had been together. He did not force her, simply lifted the burden of responsibility away from her and took it onto himself.

He set Keavy down on her feet, still holding her, and then pulled her very close and looked into her eyes. "I want you to stay," he said, his voice steady and firm in spite of the sharply rising tension in his body. "I do not ever want to spend one more night, one more day, one more heartbeat away from you . . . and you will forgive me if I believe you feel the same way about me."

The look in her shining green eyes, and the slight parting of her lips, told him all he needed to know.

He leaned down and kissed her, and her mouth was soft and sweet and as light as the air. Her arms felt nearly as strong as his own as she pulled him close. Yet just as he was about to draw her down to the soft grass at their feet, she stepped back a pace and managed to speak.

"Marriage," she said, her face flushed and warm. "You told me there would never again be a marriage for you. What future can there be for us if you do not ever want to marry?"

He could only pull her to him all the more tightly, pressing her head against his shoulder and kissing her hair and brows. "I fear to try," he said, struggling for breath. "But then I think of how bravely you faced your own strange marriage, and the night that followed, and then the day that followed that night . . . and if you did not fear to take such a chance, perhaps I will learn not to fear it, either."

Her answer was to melt against him, and he could feel the trust and happiness flowing from her almost as a tangible, physical thing. She raised her head and sought out his lips, kissing him again with ever-increasing desire—the desire of a woman who knows she is loved and cherished beyond any doubt, for she believes she has been told she is worth the most fearsome of risks.

Aengus knew that he should pull back from her; he knew he should not make promises he was not sure he could keep. But neither could he forget that this was no ordinary woman he held in his arms, no passing bride who pressed the length of her body against his and kissed him with all the passion she possessed. This was Keavy, brave, beautiful, elegant Keavy . . . a woman born to be a queen if ever one was, a woman who must never belong to anyone else. He must keep her beside him no matter what. He must never risk losing her again as he nearly had this night.

"Keavy, you must do one thing for me," he whispered. She straightened a bit, just enough to raise her chin, and then waited, still holding him close. He placed his lips against her cheek and went on speaking. "Wait until Samhain, and give me your answer then. Wait until the end of summer, some seven moons from now. By then you can be certain that a life with me is what you want."

She held him even more closely. "I am certain now. I need not wait so long. I—"

"Do this for me, I beg you," he said urgently. "Never again will I ask you for anything so vital. Please, Keavy. I will be here for you now and forever. But when it comes to the marriage, wait until Samhain and give me your answer then."

She sighed and tried to smile a little. "Do you think to keep up appearances, since I was just married a very short time ago? Well, no matter. I suppose it does no harm to allow the matter some time. If you asked me to wait seven moons or seven hundred, Aengus, it would make no difference to me."

He bowed his head and drew her close again. "I hope it will not, dear Keavy. I can only hope that it will not."

She raised her face to his once more, and he returned her kiss with equal passion. Lifting her in his arms, Aengus carried her to a spot of soft grass between the trees. With one hand he pulled the brooch from his own thick wool cloak and let it fall to the grass. His eyes never left her as he lowered her to lie atop the cloak and moved to cover her body with his own.

In the windy darkness of the night, the two of them together claimed each other—and this time it was entirely by choice, and this time there would be no going back.

The sun had just set in the pink-and-gold western sky, yet it seemed to be rising again to the east of Dun Gaoth as a great bonfire bloomed to life on the smooth rolling hills overlooking that fortress. Keavy stood beside Aengus not far from the high stone walls, watching as the men and women of the dun walked around the great blaze. The women carried hazel-twig baskets of flowers—yellow primrose and dandelion, sweet white apple blossom, and pink-and-white clover—while the men held cuttings from the branches of birch and willow trees, bright with new green leaves.

Her own soft pale blue gown moved gently about Keavy's ankles, stirred by the light wind, as did the ends of the yellow mantle that was draped across her shoulders and pinned by her white enameled brooch with its three ever-present golden eagle feathers. She held a small but beautifully woven basket filled with newly cut sprays of sweet white apple blossom.

Beside her stood King Aengus, as magnificent as she had ever seen him, in his deep purple tunic. His blue-and-cream-plaid cloak was so wide it had to be folded five times over his shoulder before being pinned with an enormous bronze brooch. As always, the only gold he wore was his king's torque capped with eagle heads at his throat. He held a branch of heavy gorse, thick with sharp spikes and spiny leaves and delicate yellow blooms.

The people of Dun Gaoth smiled and nodded to her and their king as they circled the great fire. They were polite and friendly enough, which was only to be expected on a happy occasion like the ritual of the spring equinox; but Keavy could sense the tension beneath their smiles whenever they looked at her.

"It is as though I can hear their thoughts when they stare at me," Keavy whispered to Aengus. " 'When must we go to war?' they are thinking. 'How soon will we have to fight a real battle, not a ritual one, because the king has rescued you?' "

Aengus glanced down at her. "Everyone knows that I could not let you be taken away against your will. They would expect nothing less from their king."

"But it was not entirely against my will. You know that."

He turned to look directly at her. "Was it truly your wish to leave this place, perhaps never to return?"

It is never my wish to be away from you! But she could not say the words aloud. Keavy searched for a response, and to her dismay she could not find one. "I don't . . . I suppose . . ." She sighed and looked back at the fortress—and there, standing together in the deep shadow of the curving wall, were Coilean and Maille.

She touched her fingers to Aengus's arm. "I will be back. I have someone to speak to, if I may."

He looked a bit surprised, but then looked toward the fortress. "Ah, I see. Well, perhaps you can learn why they do not want to join the others," he said, and smiled. "Go, Keavy. I will not move from this spot until you return."

She smiled back at him, then turned to go, still carrying her beautiful basket.

Coilean moved a few steps from Maille as Keavy approached, as though he feared someone might notice his interest in the young servant girl. Maille looked pale and nervous but as pretty as Keavy had ever seen her; her dark hair rested in a single thick, neat braid down her back on the nicely woven dark brown wool of her simple servant's gown. And Keavy could not help but smile at the very simple embroidery Maille had attempted to stitch in bleached wool thread on the sleeves and neckline of the gown.

Maille clutched a little bunch of pink clover, while Coilean held a twig of birch with a few limp green leaves hanging from it.

"Why do you not join the others?" Keavy asked. "Such a beautiful evening, this night marking the midway point of springtime. Everyone is dancing 'round the fire. Before long we will all sit down for a feast and some music and singing."

Coilean shot her a cold glare. "I know too well what the entertainment will be."

Keavy sighed, and she turned to smile at Maille. "Even if he does not want to join the celebration, will you not come?"

But Maille only turned to Coilean again, and tears began to flow. Finally Coilean raised his head to speak to Keavy.

"It is well that *you* are able to have the man you love," he said. "And it is certainly very well that the *king* is able to consort freely with the woman he loves. But we two are not so fortunate. We can never marry, thanks to the satires that are now such popular entertainments. I am naught but a source of ridicule for every man, woman, and child in this fortress. My parents always said they would never allow us to marry anyway—but even if they did allow it, the ceremony would only be another chance for everyone here to gather for another round of laughter at my expense! Why would either one of us want to subject ourselves to that?"

Keavy could only shake her head. Maille began sobbing in earnest and hid her face against Coilean's sleeve. "Coilean—someday you will learn not to wait for others to give you permission to do what is important to you. Nor to sit back and do naught but blame them when things do not go the way you wish. If you truly want to win the woman you love, you will have to fight for her. You will have to—"

"*You* are the *last* one to tell *me* what to do!" he said in a hiss through clenched teeth, mindful of the nearby crowd even in his anger. "*You* should never have come here! *You* have brought nothing but trouble! *You* should go back to Dun Mor where you belong and never trouble us here again!"

"Oh, Coilean!" Maille cried, growing even paler with shock. "Please don't say such things! Not to her—not to Lady Keavy!"

Keavy straightened and gave Coilean a cool stare. "Someday, Coilean of Dun Gaoth, you will learn that the world is a larger place than you know. Much larger than just you and your problems and your weaknesses."

Before he could respond, Keavy turned to Maille. "Perhaps you will join us in the celebration, even if Coilean will not. You are both welcome there. Good evening to you."

"Good . . . good evening to you, Lady Keavy." Maille sniffled.

Keavy turned away from them and started back toward the bonfire once again, feeling Coilean's furious glare on her back with every step she took.

She was very glad to return to Aengus's side and watch the dancers continue to circle the bonfire, waving their flowers and branches over it, but she could only shake her head as she came to stand beside him.

"What is it?" he asked gently, moving aside the heavy spiked branch he held. "Is he still sulking?"

"He is. And I fear it will never stop."

"Why should it matter to you what Coilean does? He is not your husband. He cannot affect your life anymore."

"Oh, but I fear he will always affect it, in one way or another. These events were set in motion when I agreed to marry him. Once started, it is very difficult to bring them to a stop."

Keavy glanced back toward the fortress, which was beginning to disappear into the rapidly deepening dusk. "Maille fears she will never have the man she loves, for she is only a servant and has nothing to say about the matter. But her man is a weakling caught up in forces he does not have the courage to face. He may well lose the woman he says he loves because of his own weakness."

She turned back to Aengus. "And I fear that I too will end up as Maille has—never having the man I love."

Beside her, she could feel him straighten and then frown down at her. "Do you mean to say that I am not strong enough to fight for you? That I am anything like Coilean? Because let me assure you, Lady Keavy, I am—"

"It is not you who is not strong enough. I am the one who lacked the courage to return home, and in so doing give two groups of men one less excuse to go to war. And now it seems that war is inevitable—real, killing war, not just the ritual battles that are more sport than genuine warfare. Men die in true warfare—men die, and so do kings."

She looked away, unable to say any more, and one of her tears fell onto the white apple blossoms.

Aengus reached out and touched her damp

cheek. Keavy could sense the tension within him as he spoke. "I will promise you this," he said. "It will not be Dun Mor that takes you away from me. But there are far worse things than battle."

She looked up at him, and was puzzled to see something almost like dread in his eyes. "I cannot think of what that might be," she whispered. "I hope never to know it."

"I hope you never know it, either." Then, with a quick smile, he touched her arm and looked out at the bonfire. "Watch now. The light is nearly gone. And when the night has fallen . . ."

They watched the people circling around the fire, even as the last light faded from the world. As the deep darkness settled over all, the dancers stopped and stood still, facing the snapping flames and waiting in silence.

Keavy watched as one of the druids stepped up and bowed to Aengus. He then walked toward the great blaze, and Keavy and Aengus followed just behind him. The breathless men and women at the fire made way for them, then watched as the king and his lady and his druid took their place among the dancers as the flames leaped and snapped.

The druid began to speak. "Here on this night of midspring, when darkness and light visit us in equal measure, we gather together to build the sacred fire. We mark this time so that all who see this fire will know what night this is.

"Each of you holds an offering of this season of year: sweet clover, bright blossoms, new leaves.

Step forward now, and give them to the flames, that the sweetness of these offerings might be sent up and out upon the winds to reach all those throughout the kingdom, and even reach those gods and goddesses who still walk among us both here and in the Otherworld. Give your gifts to them now, that such new flowers and leaves might appear every spring, now and forever."

One at a time, moving sunward around the circle, the men and women tossed their primrose and clover and willow and birch into the flames of the bonfire. The last woman to make the offering was Keavy, who threw her delicate sprays of white apple blossom into the fire, and the last man was Aengus, whose heavy branch of yellow flowering gorse caused the flames to roar and leap.

They stood together beneath the dark night sky, lit by the fierce glare of the fire. Keavy was comforted by the warmth and strength of Aengus standing close beside her—but she could not help stealing one last glance behind her at Coilean and Maille, and was left feeling cold at the sight of Coilean still glaring at her as fiercely as the fire burned.

Chapter Twenty

A few days after the spring ritual, Keavy walked in the soft morning light on the well-worn pathways of the fortress yard. Beside her was Maille, while some ten other servants and craftsmen trailed along after.

"What are we to do, Lady Keavy?" Maille asked, hurrying a little to keep up with Keavy's long strides. "Why have you asked us all to come out here with you?"

Keavy smiled at her little army of workers, and brushed one long silver-blond braid back behind her shoulders. "The fortress is quiet these days, for the men spend so much of their time riding out on the patrols watching for . . ." To her surprise, she found the words hard to say.

"For the men of Dun Mor," Maille finished. "Oh, I hope they do not come, lady; it frightens me to think they could take you away."

Keavy stopped and smiled at her little assembly. "Do not worry, Maille. Your king and his patrols will see that no one comes near Dun Gaoth. Now, then—as I was saying to you, the dun is very quiet these days. That allows us a chance to walk through it and make whatever repairs we can, and clean what we can clean, and replace what needs replacing."

The servants only stood and stared at her. Their lack of enthusiasm for the extra work she proposed was plain on their faces. Keavy placed her hands on her hips. "Dun Gaoth is such a strong place. Do you not agree that it deserves the brightest and most tightly bound straw on its roofs, the strongest doors on the quietest hinges, the finest and most abundant foods for its people and its guests, and the cleanest and most beautiful furs and cloaks and cushions and cups in its houses and hall?"

The servants and craftsmen all turned to look at each other. "Of course we agree, Lady Keavy!" Maille said brightly, elbowing the men beside her.

"Of course," the rest of them mumbled. "Of course."

"I thank you all for your enthusiasm," Keavy said with a grin. "So if you will follow me, we will begin."

Keavy led them through the dun, looking at this house and that shed or outbuilding. With the craftsmen she made decisions on whether a new roof was needed, or more clay daub on the walls, or whether the hinges should be greased or a new door constructed. She left a few of the servants and craftsmen at each place with their tasks assigned, and finally she left Maille at the hall to inspect all the copper plates and cups and bowls and bronze cauldrons and iron utensils to see how many needed repair or replacement.

With the work well under way and all of her helpers busy, Keavy finished the walk-through by herself. The last place she inspected was a low shed where horses for the king and his men could be sheltered—and she was startled to see Coilean inside, attempting to saddle a quiet black pony, an animal so advanced in age that its muzzle was turning gray.

"Are you going somewhere, Coilean?" she asked, stepping inside the shed.

He glanced up at the sound of her voice. Instantly his eyes turned cold. "I am going for a ride," he said. "I have been closed up here for far too long. I am in need of some inspiration for my poetry."

"Indeed you are," Keavy murmured, trying not to smile.

But he only looked up at her again, glaring across the pony's back. "It's too bad the army of Dun Mor doesn't just ride to the gates and take you away."

She was surprised at such continued hostility, even from him, but kept her voice calm and looked steadily at him. "Many of us fear they will indeed ride to the gates—but the king will not let them take anyone away who does not wish to go. It is a surprise attack that has the people frightened."

"Perhaps they would have no need to attack if you were gone."

"It is too late for that. The decision has been made by your own king. I am to stay. He will not have it any other way."

He shot her a murderous look as he went on struggling with the saddle. "Our problems would be over if you were gone. I could begin to recover what dignity I had. So could my family."

Keavy forced her temper to remain cool. "And what of Maille? What will happen to her if I am gone?"

"Once you are gone and forgotten, all will go back to normal! Maille is a servant in the king's house now. She will not be sent away."

Keavy studied him, and moved a step closer. "You seem very sure of yourself this day. Far more than usual. What is it that you mean to do?"

He caught his breath and gave her a startled look, but then went on readying his pony. "I have decided to take your advice. I mean to put things right once and for all. To put them back the way they were." He scowled grimly as he went on working. "I did what they wanted. I married you, the woman who was supposed to be the ideal wife. Now all is ruined and you are to blame. I want justice."

Keavy took another step toward him, her gaze level with his. "If you are threatening me or the king, I remind you that you will be the one who pays the price."

"It is no threat. I want only justice, for myself and for my family."

"And for Maille?"

"For Maille, too. I want her and she wants me. And we will have each other as we always should have."

"Then fight for her, Coilean! Stand up to your family like a—"

"My family is not the true problem! You are!" Still glaring at her with malice, he untied the pony and pulled the reluctant animal out into the yard. There he climbed awkwardly into the saddle and started the pony walking toward the tunnel through the wall.

Keavy could only stand and watch him go. She would have to tell Aengus about this, of course, but no doubt it was just more of Coilean's complaining and bitterness. He had never been known to ever actually take action about anything. Surely it was nothing to be seriously concerned about. After all, what could a man like Coilean do on his own?

Three days later, as the fresh winds blew fast-moving clouds through the late-morning sky and light and shadow took turns flying across the grounds, Keavy walked over the pathways of Dun Gaoth with King Aengus at her side.

"Your craftsmen have done wonderful things in a very short time," she called, hurrying him from one house to another. "See how smooth and clean these walls are now, with their new layers of clay. Look at the roofs, there and there, and see how bright and golden they are with new straw. Now, this house, you see, has a whole new door, and this one new shutters on the windows. And the hinges on every door and window are greased and silent now. No more awful creaking and groaning all day and all night!"

She pointed from house to shed to hall. "The cobwebs are cleared from the rafters. The cauldrons are patched; the copper plates shine. Even the weeds have been pulled from the doorsteps. Your fortress was beautiful before, King Aengus, but now it is fresh and clean and new again."

Keavy looked up at him, enormously pleased with the results of her efforts. But he seemed entirely distracted, almost as if he had not been listening to her at all, and kept looking toward the entryway in the wall.

"I am sorry," she said quietly. "I am going on about a little springtime cleaning, while you are expecting someone or something. What has happened?" Then her eyes widened. "Is Dun Mor returning? Have they been seen? What . . . ?"

He finally turned back to her and smiled tightly. "There are no men of Dun Mor anywhere near here. The patrols are watching very closely. There are at least two of them out at all times, and usually three."

"Then . . . who are you expecting?"

Aengus took her arm and began to walk with her toward the back of the fortress. "One of the families here is expecting . . . a guest. Several guests. I simply wanted to see that they arrived safely."

"Oh—guests! How wonderful! It is always wonderful to have visitors. Where are they from? What family is expecting them?"

"They are from—I believe—the fortress of Cahir Cullen, far to the north. One of my men, Finbar, is expecting them."

"I am so pleased! There is nothing more fun than having guests. Well, almost nothing." She smiled up at him. "I am glad that so much of the work and repair was completed, just in time!"

"I must thank you for seeing to it all. I may have neglected to tell you so, but I am grateful for your efforts here. Grateful to you for caring so much about my home."

She stopped, making him stop, too, and looked up into his hazel-gold eyes. She was puzzled by the apprehension she saw there and by the tension and distraction evident in his manner. "Of course I would care about your home. I could do no less, for—"

She stopped as his head jerked up and he looked toward the entryway. Keavy looked, too, and saw servants and horseboys gathering near the tunnel, watching as riders began filing in one at a time, eleven in all, plus three pack ponies. And from outside the walls came the sounds of mooing, bawling cattle.

"My, they've brought everything with them, haven't they?" Keavy laughed. "Servants, and cattle, and the whole family—a set of parents, two young men and a lovely young woman—ponies loaded with fine things—a whole herd of cattle—why, this looks like nothing more than—"

Keavy felt as though the coldest wind of winter had suddenly struck her. Her heart began to pound. She looked at the beautiful dark-haired, dark-eyed young woman being helped down from the pack pony by Finbar. "Like nothing more than a wedding party," she whispered, her throat beginning to close up.

She could only stand and stare at the arriving guests as realization slowly dawned. This was indeed a wedding party, here for the marriage of a man of Dun Gaoth to a woman from another kingdom. The same kind of marriage that she herself had made. And on this night, once the marriage contracted had been recited, this new and beautiful dark-eyed creature would be taken not to her husband but to the bed of the king.

To Aengus.

She began to feel hot and cold all at once. Her breath came so quickly it seemed she could hardly breathe at all. Quickly she turned and started toward the tunnel in the wall, making a wide circle around those who had gathered to welcome the guests.

Aengus tried to catch hold of her arm, but she shook him off. "I cannot stay here," she said, her voice shaking badly in spite of her best effort at steadying it. "I must go out for a time. I am sorry. I cannot watch this. It is a failing of mine. I have not the strength to watch it."

He started to follow her. "Where are you going?"

"I don't know. Outside. To the forest. Somewhere. Anywhere. Anywhere but here."

"Keavy, I cannot go with you at this moment. I must greet my guests. I must see that all is ready. But I will come and find you just as soon as I can. I will come and find you!"

But Keavy only lifted the hems of her skirts and hurried away from him, running through the dark, damp tunnel in the fortress wall and out to the open hills beyond.

Keavy sat on a fallen log beneath the sun-dappled shadows of the birches, gazing out across the stream and the hills at the distant lake. She kept her back to the great stone fortress. As much as possible, she tried to keep her breathing calm and her heartbeat steady and her mind quiet and relaxed. It was not so difficult out here in the beauty of nature, but she did not want to think of how she would feel once she returned to Dun Gaoth—returned to the house of the king.

Before long there was the sound of heavy footsteps walking across the grass behind her. Keavy closed her eyes, but made no move to go; and in a moment Aengus sat down beside her and covered her hand with his own.

"I am sorry this has happened," he said quietly. "I had hoped it would not come so soon."

Keavy steadied her breathing, and watched the glint of sunlight on the waters of the lake. "Now

I see why you wanted me to wait until Samhain—until the start of winter—to decide whether I wanted to stay with you."

He nodded. "I knew that by Samhain, there would no doubt be another marriage. Another First Night. By then you would know for certain whether you still wished to stay as my wife."

"And this is what you meant when you said it would not be the men of Dun Mor who took me away from you. I did not understand at the time—but now I do. You feared it would be a First Night ritual that would take me away from you forever."

His voice was gentle. "That is what I feared."

"I do not know how I could have forgotten that there must eventually be another marriage—and another First Night. I suppose I wanted to forget. I wanted to pretend there would never be anyone else for you but me."

"There *is* no one else for me but you."

"But that is not true, King Aengus. As long as there are brides from other kingdoms, it is your duty to have others besides me. I am sure you are the envy of every other man in this fortress. Do you truly wish to change this?"

"I cannot change it. I have not the power to change it. It is a custom as old as time."

"I see. Then that is the end of it." She looked down at the soft, grassy earth beneath her feet, and listened to the wind whispering high in the branches of the silvery birch trees. "And I see, now, what must have happened to your marriage with Deirdre."

Aengus withdrew his hand and sat quietly for a moment. "She had been told, before marrying me, that this has always been a part of the marriage ritual here. She understood that it was part of the king's duty. My duty."

But Keavy shook her head. "Deirdre's was an arranged marriage. She had never seen you, she did not know you, and she did not love you before coming here. She knew of the tradition here, it is true, but must have thought she could accept it. The head sometimes believes it can do what the heart later learns is impossible. It was far, far different for her once she lay with you in your bed and gave herself to you as your wife—before she began to love you as her husband."

"She had been my wife for only a few nights before there was another wedding and I was called upon for the ritual. We had had only a little time together."

Keavy shrugged. "A few nights is more than long enough for a wife to begin to love a husband such as you. It took even less time for me. I can well understand how she must have felt."

"But Deirdre said nothing to me of how she felt. She simply . . . withdrew."

"Indeed. What else could she do? She was a queen, and could not leave her people or her king . . . but she had to live each day not knowing whether her husband would be taking another beautiful young woman to his bed that night."

"None of them would ever have replaced her. They were no threat to her. I made sure she knew that she need not ever worry about such a thing."

Keavy smiled a little, though there was no joy in it. "You must understand, Aengus. On the nights when it was your duty to be with another, Deirdre *was* replaced. There was another woman getting your attention and your tenderness. Deirdre was powerless to do aught but stand aside and wait alone while her beloved husband did these things for a woman not his wife."

"But it was not my choice. It is an ancient ritual. It is the law. That is the only reason why—"

"Aengus, do you really believe the reason would make any difference? All she knew was that it was indeed happening, and that her feelings would never be considered in the matter. I do not know how any woman could live so. I know that I could not."

He was silent for a time. "She never spoke of it to me," he admitted at last, so softly that Keavy could scarcely hear the words. "After that First Night ritual that came just after we were married, she never spoke of it at all . . . and never again did she touch me. I believed—or chose to believe—that she had simply not found me to her liking after all.

"How could I blame the duties of my kingship for the loss of my wife? How could I change a ritual so old that its origins are lost to any man's memory?" Aengus shook his head. "Deirdre and I stayed together because it was far easier to do than to go our separate ways and start again. It is very, very difficult for any king or queen to do such a thing. We never even considered doing so."

He stood up suddenly and turned his fierce gaze directly at Keavy. "Now do you understand?" he asked, with an edge of anger and frustration in his voice. "Now do you understand why I have kept you at a distance? Do you see what life is like for the wife of a king such as I?"

Keavy rose to her feet and slowly walked a few paces away from him. "Is there nothing you can do to change this custom of the First Night?"

He shook his head emphatically. "It is not just a custom. It is the *law* in this kingdom and always has been."

"You are a king, Aengus of Dun Gaoth. Surely you could—"

"I do not have the power to change it on my own. Only the druids and the free men of the tribe have the power to change a law—any law. Especially a sacred law like this one."

"And what do the druids and the free men say when you propose that this law be changed?"

He was silent for a very long time. He turned away, and then looked down at the ground, but said nothing.

"I see," Keavy said quietly.

"The old ways have served our people well for a very long time." His voice was harsh.

"How well are the people being served if an old law costs them their queen?"

"Deirdre stayed and served as their queen."

"But she was hardly a queen to her king. And

it *is* possible for someone to die of a broken heart. Did she not go to the Otherworld much too soon?"

Keavy clasped her hands in front of her and gazed directly at him. "So you are not certain you would change this custom if you could. You are not sure you would really want such a custom to end."

Again King Aengus was silent. He could not look at her.

"Well, if you do not wish for this ritual to end, you may be sure it never will. I must say I cannot blame you. What man would not love to have such attentions to women be required of him as part of his duty, while remaining free to disregard the wishes and feelings of his wife regarding those very same attentions?"

Aengus lifted his head and stared at her, blinking. "I *would* end it if I could," he said quietly. "I do not know what else I can say to you."

"I do not know either. I can only tell you that I have not the strength to be the wife of a man whose duty requires him to give the most personal of attention to other beautiful young women. I wish I did have such strength, for I love you, and I would love nothing more than to be your wife . . . but so long as you are content to let this custom continue, I will have no choice but to go, for it hurts me far too much to stay."

Quickly she caught up her long skirts and started toward the stone fortress of Dun Gaoth, leaving Aengus standing alone in the sun-dappled birches. But Keavy had barely left the shadows of the trees before she heard hoofbeats approaching from the far side of the stream to the north.

Chapter Twenty-one

Keavy paused, still facing the fortress. The wedding party had also come from the north, but all of them were already inside and safe. Was this a late patrol, riding in after them? But that was not possible. One of the patrols had ridden in with the visitors from Cahir Cullen to the north, while the other two remained south to keep themselves between Dun Gaoth and Dun Mor.

Finally she turned around—and was horrified to see ten men of Dun Mor, led by Tiernan, the king's champion, riding their horses across the stream and surrounding Aengus with weapons drawn.

"Well, now. Look who has come out to welcome us!" Desmond said with a laugh, jabbing his sword at the air just in front of Aengus's face. "We thought we'd have to lure you out with the offer of a champion's battle, but you've saved us the trouble!"

Aengus gripped the hilt of his own sword, but

it was no use against ten men and he well knew it. Keavy tried to push past the milling horses and get to Aengus's side, but the men forced her back with the points of their swords and the flanks of their horses.

"What are you doing here?" she cried. "Why do you surround the king? I am the one you want! Take me. I will go with you. I am the one you want!"

To her shock and amazement, the men on horseback all turned and laughed at her. "That's what Coilean thought, too!" Owen said, still laughing.

"Coilean?"

Aengus raised his head to look at her, seemingly ignoring the sword point at his throat. "Keavy. Run back to the fortress. Your own men will not harm you. Go now. Go quickly. Please. Just go."

"Oh, I think not," Tiernan said, riding his horse to block Keavy's path. "Not until we are gone. And it was your own Coilean, your own recent husband, Lady Keavy, who very kindly rode out to tell us about the wedding party that would be riding here from the north five days after the equinox. He told us how easy it would be for us to follow in its wake—and that's exactly what we did."

Keavy could only gasp. "How is that possible?"

"Quite simple," Desmond said. "The patrols would either be staying with the arriving party, or watching to the south toward Dun Mor. No one would be expecting us to come down from the north. So that's exactly what we did!" He sat back on his horse, grinning broadly.

"Coilean was most helpful," continued Owen. "He explained to us how you were known to walk out near the birches and the stream nearly every day. All we would have to do is watch and wait for you—and he was right."

"Then take me! I will go with you. Let King Aengus go!"

All of them laughed again. "As Owen said, Coilean too thought we wanted you," Tiernan said. "But he is no warrior. In fact, he lacks so much as the wisdom of a sparrow. He thought only to let us take you off his hands and out of his life. It seems he blames you for all of his troubles. But you are not our concern, Lady Keavy. It is the king we have come for, and the king we mean to take."

"The king?" She tried to approach Aengus again, but Dun Mor's men and swords and milling horses kept her back. "Do you truly want to start a killing war? The men of Dun Gaoth will stop at nothing to get their king out of your hands. What do you mean to do to him?"

Desmond grinned at her. "Why, we mean to do nothing to him, except keep him as our guest for a time to show Dun Gaoth that we are not to be played with and insulted for *any* reason—certainly not by taking a woman of our kingdom away from the men who have come to escort her home!"

"See? You came to take me," Keavy said, looking from one familiar face to another with ever-rising anxiety. "You came to take me!"

Tiernan shook his head. He was not laughing now. "You are a free woman and can go where you like—and apparently Dun Gaoth is the place most to your liking. But your king will come with us."

Keavy tried another plan. "At any moment the watch will realize there are horses among these trees. Men will be riding out from the fortress to see what is happening here."

"You are correct, lady. That is why we must be going. Drop your sword, Aengus, and get on that horse."

But Aengus did not move. He knew it would not be long before his own men would come riding out to see what was going on in the trees near the stream—especially since their king was suddenly nowhere to be found. He looked up almost casually at Tiernan and smiled, making no move to go anywhere.

Desmond vaulted down from his horse and grabbed Keavy by the arm. She struggled with all her strength to free herself from his iron grip, but it was no use. "Drop the sword and get on the horse, King Aengus. Else I throw her over my horse's neck and take her with us."

And, so early, Aengus was beaten. Without a word, he let his sword fall to the grass. He stepped to the horse and swung up onto its back, his eyes flashing with anger. "Go, Keavy. They will not harm me. I am no use to them dead or wounded."

"He is right," said Tiernan, glancing toward the still-quiet fortress. "Aengus will remain our honored guest, until his people decide they want him back. In that case they can offer us a ransom."

"A ransom?" Keavy cried, pulling away from Desmond as he released her to get back on his horse. "What can Dun Gaoth offer to ransom a king?"

The men sat back on their horses and looked at her, grinning, playing with her and enjoying every moment of it. "Now, what *could* Dun Gaoth offer?" Tiernan said, as though he'd never thought of such a thing before. "That is a very good question. What would be enough to ransom a king?"

"How about gold?" Owen suggested.

Tiernan nodded. "Gold is the traditional ransom for a king. But the halls and homes and women and warriors of Dun Mor are already gleaming with as much fine gold as we could want."

"Cattle," Desmond said.

"Cattle make a fine ransom, too. But our pens and pastures are filled with the strongest bulls and the best milking cows. There are so many calves we have to slaughter half of them every year at Samhain." He shook his head, gazing at each of his men. "Is there nothing else? What could be large enough, grand enough, and valuable enough to ransom a hostage king from a large and wealthy kingdom like Dun Mor?"

Owen glanced at him. "There is a very fine valley right between our two kingdoms," he said. "I seem to remember riding through it once or twice. Dun Gaoth claims it is theirs."

Tiernan's eyebrows lifted, as though he were astonished. "Why, there *is* such a valley, isn't there? I don't know how I could have forgotten it. And a beautiful, lush place it is, too. I believe our king *would* accept such a place as ransom for King Aengus. It is for you, Lady Keavy, to tell your people that he will accept no less."

They reined their horses around and walked them back across the stream. Desmond had the reins of Aengus's mount pulled over the animal's head and led it alongside his own horse.

Fear and anger rose in Keavy's chest at the sight of them forcing Aengus away. "King Aengus was right about you all along, Tiernan! You and all of your men! None of you cares about your people—not me, or whether I ever come home or not. You just wanted someone else's land and saw me as a way to let you take it!"

But the warriors only laughed again. "You demanded to be allowed to go where you wished and live where you chose," Tiernan said. "Now that we understand that and have left you to it, you have no cause to complain. And if you had never left Dun Mor, and happened one day to visit a beautiful valley that King Ross had fought and won for you, you would never think of how he gained it."

"That is the way of the world, Lady Keavy," continued Desmond. "Your new king knows this and so does ours. Now, step back out of the way. This is no longer your concern."

"They will find you," Keavy said as they started to ride off toward the north. "The men of Dun Gaoth will be after you in a heartbeat. You cannot possibly escape them."

"Oh, but I think we can," called Tiernan as they galloped away. "We have a plan for that, too. Good day to you, Lady Keavy!" And Keavy could do nothing more than watch as Aengus disappeared with his captors over the grassy hills toward the lake and the heavy forest beyond.

As the full moon rose in the dark eastern sky, a group of riders gathered outside the walls of Dun Gaoth and walked their exhausted horses one by one through the narrow tunnel and onto the fortress yard. Keavy stood with the rest of the anxiously waiting people standing on the torchlit grounds, and hurried over with them to the riders who entered. "Did you find him? Did you find the king? Where is King Aengus?"

But everyone knew the answer even before the men on horseback looked down at them and shook their heads: the king was gone, and his men had not been able to find him.

"We followed their tracks. They had only a short lead," Parlan said, sliding down from his tired, sweating horse. "But just past the lake they divided into two groups. We split up, too, and each followed one lead—only to find that each of their groups had divided again. All we found was one loose horse, set free as a distraction. The rest of them got away."

He clenched his fists as one of the servants led his horse off. "We never thought to look for them coming from the north. But we should have."

"How did they know where and when to find the king?" cried one man, his voice rough with frustration. "Maybe *she* told them!"

To Keavy's horror, the entire crowd turned to stare at her. But she raised her chin and stared them right back.

"It was not I who betrayed the king. I would never do such a thing. It was one of your own. It was Coilean!"

"Coilean!"

"Why would Coilean try to do such a thing? Why would he betray his own king?"

Keavy took a deep breath. "He did not think he was betraying the king. He is such a fool, he thought he would be handing *me* over to Dun Mor and seeing the end of all his troubles as they dragged me back home. Dun Mor merely used him—and me—to get what they wanted, which was a chance to find the king alone."

There was a low muttering from the crowd. "Coilean is such a half-wit, I'm inclined to believe her story."

"It would make no sense for Keavy to betray King Aengus."

"Everyone knows how much Coilean despises her."

"Everyone knows what an ignorant fool he is!"

"No wonder he's closed up in his house, refusing to come out. We will have to deal with him later."

Keavy closed her eyes.

"What will we do now, Parlan?" someone shouted from the crowd.

"You are the king's champion. It is up to you to lead his men in the fight to bring him home!"

"Bring me a horse, and I'll go to Dun Mor right now and get him out myself!"

The crowd shouted in agreement, and moved to stand close to Parlan and his men as the horses were led away. "Listen to me!" Parlan cried. "We will bring our king home. But we will need our every strength, our every man, our every sword and spear and sling and javelin to do so. We must make ourselves ready and ride out in force."

One of the druids stepped forward. The crowd parted to make way for him. "Should we not wait for them to send a messenger to ask for their ransom?" said the druid.

"I agree," said a second druid, stepping out of the shadows. "Surely this is why they have taken him. Why would they take any king, or any man of high rank? First to serve us a bit of humiliation, and after that to force us to pay them some exorbitant price to get our king back."

"It is ever the way of things," said the first druid, nodding in agreement.

But Parlan only fixed the two of them with a cold stare. "Most times what you say would be true. But not now."

Instantly there was a wave of agitated voices from the crowd. "Are you saying they will harm him?" someone shouted.

"Or kill him?"

"Why would they do that?"

"He is of no value to them as a hostage if he is dead or wounded!"

Parlan raised his hands to silence them. "You are right. A dead king, or one who is maimed and no longer fit to be king, cannot bring a king's ransom. But think on this: what ransom would Dun Mor want?"

"Why . . . what any kingdom wants!"

"Gold!"

"Cattle!"

"Weapons!"

"They have all those things in far greater numbers than we do. Not that they wouldn't take more, but their fortress is already crowded with such things. They are a larger kingdom than we. Why would they go to the trouble of taking a king unless they were holding him for something of far more value to them?"

The people all looked at each other, momentarily puzzled. "The valley," Keavy said, stepping forward to stand before the king's champion. She had remained silent, waiting to see the people's reaction but now she spoke. "Parlan is right. Aengus knew they would try to take it. And they spoke of it today when they took him away. They hope to ransom him for the valley."

Parlan glanced at her and nodded. "They want

that valley, and they will do anything to attain it."

The first druid stepped forward again. "Could we not offer them the valley for Aengus's life? Is it so important?"

The crowd fell silent. Keavy straightened, as did Parlan. "Offer them the valley?" he said. "Give away our kingdom, piece by piece? And what will we do when we have no more land to give them?" He shook his head. "Aengus did not become our king to see bits of his land parceled out to his enemies like gold trinkets or fine heifers. He would have fought to the death to protect that land, and he would do no less now."

Keavy drew a deep breath. "What are you saying?"

Parlan looked out at the anxious crowd. "I am saying that Dun Mor will do their worst. They took King Aengus to hold him for ransom, to get that valley for themselves—and when we will not exchange it for our king they will kill him and force us into battle."

Keavy felt cold all over. Someone beside her shouted, "Then we must ride to the gates of Dun Mor right now and get Aengus out by force!"

The crowd began shouting in agreement. "We should go right now!" "I'll go!" "I'll go!" "I'll ride straight into that place and kill them all to get our king!"

"Think!" cried Parlan, raising his hands as he tried to get the crowd's attention. "Think of it! Nothing would end the life of Aengus faster than for us to do exactly that—to attack them in the very walls of their home!"

"What else can we do?" shouted another man. "This is intolerable!"

"We will do what we must—to save both our king and our land," answered Parlan. "We will do what Dun Mor will understand. I will send a messenger tomorrow to tell Dun Mor to meet us at the valley in four days' time. They will bring Aengus with them, and we will have a battle to see who will win both him and that valley. They will understand this. They will not feel threatened by the tradition and ritual of such a battle. *That* is what we can do. That is what we *must* do."

Keavy hurried inside the king's house and shut the door tightly behind her. Quickly she turned to face Maille and Elva where they stood against the glowing hearth. "Where is Seanan?"

"At the hall," answered Elva, "waiting on the men gathered there. They will be there most of the night, I think."

"Good." Keavy pushed herself away from the door and went to stand near the warmth of the fire. "We have a lot to talk about. And a plan to make."

"A plan?" Maille asked in a quiet voice. "What do you mean?"

Keavy looked closely at her. For the first time she realized just how calm and poised the young servant girl was on this very strange night. "Maille, I am so sorry for what Coilean has done. He is in his house and will not come out, according to the men in the yard."

"He has no face to show in this fortress any longer. Nor to me," Maille said. Her eyes were bright with tears but her voice remained quiet and steady. "He tried to have you taken away."

Elva took a step forward. "He is lucky the men believed him when he said he did not betray the king, but only thought he was betraying you, Keavy." She shook her head. "I'm sorry to say so, Maille, but we are lucky: he is such a fool that they must have felt sure he lacked the wit and courage to actually give Dun Mor the king."

"His reputation worked to his advantage this time," Keavy said. "They might well have killed him otherwise."

Maille closed her eyes. "I'm so sorry, Lady Keavy. I don't know what made him do such a thing. I only wish I could have stopped him."

"It is in no way your fault," Keavy reassured her. "Try not to think of it again. There are other things I need from you right now."

She paced around the circular hearth, and both women turned to watch her. "What is that you want us to do?" Maille asked.

"I need you to help me pack."

"Pack?" Elva took another step toward her, frowning. "Whatever do you mean?"

Keavy walked to her sleeping ledge and began looking through her stacks of colorful gowns and long rectangular cloaks. "I'm going back to Dun

Mor. I have to. I'm the only one here who could ever get through those gates."

"Through the gates!" Maille hurried over to the ledge. "Then . . . you're leaving us forever? You're going back to the home of your parents?"

"Not at all. But that's what I will say when the watchmen at Dun Mor ask me why I am there. And once inside, I will find a way to free King Aengus."

Maille and Elva looked at each other as Keavy continued to sort through her clothes. Then they each placed a hand on her shoulders and gently but firmly pushed her back, until she abruptly sat down on the fur-covered sleeping ledge.

"My lady, you must listen to us," Elva said, in her low and dignified voice. "It matters not at all what you think you will say to the watchmen at Dun Mor, for you will never get outside the walls of Dun Gaoth at a time such as this. Aengus's men will never allow it."

"They will have to let me go," Keavy said stubbornly. "The king said I was not a prisoner here and that I can—"

"They know what happened the last time you rode out alone!" Maille said. "What do you suppose would happen to them if the king returns and finds that they again let you ride out alone across the country?"

"And even if you could get to Dun Mor, surely you do not believe the people there would ever let you near King Aengus." Elva straightened, and folded her hands. "They know your feelings for him. They would fear you would somehow try to free him—and they would be right."

Keavy stared at the two other women for a moment—and then smiled. "I suppose you are right," she said, raising her hands a little in surrender. "But I must do something! If Aengus can be freed, then there will be no battle fought to get him back."

"Dun Mor wants that valley," Elva warned, "and so does Dun Gaoth. Sooner or later there will be a battle for it."

"No doubt there will be, sooner or later. I have no power over what two determined armies might choose to do. But if I can bring Aengus home now, at least he will not be a prisoner at the center of it who could be killed at any moment if the battle goes wrong. Parlan's course is the right one—but it is still a risk to Aengus that I cannot accept." Keavy looked at her two friends, who by now were hanging on her every word, and slowly nodded her head. "I have another idea. And I'm still going to need your help."

Chapter Twenty-two

As Maille and Elva waited beside the hearth, Keavy set aside the leather screen that guarded Aengus's sleeping ledge and walked inside the quiet, shadowed space where he had slept . . . and where Keavy had spent the most fateful night of her life.

She ran her fingers over the neatly arranged furs, closing her eyes as powerful memories came rushing back with a force she had never expected. She could all but see the king lying there in these same furs, smiling up at her with his hazel eyes gleaming, inviting her to slide in beside him and stretch out against the heat of his body and rest her head on the warmth of his smooth bare chest—

Keavy pulled her hands back and bit her lip to break the spell of the memories. She had a task to do—a very important task, one at which she must not fail if she ever hoped to see Aengus here in this place again.

Reaching beneath the cushions, she drew out

an iron dagger sheathed in brown leather. No man—no *king*—would sleep without a weapon at hand, and she had been certain she would find one here. Keavy held it carefully and took it back to the hearth, where she placed it on the stones in the light of the flickering flames.

Maille and Elva came to stand behind her as Keavy rested her fingertips on either side of the weapon. She gazed down into the fire. "From this night on I am no longer the guarded woman who seeks only security and comfort and pleasant, safe routine. From this night on I will be the maiden of the winds, the free spirit who faces life the way an eagle faces the wind and is unafraid to go wherever the drafts of life might require her to go. I swear on this, the weapon of King Aengus of Dun Gaoth."

She picked up the dagger and pulled it from its sheath. "Elva, I need your help."

As Elva slowly took the dagger by its smooth bone handle, Keavy caught up one of her long silver-blond braids and held it out just above her shoulders. "Here. Please cut it. Cut it off."

She had thought the women would protest—especially Maille—but the only sound in the house was the low crackle of the fire. Elva raised the knife, rested its sharp edge against Keavy's shining hair, and cut through the braid.

In a moment the other braid was gone, too. Keavy shook her head, running her fingers through her short and newly freed hair, feeling strangely light and free. She glanced at the two long braids trailing from Elva's hands. "Throw them on the fire."

Now Maille hurried over, and with great care took the long, shining braids from Elva. "Oh, please do not. I think I understand why you must cut them—but they are far too beautiful to throw on the fire. I will tie them off with strips of linen and put them away for you." And before Keavy could answer, Maille had taken the braids to Keavy's sleeping ledge and disappeared with them behind the leather screen.

Keavy drew a deep breath, took the dagger from Elva, and set it on the hearthstones. "I'm going to need some different clothes. Could you go to the servants' house and see if you can find something for me?"

"Of course." The older woman smiled at her—almost—and then left the house.

"Maille, next I will need a long, wide strip of linen. Is there anything like that here?"

"I believe there is. Let me see." Maille walked to the far side of the house where she made her bed in the straw, and began sorting through the baskets of wool waiting for combing and the pieces of cloth she was weaving. "Here is a fine piece, even if I am the one to say so. I wove it myself, and I've even started a bit of embroidery on it."

"I've been very proud of you. You have indeed been making some beautiful things."

"You're the one who taught me. I'm grateful to you for that."

Keavy smiled at her. "I can only hope so, because I may be asking a great deal of you very soon." She unfastened the small bronze brooch that held the folded neckline of her gowns closed, and let the garments fall from her shoulders. Quickly she took the piece of linen from Maille and draped it around the back of her neck, crossed it over her breasts and behind her back, and then tied it off snugly in the front.

"There," she said, "it's really quite comfortable. Next I will need a piece of cord or leather long enough to tie a knot. And it must be old and worn, not new and pretty."

Maille searched throughout the house again, and before long came up with a few pieces of brown leather cord that had once been used to bind the old cushions together. "I think these will do nicely," Keavy said, and gathered her astonishingly short hair into a tail that just brushed the top of her shoulders. Holding on to the hair, she waved Maille over, and held very still as Maille tied it off securely with the leather cords.

Just as Keavy lowered her hands, the door opened and Elva hurried in with what looked like some old pieces of woolen and linen fabric draped over her arm. "I believe these will do for you," she said, handing the garments over to Keavy.

"Oh—these will be perfect." Keavy held up the dark brown, coarse woolen cloak, looked at the greenish copper brooch hanging from a ragged hole in the fabric, and grinned at her companions. "I feel as though I've just been handed the most beautiful and delicate of embroidered gowns. These clothes are going to be just as important to me."

Turning her back on the light of the hearthfire, she let her own gowns fall the rest of the way to the floor and quickly stepped into the long, heavy, dark brown woolen trews and tied them around her waist with a piece of flax rope.

Elva handed her the worn linen tunic. Keavy pulled it on and was pleased to see that as it settled over her firmly bound chest it left her with a smooth and quite unremarkable silhouette. She threw the ragged dark cloak over her shoulder and carefully pushed the pin of the little copper brooch through the parts of it that were not too threadbare to rip out. Last came her own simple folded leather boots, and her new outfit was complete.

Keavy drew the top of her cloak up over her head so that it at least partly hid her face. "There," she said, standing in profile to Elva and Maille. "What do you think?"

Elva walked around to study her, frowning a bit, and then pushed back the top of the coarse woolen cloak from Keavy's head. After scrutinizing Keavy's face as though she had never seen it before, Elva turned to the hearth and began running her hands through the cold ashes near the edge. Once her hands were coated, she reached up to Keavy and began brushing the soot and ashes over Keavy's soft skin.

Keavy shut her eyes tight and let Elva work. "There. That's better. Though even like this your face is too pretty. Oh, and your fingernails! Let me see. Good, good, not too long, we won't have to cut them—but you had best rub a little ash into those lovely hands. There, that's it."

Maille walked up to Keavy, grinning ear to ear, and handed her a polished bronze mirror. Keavy examined her hazy reflection by the fire's glow, and soon she was smiling as brightly as the servant.

She placed the mirror on the hearthstones and walked around to the far side of the house, where Seabhac rested in the quiet shadows. There she pulled on the heavy leather gauntlet and invited the hawk to step up on her fist. Slowly Keavy stood up with the magnificent bird and faced Elva and Maille across the low flames of the hearthfire.

"You were right," she said to them. "A group of men, even a few men, appearing at the gates of Dun Mor would only get King Aengus killed. Better to kill their hostage than to let him be rescued, especially a hostage who has brought such humiliation. But a pair of serving women riding with the son of one of Dun Gaoth's warriors, bringing their king a few small things he might wish for to pass the time—especially his pining pet hawk, who must see her master else she may die, poor thing—now, that, surely, might make them laugh. What sort of king would draw such visitors? No, such a paltry expedition would raise no suspicions at all."

Seabhac cocked her head at Keavy's words and raised her wings a little, but then the bird settled back on Keavy's gloved hand and sat quietly, blinking at her three companions by the flickering light of the fire.

The next morning, so early that the eastern sky showed only deep darkness and the waning moon still rode high in the west, three women rode their ponies toward the tunnel in the fortress wall. Two were servants, in plain garb and riding bay geldings, while the third was clearly a person of the noble rank with her fine gray mare, beautiful green-and-white-plaid cloak, white enameled brooch, and fierce goshawk riding on her arm.

"Lady Keavy," said one of the watchmen up on the wall, "I can see that it is you, even in this darkness with your cloak up over your head. Where do you and your serving women mean to go before dawn?"

"The dawn is nearly here," Keavy called up to him, "and we mean only to go out for a short time before beginning our day's work. We can get some watercress, and perhaps some dandelion and primrose as well."

She looked down at the hawk, and shook her head. "Poor Seabhac is pining for the king. She will scarcely eat at all. I thought that letting her see the wild forest again might tempt her a bit and make her recall her days as a hunter." Keavy sighed loudly. "When the king returns, he will surely want to see her. I would not want to have to tell him that while he was gone, the hawk would not eat and so she—"

"Go, Lady Keavy," said the watchman. "I trust you will not go far with two serving women and a wild bird. We will watch for your return."

Keavy inclined her head in gratitude. Then the three women rode off into the darkness, into the east, out of sight of the fortress, where Keavy pulled the brooch from her cloak and let the fine plaid flutter to the ground. There all of them turned to the south and rode as fast as they could go.

Though they had left before dawn and ridden as steadily as they could, it was very late in the afternoon before the three servants from Dun Gaoth approached the massive wooden gates of Dun Mor. Keavy knew they had been seen at least once or twice by King Ross's patrols, but as she had hoped, two female servants riding with one young male servant—and all of them with leather bags overflowing with clover and watercress and bright yellow dandelion and primrose swinging from the wooden frames of their saddles—attracted no more than fleeting attention.

She wondered what they made of Seabhac, but was beginning to realize that people did not always see what they did not expect to see. And who expected to see a fierce wild goshawk riding passively on the arm of a youth? Keavy grinned to herself and made certain that the top of her coarse, heavy cloak was securely pulled up over her head and face.

The gates of the massive fortress of Dun Mor, with its two grass-covered earthen walls, stood partly open so that the servants might come and go and carry out their daily tasks of fetching water and working in the fields. But, as Keavy had known they would, the watchmen standing near the open gates challenged her and her servants immediately.

"Stop, there! I don't recognize any of you. What do you want here?"

Elva glanced once at him, and then kept her eyes down and spoke politely. "We are servants from Dun Gaoth. I am Elva, and this is my daughter, Maille, and the boy Kevan."

The guard's eyes narrowed. "From Dun Gaoth? What are you doing here?"

"We were sent to bring King Aengus a few small things he might wish for, to pass the time while he is your guest."

The guard laughed and started to walk back inside. "Let us know when they want to send someone with the ransom. Until then, go back where you came from."

"Wait! Oh, wait, please!" Maille urged her tired pony up toward the guard. "Surely you would not deny a hostage king a few personal comforts! What would your own king say if he knew you had tried to do such a thing? We have brought him herbs to make his favorite tea, and some of his own garments, and . . . and something very special."

She waved toward the hooded Keavy, who sat very still on her gray mare with Seabhac on her arm.

Finally the guard's attention turned to the hawk. He blinked, frowned, then blinked again. "What . . . what is that?"

Keavy's eyes flicked to Elva, who spoke. "I am sorry. The boy cannot speak. But I can tell you that this bird, injured during a hunt, has become tame and is a great favorite of King Aengus's."

"A tame hawk," repeated the guard, staring at the magnificent creature that was content to sit quietly on a servant's arm and had allowed its eyes to be covered with woolen wrappings. "A tame hawk!"

"Oh, but sadly the poor thing is pining away in the king's absence and will not eat," Maille said. "Surely you could let us take her to visit Aengus so that she will not die."

"And perhaps your own King Ross would be amused at seeing her, too," added Elva.

The guard grinned, no doubt thinking of how his king might reward him for bringing in such unusual entertainment. "All right, then. Inside with you. But only for a short time. You'll all be gone before dark."

"Thank you," Elva said, and all three women rode together through the gates of Dun Mor.

How strange it was to follow a guardsman across the grounds of the place that had been her home for all of her life, and have not one person recognize her! Though she kept her hooded head down low, Keavy caught many glimpses of people she knew. There was Doreen, her young friend and apprentice, walking by with a huge basket of wool. There were Desmond and Owen, leaning against the doorway of the king's hall and staring at her hawk. Oh, oh, and there was her mother—so busy chatting with a little group of equally talkative women that she took no notice of a few outsider servants walking across the yard.

The guard led them to one of the smallest and oldest of the many round houses. Keavy was dismayed to see the poor condition of the roof and the mud and weeds around the doorway. But of course she said nothing, and kept her eyes on the ground as the guard pushed into the dwelling.

"Servants from Dun Gaoth, come to see you," the guard called into the house. "You can have a short time with them, if you wish." He glanced back at the servants and then stepped away from the door, pointing. "Remember, you lot leave before dark."

Slowly the three servants walked inside, blinking in the dusty dimness. She stood behind Maille and Elva, and Keavy cautiously raised her head just enough to see Aengus sitting on a sheepskin thrown down on the straw. He had a *fidchell* board in front of him and sat across from another of King Ross's men, one who had apparently been assigned to play board games with their hostage for the afternoon.

Quickly Keavy's eyes flicked over him. He appeared to be well enough. There was a half-filled plate of food beside him in the straw, his clothes were clean, and his soft brown hair and beard were neatly combed. But then, as he stood up to greet his visitors and his dark green cloak fell back from his shoulders, Keavy saw that his left arm was heavily wrapped with a linen bandage halfway between his shoulder and his elbow.

She gave a little gasp, then quickly ducked her head. But as she cautiously peered up again, she caught sight of his hazel eyes—and it was clear, by his briefly shocked expression, that he had recognized her instantly.

Right away his relaxed smile returned. "Why, it is so good of you to come to me! Elva and Maille, I do know you—but this young lad is not familiar to me, I am afraid."

"King Aengus, this is the boy Kevan," Elva said calmly, as she and Maille set down the leather bags they had brought. "He cannot speak, and so prefers to work alone most of the time at Dun Gaoth—but we found that he was the only one whom the bird would suffer to carry her."

"Such wild creatures do what they will," murmured Aengus, his eyes gleaming. "Elva and Maille, I thank you so much for coming here. Would you be so kind as to leave me now with Kevan and Seabhac? I'm sure King Ross's men will be only too glad to show you to the servants' place so that you might eat and refresh yourselves."

Both the guard and the *fidchell* player started

for the door. "Come with us," the guard called. "We'll be back for the other one before dark."

The door creaked shut, leaving Keavy and Aengus alone together in the dim light and rapidly lengthening shadows.

Chapter Twenty-three

Keavy set the hawk down on the straw beside Aengus's sheepskin cover, and quickly held a finger to her lips as she looked up at him. "Quiet, quiet," she whispered. "They may well be listening, watching . . ."

"I do not care," he said, and she could see his eyes drinking in the sight of her. He tried to hold himself away, to treat her like the nameless young servant she was supposed to be—but he caught her in his arms and pulled her close, leaning his head against the rough hood of her cloak. "I do not care! Ah, Keavy, Keavy," he whispered. "You should not have come. It is so dangerous for you. Such a risk you and the other two have taken!"

"You forget, this was my home. I know these people. They would not harm me or any of the women who might ride with me. It is you we are worried for."

She drew back and ran her fingers over the heavy bandages around his left arm. "What happened? They said they would not harm you. Did you fight them?"

He smiled a little wryly. "I am sure that Dun Mor offers none but the finest hospitality—but surely you did not think I would not at least try to break away from my hosts? This happened not long after we entered the forest. After that they bound my hands, and I am sad to say that I could give them no more trouble."

"How badly are you hurt?" Keavy could not keep her fingers from his wound, as though somehow she could heal him with only a simple touch.

He tried to flex his arm, and grimaced. He could move it only about half its normal range. "They did their work well enough. I am only sorry I was not a little faster."

"You could not have escaped. There were too many of them. I am just glad . . . I am just glad you are alive."

Aengus reached out and carefully folded back Keavy's rough cloak until it rested on her shoulders. With infinite gentleness he touched the soot rubbed into her face, and the newly cut ends of her hair. "I will not be undoing your golden braids again, I am afraid. Not for a very long time."

Keavy's eyes suddenly burned with tears, but she raised her chin and looked into his eyes. "I had to do it," she said, forcing her voice to remain steady. "We feared for your life. There is going to be a battle—both sides are angry and determined to have one. A hostage king could well meet with a terrible accident—"

He stopped her words with the softest and gentlest of kisses. "Dear Keavy . . . you are as courageous as you are beautiful. And never have I seen you looking more beautiful than you do right now."

She returned his kiss and then held him close, thinking that all of her life until now had led solely to this moment—and knowing that whatever happened in the next few moments would affect all the rest of it as well.

"We have come to take you home," she said, looking up at him.

"Home?" He grinned, trying to keep from laughing. "Do you think your people here will simply let me walk out through the gates and wish me well as I start my journey home?"

"I do not think they will let you *walk* out." She looked directly into his bright hazel eyes.

"Then how will I get out?"

"There is another way. Another way for a king such as you."

Instantly his face grew serious. "You cannot mean for me to . . . Surely you don't believe—"

"But I do believe," she whispered, embracing him again. "I *do* believe—and you must believe, too."

He closed his eyes. "Keavy . . . I told you, I cannot do that thing any longer. That was long ago, so very long ago. It will never happen again."

"It *will* happen again. It will happen now. It will

happen because it must, and because this time I will be here to help you."

Before he could say anything more, she reached up and pulled out the bronze brooch that held his dark green cloak, and then pulled away the cloak and dropped it to the straw along with the brooch. She untied the brown leather belt over his tunic and then drew the tunic up over his head. In a moment the belt and the tunic joined the cloak down in the straw.

Next came his folded brown leather boots, and then, after another gentle kiss, she untied the slender leather belt that held his trews and then slid them down over his hips and drew them off over each foot.

Now he stood naked and proud before her, and though Keavy knew she must keep her focus on the task at hand, she was aware of almost nothing else save her rapidly beating heart, her quick, shallow breathing, and, most of all, the rising heat and tension within her own body. But she closed her eyes for a moment, took a deep breath, and then led Aengus to stand on the sheepskin beside Seabhac.

Keavy moved to stand behind the king and placed her hands on his shoulders. "Now, then," she began, her voice soft and low. "Look down near your feet, and see the beautiful creature resting there. Look into her eyes, her bright, sharp, fierce hunter's eyes, and see the world through them—through the eyes of a winged master of the skies."

Aengus's head moved down as he gazed at the hawk. His breath came deep and slow, and she could feel him beginning to let go and allow her words to direct him. "You have seen the world this way before. You have done this thing before. It is easy for you, for it is your nature to rule your kingdom the way an eagle rules the sky. . . . Look at the world with the eyes of an eagle, for that is what you truly are."

He raised his head and made as if to glance back at her—and Keavy caught sight of his eyes, large and bright and golden and fierce, with a gaze so sharp it seemed to go right through her.

Keavy closed her eyes and thought back to the words she had heard him say on their first night together. *"Let your heart fly again, as it did long ago. Let your heart fly, and you will have wings."*

Quickly she ran her fingertips beneath his arms and raised them up in a graceful arc with his fingertips trailing downward. "Flight," she whispered. "These powerful, great wings will let you take flight on the currents of the sky. Look down at your companion, Seabhac, and see the great wings that are always a part of her—raise your wings even as she raises hers and let the air take them, let the winds hold fast to the feathers that allow you to take flight."

Even as Keavy spoke, the goshawk returned the king's sharp gaze and raised her wings as best she could. And in a breath, in a heartbeat, Keavy realized that instead of smooth warm skin beneath her fingers she felt the beginning of soft, slick, tightly packed feathers.

"Now the rest," she said quickly. "Become as Seabhac and take all these things for yourself. Piercing talons, sharp, curving beak, body light as air! Become the eagle that you truly are. Become the eagle!"

Keavy took her hands away and stepped back from him. In the breathless silence she could hear Aengus whispering to himself, whispering strange words she had never heard before and could not hope to understand.

Then suddenly there was silence again.

She closed her eyes, fearing to look—but when the house remained quiet for several heartbeats, she reached out one hand to touch Aengus. She found only cool air where he had stood just a moment before.

Keavy made herself open her eyes. There, at her feet, standing on the sheepskin with outstretched wings, stood a glorious golden eagle.

Keavy caught her breath. For a moment she could only stare down at the creature, caught up in surreal amazement at the knowledge that this thing had truly happened. But then she realized that, very much like Seabhac, the golden eagle could raise its left wing only about half as high as it should go. The king had been wounded in the arm, and the transformation had not healed him. The eagle was just as crippled as the king.

But as the great bird stretched his wings again and flapped them strongly a few times, Keavy knew that he would stop at nothing to fly—and to escape.

She became aware that the light outside was growing lower. Quickly she hid Aengus's clothes beneath heaps of straw and then caught up one of the leather bags they had brought with them and threw it over her shoulder. She pulled her hood up over her head, grabbed her gauntlet, pulled it on, and coaxed Seabhac up onto her fist—and then hurried to the door and pushed it open to the fading twilight.

Keavy gave one last glance at the great bird behind her. "Fly, king eagle," she whispered. "Leave this place and fly home." Then she turned and left the house, keeping her eyes cast down and the hawk on her fist held high.

As casually as she could, Keavy walked across the grounds to the gates. Maille and Elva were already waiting there with the horses and the guard, who apparently intended to make good on his promise to see them all gone before dark.

From beneath the hood she caught sight of the many people who were still out on the grounds, and then looked down at Seabhac. Keavy spoke softly and politely to the hawk and then gave her wrist a small wave as she walked—and the bird complied by raising and flapping her wings and giving a piercing cry.

As Keavy had hoped, all heads turned in her direction. No one paid any attention to the house where Aengus stayed—the house where the door still stood open, the house where a golden eagle with outstretched wings moved one small hop at a time across the doorway and outside.

"Are you sure your king would not like to see the tame hawk?" said Elva to the guard, as Keavy came to stand beside her with lowered head.

The guard only scowled and waved his hand, dismissing them. "It's nearly dark. The king has other business. Get on your horses and go."

"Very well, then. We thank you for allowing us in. Come, Maille, Kevan—we must be going now."

The three of them mounted their horses. Keavy stole a glance back just in time to see the eagle raise his wings and attempt his first leap into the air—and crash back down again.

The strange motion in front of the house caught the attention of one of Don Mor's inhabitants. Then another turned to look. Then the women standing near the hall stopped talking and looked behind them—and all at once it seemed that everyone in the entire fortress stood staring at the great golden eagle that half ran and half jumped across the grounds, struggling to fly in spite of its badly injured left wing.

Some of the people stepped back, startled at seeing a fierce wild bird suddenly appearing in their midst, while others hurried for a closer look. A few laughed at the odd and unexpected sight. Most just stood and stared.

Fly, beautiful eagle! Fly! Keavy wanted to cry out to him, but she could only watch in horror as the great bird fought to get into the air. Then her blood ran cold as one of the druids stepped out of the king's hall to see what was going on, and she saw him look from the eagle to the open door of the house and back to the eagle again.

"Get it! Get it! Catch the eagle!" the druid cried. When everyone simply turned to stare at him in confusion, he shouted out again: "It's the king, you fools! Don't you understand? It's King Aengus! He's escaping!"

Keavy thought her heart would stop as a few of the men—whether they believed the druid's words or not—turned and started after the crippled bird.

But the eagle would not give up so easily. Forcing its wings to work, screaming in pain and defiance as it leaped across the yard, it finally climbed into the air just as his captors began to close in. The bird's talons brushed the top of Dun Mor's earthen walls as it took to the sky at last and flew away above the treetops.

Instantly Maille and Elva and Keavy sent their ponies trotting out of the gate and urged them into a gallop as soon as they found the road. The eagle cried out to them from far above, and the three of them followed it north, followed it on the way back home to Dun Gaoth.

Night was not long in coming, and the three women rode as fast as they could on their tired ponies through the darkness of the forest. Keavy struggled to guide her gray mare, balance Seabhac on her fist, listen for the hoofbeats of pursuers behind them, and, most of all, follow the cries of the eagle flying just ahead.

But no one did follow them. The three lowly servants were of no interest to the warrior men of Dun Mor, and they could not catch a flying king. This matter would still be settled on the battlefield, just as Keavy had feared—but at least now Aengus was no captive whose life could well be taken during that battle if Dun Mor's warriors thought it would serve their purpose.

The eagle cried out one last time. The sound came from within the trees only a short way ahead. The women walked their ponies carefully through the dark wood as a few hazy stars appeared and disappeared among the clouds and the tops of the trees. Then suddenly Keavy's gray mare threw up her head and stopped, facing straight ahead with her ears up, and in a moment the other two horses did the same. From the trees just ahead came a pleasant voice.

"Good evening to you, ladies. I cannot tell you how pleased I am to see you all—and I will be even more pleased to see the bag of clothes that I know the Lady Keavy is carrying."

"Aengus," Keavy said softly, finally letting go of her breath. She slid to the ground and placed Seabhac at the base of an oak, pulled off her gauntlet, then hurried over to the trees where Aengus waited.

He peered out at her from behind the trunk of a tree, his eyes shining. He had as pleased a smile on his face as Keavy had ever seen on anyone. He stood tall and proud, with his fair skin glowing and his golden-brown hair streaming down over his shoulders. She slipped her leather bag off over her shoulder and handed it to him. "You are a glorious sight, King Aengus—but the night wind is cool and you may wish to put these on."

He took the sack from her, still grinning, and then caught her hand and pulled her close, embracing her as though he would never let her go.

"Thank you," he whispered into her ear. "Thank you."

Though the night was indeed cool, Aengus's skin was smooth and warm, and Keavy drew enormous comfort from the great strength of his physical presence. "Do not thank me," Keavy said, resting her head on his shoulder. "I only told you what you already knew. You have always been the eagle and you always will be."

He drew back a little, just enough to gaze down into her eyes and smile again. "What a fine pair we make! The naked king and his servant-boy queen. But no matter. There are no clothes fine enough to make me feel more like a king than I do right now, no gowns or gold that could ever make my queen lovelier than she is at this moment."

At his words, Keavy let go of him and turned away. "I am very glad that you are safe now—but I wish you would not speak of me as being your queen. We both know that such a thing can never be."

For a few moments there was only the quiet of

the forest and the soft sounds of Aengus putting on his trews, boots, tunic, and cloak. At last he stepped out from behind the tree and reached for Keavy's hand once more.

"You know that I will have no other for my queen but you." He tried to smile. "Would you have me live alone for the rest of my days?"

Keavy only set her jaw and looked away. "Aengus . . . I have told you, I cannot be your queen—cannot be your wife—cannot be anything at all to you, not even a servant, so long as this custom of the First Night continues. I would never know when you might bring another woman into your bed simply because it is your duty or . . . Law or no, custom or no, I know that I simply do not have the strength to live that way, and there is no use putting both of us through such torment."

Aengus placed his hands on her shoulders. "You must understand. I would end this custom this very day if I could, but I do not have the power to do so. The druids and the free men of Dun Gaoth would all have to agree to change the law of the First Night ritual. And I do not know why any of them should want to change the most ancient and sacred of laws."

"And I do not know why any man should want another to sleep with his wife, on the First Night on any other night."

Aengus sat back and folded his hands in his lap. "You heard what the druids said on the night you were brought to me. The First Night ritual was not begun as a way for a king to have more women in his bed. It was taught to all the kingdoms of Eire—so long ago that countless generations have now passed—by the gods of the most ancient time, when they walked the land just as men do now."

"Yet why should the gods instruct the people to adopt such a ritual? Did they not know how troubling it would be?"

Aengus shook his head. "I believe their intention was a good and kind one, meant to prevent the cruel and thoughtless handling of young women at a time when they should be treated with the utmost care. It was a very strict law, and any tribe which did not hold to it risked suffering the consequences: Their crops might fail, their cattle might die, their children might fall ill. And so no one had any wish to do away with an old and revered law that allowed the gods to be obeyed and women to be treated with respect."

Keavy nodding. "But many other kingdoms—Dun Mor among them—allowed such laws to fade away long ago, and they have prospered. All things change in their time, King Aengus . . . even laws handed down by gods at a time when life in Eire must have been very different. And I suppose it is a rude statement, but it occurs to me that with the strong bold women who live among us now it is probably far too late for most of them to require any special treatment in the bed of a king."

She could sense Aengus's amusement, even in the darkness. "Some do not, it is true . . . but the gods meant to make certain that any women who remained untouched until the night of her wedding could be certain of being treated with the greatest care and respect."

Keavy closed her eyes as the memories came flooding back. "But surely, King Aengus," she said at last, "surely those men whose brides are sent to the king would not object to seeing this law done away with."

He only shrugged his shoulders. "Lady Keavy—the men of Dun Gaoth have always been willing to place the gods, and the laws of the gods, above their own wishes. We are among the oldest of the kingdoms of Eire and we believe we have lasted because we have respected the teachings of the gods, not ignored them. If the free men and the druids of Dun Gaoth all vote to strike down the law of the First Night, then struck down it will be—but in no other way can it be ended."

Keavy closed her eyes. She knew there was nothing else she could say.

Out of the darkness came a little flare of light. Elva had struck a spark with her pieces of flint, and managed to get a fire going within a little ring of stones she and Maille had constructed. Before long the four of them were gathered around a fire eating warmed bread and smoked beef and boiled dried apples.

"Are you sure they won't come after us this night?" Keavy asked. "It would not be difficult for someone up in the hills to see our fire, small as it is."

Aengus shook his head and helped himself to another strip of beef. "They will not bother chasing after us tonight. There will be nothing but an all-out battle this time. I would expect to see them at the valley the day after tomorrow. That is the place they intend to take, and that is the soonest they can be ready."

"Aengus," Keavy said, gazing into the fire. "It is a simple fact that the men of Dun Mor outnumber the men of Dun Gaoth. Can you possibly hope to defeat them in a battle to the death?"

She had expected him to ponder this, and perhaps even to be pessimistic about his chances against a larger army; but he only looked at her and grinned, his teeth white in the light from the fire. "I have found my heart and my strength again, thanks to you," he said, and he reached for her hand. "I welcome the battle to come. I welcome it! I am fighting for my home and my kingdom and the woman I love. They cannot bring the battle soon enough for me!"

It was good to see him so vital and alive once more, as though the years had simply fallen away from him—but the question of numbers tormented Keavy. "I fear to see you face an army larger than your own. Tell me, please—what do you mean to do when you actually face those men across that valley?"

He shrugged, and went on tearing off more strips of beef. "They are not so many more. I will have to do the best I can. That is all any man can do."

"Is it?" she pressed.

He remained silent.

At last he looked up at her and slowly nodded. "Perhaps you are right. Perhaps I should look further. . . . But where?"

Just then Maille walked over from the fire with another dish of beef and bread and butter—and Aengus sat up and stared at her as though he'd never seen her before.

"What is it, my king?" Maille asked, startled and flustered by suddenly finding his full attention directed at her.

"I am going to need your help," Aengus said, smiling. "Yours—and Coilean's."

"Coilean's? Oh, King Aengus, I don't understand—but I will do whatever you might ask of me."

"I know you will, Maille. I just hope that Coilean will agree as well."

Maille's eyes flashed. "I assure you, King Aengus, he will do whatever you ask and do it gladly . . . or else he will have to deal with me!"

All of them laughed, much to Maille's momentary amazement, and soon all four were sitting comfortably around the little fire, glad of one another's company against the dark night and the thoughts of the battle to come.

Chapter Twenty-four

Two days later, as the midday sun lay hidden behind swiftly moving black and silver clouds, the two armies lined up along the opposite side of the beautiful valley and turned to face each other.

To the south were the men of Dun Mor, with nearly two hundred fully armed fighting men. To the north were the men of Dun Gaoth, with a force of perhaps one hundred and fifty. Solemn druids stood behind each army to watch for signs of good or ill that would come about during the battle, as well as to note which men fought well and which did not. At the head of the army of Dun Gaoth rode Aengus on his tall, pale gold stallion, his blue plaid cloak flying out behind him in the wind and his gold king's torque with its eagle heads gleaming in the sun.

Behind the lines on both sides, he knew, were as many able-bodied men and women and servants as each fortress could spare. They would serve as support for the fully engaged armies, bringing food and water to the warriors, caring for the wounded, and even shouting encouragement from the sidelines as needed. His own servant, Seanan, had been charged with bringing enough of the kingdom's long-hidden gold to ransom any high-ranking warrior, should it come to that.

Aengus very much hoped that none of the women and servants would be needed this day, though he know Keavy was surely among them. His fingers tightened on his thick leather reins as he looked across the bright green grass and white-blossoming apple trees to the hostile army just below the opposite ridge. The men of Dun Mor began beating their wooden shields with the bone hilts of their iron swords and shouting out insults to their waiting foes.

Parlan rode up alongside him. "They will attack at any moment."

Aengus nodded. "It is time." He swung his stallion around, rode him between the lines of his men to a place high on the ridge behind them, and raised his hand in a signal.

Immediately the army of Dun Mor charged down into the valley and dashed through the low-hanging branches of the apple trees, sending out a fall of white blossoms and shouting as they ran; but just as they reached the center of the valley and began trampling through the stream, their champion shouted out, and all of them came to a sudden stop.

Their attention was riveted to the top of the

ridge behind the fighters of Dun Gaoth. Standing now with Aengus was a strange mob of what looked like servants or slaves: the rock men!

Well over one hundred of the rock men waited now with King Aengus—young men, old men, and men of every age in between. Even some women stood among them. All wore coarse, dark woolen garments and carried tools of wood and iron that they brandished just like swords and spears. They were rough and untrained, but they appeared fierce and determined—and their added numbers almost doubled the size of Dun Gaoth's army.

The strangest sight of all was the man who rode at the head of this unlikely army, the slight young man who sat precariously on the back of his grizzled old pony, clutching the crossed wooden frame at the front of his saddle with one hand and the flax-rope reins of his pony with the other. The man pulled his pony to an awkward stop beside King Aengus and, after two tries, managed to drag his iron sword out of its battered wooden scabbard and raise it before his king.

"The men of the rock lands are here to serve you, my king," said Coilean. "As am I."

Aengus grinned at him. "I believe you have changed, Coilean," he said. "And I am very pleased to see it."

Coilean shrugged. "I know nothing of how to handle a sword."

"Then we will teach you. Parlan will begin your training tomorrow."

"And I am the worst horseman in the kingdom."

"Yet you rode out to find and summon the rock men when I asked you to do so. You were able to convince them to come and help in the fight. You have been a great help to everyone in your kingdom this day."

"It was the least that I could do to try to make things right," Coilean said quietly. Then he smiled a little. "Besides, it was not all my doing. I had enough sense to take Maille with me. They were her people, for she was born among them. She was a great help to me in persuading them to do this—to help you fight to keep this valley for Dun Gaoth instead of letting strangers overrun it."

Aengus nodded. "You were wise to let someone with knowledge help you. I shall thank you both—and the people of the rock lands, too—at the end of this day."

He reined his stallion around and nodded to Parlan. Together they rode down the steep grassy side of the valley to face the army of Dun Mor, but their enemy made no move to attack as the men approached. They stood waiting in sullen silence, glaring and glowering at Aengus and at all of Dun Gaoth's suddenly sizable army.

"Why, good day to you all," Aengus called, halting his stallion in front of them. "How kind of you to come and visit this beautiful valley that belongs to Dun Gaoth. I suppose you were merely out for a day's hunt and thought to gaze upon the loveliest region in all of Eire—the region that belongs to my people."

At those words, there was a great deal of low and angry muttering among the fighters. Most of them stayed where they were, except for those who began parting ranks to allow King Ross and his champion to ride through.

Aengus gave his best smile. "Thank you for coming to my valley this day," he called to them. "Now, I have some folk I would like you to meet." He turned and signaled to the rock men waiting on the ridge, and then sat back to watch as Coilean led all of his newly commissioned soldiers down into the valley to stand behind him.

King Ross glared at the rough and ragged assembly. "What sort of battle is it when you must bring in others—the lowest-born at that—to do your fighting for you?" He sneered at Aengus and started to ride away. "You and yours are not worthy opponents for fighters like my own men! We will return when you have the courage to fight your own battle."

But Aengus only laughed. "Is that any way to greet the folk who rule this valley?"

King Ross stopped his horse and looked over his shoulder. "What do you mean?"

Aengus waved his hand at the rough-clad men and women who stood still and solemn beside him—and who stared up at him now with expressions of amazement and disbelief. "These people have lived on the poorest of the lands for longer than any can remember. I thought they could serve me better by living in this valley and guarding it for me."

"You want us to stay here?" one of the old men asked. "We can live here?"

Aengus nodded. "You can live here for as long as you like. You would serve me well by doing so."

King Ross was outraged. "You cannot be serious! These people are the lowest, rudest, most ignorant sort. They cannot guide their own lives, much less rule a part of your kingdom for you!"

"They have managed to live where no others could—they must have some measure of wisdom if they could do that. But I am not leaving them to fend for themselves. I will be sending one of my men to live among them and give them whatever help Dun Gaoth can offer."

Ross frowned again. "What man?"

"Why, Coilean, of course. Coilean was the one who led them here."

Ross set his jaw, and then glanced at Coilean with the utmost contempt. "This man is a traitor who tried to betray the woman you say you love. He made it possible for us to take you as hostage. I suppose he deserves to live among the worst of your people."

"Coilean was a young and foolish man who has had an awakening. I believe he deserves another chance. And let me assure you—if you believe you can ride in when you please and drive these people out, you will find them tougher to deal with than you might imagine. You will also find every last man of Dun Gaoth at their backs the instant you move to attack."

The rock men all turned to look directly at King Ross and his champion, shifting their rusted iron fire pikes and old wooden shovels and chipped stone knives in their hands. They did not threaten, but neither did they show any sign of backing down.

Ross jerked his horse's head around. "May your new subjects bring you much pleasure, King Aengus. I can only advise you not to get downwind of them whenever you do come to visit." And with that he started to ride away.

But they had gone only a few paces when the men of Dun Mor suddenly stopped again. Their horses snorted and began shying nervously, refusing to go forward. Something small and dark flashed past Aengus's head—and then another, and another, and another. His stallion reared.

Aengus got his horse under control and managed to look up—and saw the whole of the valley covered with an enormous flock of birds, birds of practically every type that had ever lived in Eire. Aengus saw larks and wrens and sparrows, ravens and eagles and hawks. Though the air was crowded with them, none made any attempt to attack the others. They darted about, calling and crying and shrieking and singing, until the valley was filled with their flying wings and incessant songs.

There at the top of the ridge, on the north side of the valley just a short way from his own astonished army, stood Keavy, beautiful in a flowing pale yellow gown with a deep green cloak floating out behind her on the wind. On her fist stood Seabhac, flapping both wings and crying out to the many birds that filled the valley.

Aengus shielded his eyes from the flashing, darting birds. He saw Keavy raise one arm, and to his relief the creatures began to leave the valley and fly back into the surrounding forests. Soon there were only little groups of wrens remaining, flying and fluttering all around Keavy at the top of the ridge.

Aengus swung down from his horse and tossed the reins to one of the rock men. He started toward Keavy, climbing up the steep, grassy sides of the valley—but before he could reach her, she raised her right arm and held it out as Seabhac leaped up into the air.

Aengus stopped, transfixed by the sight. He turned to follow the bird's flight as she traveled nearly the length of the valley and then climbed high on the currents to circle overhead.

"She flies again!" he cried, making his way up to Keavy and stopping just a few steps down the hill from her. "I never thought it possible . . . but I should have known that if anyone could heal her it would be you."

"She does indeed fly again, through the kindness of a king," Keavy said, lowering her gauntleted arm. The dark green and gold-wire embroidery on the sleeves and neckline of her gown glinted in the sunlight. "You allowed her to stay in your home for as long as she needed to stay, feeding her and sheltering her until she was ready to fly again on her own."

"Do you think she will ever return?" he asked, watching as the hawk continued to circle high above them.

"I believe she will," Keavy said, smiling. "It would not surprise me to see her come down to the walls of Dun Gaoth from time to time and accept a bit of meat from the king who was her benefactor."

"And from the queen who saved her life." Aengus shook his head as he gazed up at her. "Truly I have never seen anyone so beautiful. Even your shining braids are in place once again."

She reached up to touch her knee-length silver-blond braids. "Maille saved them for me. It was a simple matter to attach them with a few linen wraps."

"Someday your own hair will again grow just as long . . . and I want to be with you when it does."

Keavy stood tall. Her deep green cloak, fastened by her white enameled brooch with the three golden eagle feathers, billowed out behind her in the breeze. "I am very happy, King Aengus, to see that the two kingdoms that have been my home have chosen not to fight each other. And I am happier than I can tell you that the rock men and their families will have this beautiful place to live from this day on. It was a wise decision by a wise king."

"I thank you, Lady Keavy."

"But now I have one last decision to make. I must choose where I will live from this day forward. I must choose between Dun Mor and Dun Gaoth."

Aengus looked into her shining pale green eyes. "There is nothing I want more in life, Lady Keavy, than to have you make your home at Dun Gaoth as my beloved wife and queen."

She closed her eyes for a moment, and then gazed down into the valley once more. "There is nothing I would love more than to accept your offer, King Aengus. But as I have told you, I know that I could never live as your wife so long as the custom of the First Night continues. I know you cannot end it on your own. Yet I do not want you to believe that I am the only one who might feel this way."

Keavy turned to look behind her, down on the forested plain beyond the valley, and raised her hands. In a moment nearly all the women of Dun Gaoth stepped up beside Keavy until they formed a long and colorful line along the very top of the slope.

Nearest her stood a young dark-haired woman who seemed familiar to Aengus, though he could not think of who she was. The girl was only as tall as Keavy's shoulder, and round of figure and full of face, though she carried herself with dignity and pride. She wore a fine gown of dark red wool, and her hair was neatly plaited in a pair of shining dark braids capped with copper spheres. Then Keavy turned to smile at her, and with a start Aengus realized who it was.

Maille, the servant girl.

As both of the kings and both of their armies looked up at the ridge, Keavy spoke directly to the assembly of women. "Now is the time for us to speak with one voice to the king, and his druids, and his free men. Tell me, my sisters: could you be happy as the wife of a man required to perform the ritual of the First Night?"

And one by one, loudly, clearly, so all in the valley could hear, the women answered.

"I could not."

"I could not."

"I could not."

When every one of them had answered, Keavy nodded. "Yet this decision is not one that can be made by the women. It is left to the free men and the druids of Dun Gaoth to decide. And so it seems to us, the women of Dun Gaoth, that you men must make a choice."

She turned to face the men in the valley once again. "I am told that the law of the First Night was given to us by the gods, so long ago that the years since then cannot be counted. I am told that the men of the tribes obeyed the gods and followed this law, and that the men of Dun Gaoth continue to do so today.

"It is vital to respect the gods. It is vital to respect the law. Yet I would say to you that we have learned many things since those ancient days when the gods walked the earth. We have learned to use copper and bronze and iron for tools and weapons, instead of only stones and bones. We have learned to keep tame animals at home, instead of only hunting them. And we have learned much about how men and women treat each other, and of how sacred is the bond between a husband and a wife. It is a bond that none should ever interfere with. Not even a king. Not even a god.

"Here is your choice: Either the custom of First Night continues as it always has, or Dun Gaoth can think instead of the hearts of the women whom it affects. And as well, you can think of one who might be queen, who loves both your people and your king.

"If you choose to continue the custom, then I shall thank you for your hospitality and return with King Ross to my family at Dun Mor and whatever fate awaits me there. You, however, must live with knowing that this custom persists in spite of the ill-feeling it causes among your women who have little choice but to tolerate it. Men of Dun Gaoth, I cannot imagine that you face this custom with any more eagerness than do the women. All of us await your decision."

The men of Dun Gaoth all turned and immediately began to talk among themselves, sending up a low murmuring throughout the valley. As they did, Aengus walked to the top of the hill and offered his hand to Keavy. She placed her fingers atop it and smiled. "I will give you my thoughts now," he said, in a voice that carried to everyone in the valley. "Perhaps there was a time when the custom of First Night had its place—but this is a new and transformed time, and my kingdom has need of a strong, wise, and gracious queen far more than it needs this custom. Indeed, there is a great longing for such a woman—one woman—to take her rightful place here."

He looked at Keavy again. "No matter what happens, I hope there is no doubt of my own desire in this matter."

"No doubt," she answered, and smiled at him once more.

Aengus released her hand and took a few steps down the slope. "Men of Dun Gaoth!" he cried out. "Warriors and druids! You have heard what the Lady Keavy said. You have heard what the women of Dun Gaoth feel. Make your own wishes known now. If you believe the time has come for the custom known as First Night to end, you have only to walk five paces toward me."

For a moment no one moved. The men all looked at one another, and then up at the many women who stood tall and silent and looking down at them from the top of the ridge. Finally, a few at a time took the five steps, and then a few more, and then the entire army, followed by the druids, moved toward King Aengus and stood at the base of the slope looking up at him.

"The free men of Dun Gaoth have made their feelings known," said Finnian, one of the druids. "I daresay that the many husbands at Dun Gaoth have no more wish to see this custom continue than do the wives."

Aengus faced them all and raised both hands. "Then, as of this moment, the custom of the First Night belongs to our ancestors."

Keavy closed her eyes as the men and women all cried out their approval, feeling as though she could soar as high as Seabhac all by herself.

Aengus took Keavy's hand once more and raised it up before his people. "Then I say to all of you now—those of Dun Gaoth and those of Dun Mor—we can still have a battle this day, if you wish. But I believe I can make you a better offer. Instead of a fight to the death, you can witness the marriage that will create an alliance between both our kingdoms. Which would you rather have?"

Down in the valley, King Ross and his men looked again at the army that now greatly outnumbered them. "Are we invited to the feast?" someone shouted, and the rest began to laugh.

"What sort of wedding would there be without a feast?" Aengus answered, grinning back at them. "There is food in plenty here. Let it be used for celebration instead of sustaining weary fighters. And nearly all the folk of both kingdoms are here. Let us all join in feasting and music and poetry instead of tending to our dead and wounded kin. Let us share and become one family. What say you to this?"

The army of Dun Mor began setting down their wooden shields and replacing their iron swords in their scabbards. "Well, then, bring on the food! I'm starving!" King Ross shouted, and from that moment on all thoughts of battle were forgotten.

Chapter Twenty-five

The happy men and women from two kingdoms—now the guests of the folk once known as the rock men—made short work of turning the beautiful valley from a battlefield-to-be to a scene of celebration.

Fleeces and woven wool saddle pads were thrown down in several rows on the bright green grass near the stream, beneath the overhanging branches and sweet white blossoms of the apple trees. The pack ponies, laden with food, were led down to where the servants built fires and the cooking began. A little distance away, horses grazed in peace and drank from the crystal-clear stream.

Before long each guest was seated with a gold plate and cup—even the rock men and their wives, who soon joined in the merriment as though they had been accustomed to such luxury all their lives. At the head of the gathering, Keavy sat beside Aengus, and just a short way down the row were Maille and Coilean.

Keavy was delighted to learn that her own parents had made the journey with the other folk of Dun Mor. "Of course we would come!" her father insisted. "In part because the fighters might need us . . . but also because we knew you would be here, and because we feared for you."

"Yet I see all has ended well," her mother said, looking over her shoulder at yet another collection of gold cups and plates and brooches and pins that servants guarded near the stream.

"So it has," Keavy said, smiling at them both.

"Lady Finola," Aengus said, watching Keavy's mother with a glint of humor in his eye, "I see you have spotted the *coibche* that I intend to offer for your daughter. Does it meet with your approval?"

"Oh," Finola said under her breath. "It does, it does!" She elbowed her husband in the ribs. "Look at it, look at it all! So much better than the last time. There is far more, and oh, it is—"

"I think it is wonderful that our daughter has made so fine a match," Egan said, and he smiled gently at Keavy.

"Oh . . . why, of course. I feel the same way." Finola, too, smiled at her daughter then with shining eyes—though she could not quite resist another glance at the very fine *coibche* that would soon be going home with her.

Aengus signaled to one of the druids. "Are both contracts ready?"

"They are, my king. Do you wish to begin?"

"I do." He got to his feet and turned to face the assembly, calling out to get everyone's attention. "People of Dun Mor! People of the valley! People of Dun Gaoth!"

When the many conversations finally stilled and everyone turned to look at him, Aengus held his gold cup high. "It is my pleasure to tell you that there will be not one wedding this day, but two," he said. "The contracts are prepared, and the other bride and her prospective husband are both here."

The crowd murmured its approval. "Who is it, King Aengus?" someone called.

He grinned, and then walked down the row of guests to the place where Coilean sat beside Maille. He took them both by the hand, raised them up, and took them to stand with him and Keavy at the head of the gathering.

"Coilean of Dun Gaoth. Maille of the people of the rocks," he said. "Do you wish to marry this day, and then remain in this valley as my emissaries to help these people make a home here?"

"Indeed we do, King Aengus," Coilean said, standing taller than he ever had in his life.

"Indeed we do," said Maille politely, looking as poised and pretty in her fine red gown as any young woman of high birth.

"Then let everyone know this: Maille, you are no longer one of the rock men. Neither are you a servant. You are a skilled craftswoman of Dun Gaoth, and of the Valley, and as gentle a lady as any I have ever known. And I thank you for your service to this kingdom."

"I thank you, King Aengus—and the Lady Keavy," Maille said softly, and her eyes shone as she looked from Aengus to Keavy and finally back to Coilean.

Aengus searched the rows of guests until he found Dallan and Sorcha. "Does this match meet with your approval?"

Coilean's parents looked at each other with something like relief. "It does, King Aengus," Dallan said, standing up. "It seems clear to us that this woman is a worthy match for our son."

"And I agree," said Sorcha. Aengus nodded to them, and just as Dallan sat down again Aengus heard her whisper loudly, to him. "I am so glad he has finally forgotten that servant girl! I never could remember her name. I am sure this one will be much better for him."

Dallan looked surprised. "But didn't the king say this one was from the rock men?"

"Rock men? Look at her! She is no servant, no rock man's daughter. I'm sure this one is much better suited to our boy."

Aengus and Keavy could only look at each other and try their best not to burst out laughing.

"Dear Keavy," the king said, his eyes bright. "I have a gift to give you before the contracts of marriage are read." He reached into a leather bag at his waist and drew out a gleaming circle of gold.

It was a torque very much like his own, only smaller and lighter. It was made from a slender bar of twisted gold curved into a circle with a little space left between the ends, but where Aengus's torque was capped at the ends with the heads of eagles, this one had been finished off with the beautifully wrought heads of goshawks.

"This is a queen's torque," Aengus said, gently slipping it around her neck, "made for you, the queen of Dun Gaoth, the bringer of healing and harmony and the love of my life. Now, if you will, Queen Keavy, come stand with me beneath the apple blossoms, where you will become my wife for this day and for all the days to follow."

By way of answer, Keavy kissed him lightly and gently, and then stood back and smiled. "I will come and marry you, King Aengus, for this day and all the days to follow."

He reached for her hand and lifted it up. Behind them Coilean took the hand of Maille. The four of them made their way to the sparkling stream beneath the white blossoms of the apple trees, standing before the druids there as larks and sparrows flew merrily around them, and Seabhac soared high overhead, crying out a greeting to all who gathered in friendship and love on the green grass of this most beautiful and pleasant valley.